GAMES OF OBEDIENCE

Games of Obedience

Frances Allen

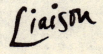

Publisher's message

This novel creates an imaginary sexual world. In the real world,
readers are advised to practise safe sex.

Typeset by CBS, Martlesham Heath, Ipswich, Suffolk
Printed and bound in Great Britain by
Mackays of Chatham plc, Chatham, Kent

HEADLINE BOOK PUBLISHING
A division of Hodder Headline PLC
338 Euston Road, London NW1 3BH

Games of
Obedience

Chapter 1

'What's the time?' asked Kate anxiously, as she sat in front of the dressing table mirror applying her make-up.

'Don't worry,' said her friend Lizzie. 'It's not ten yet and you don't have to be there until ten-forty-five.'

Kate let out a sigh of relief. James was a stickler for punctuality at all times. She couldn't even begin to imagine what might happen if she were late for their wedding day. Finally, deciding that there was nothing else she could do with her face, she stood up and Victoria, who together with Lizzie would provide the only friendly faces at the brief ceremony, held out the dress. It was exquisite, an ivory-coloured Edwardian dress made from silk and trimmed with lace. The top skirt was gathered at the back and finished with a bow forming a stylish bustle. Once it was on, Kate glanced in the mirror. As usual she wasn't satisfied with what she saw. 'Is it simple enough?' she asked her friends.

'He doesn't want you turning up for the wedding in a blouse and skirt does he?' asked Lizzie sharply. 'You look absolutely gorgeous and I'm green with envy.'

'I didn't think you liked James,' said Kate.

'I'm not jealous of *him*. I'm jealous of the way you look.'

'I think James would prefer it if I had a fuller figure,' said Kate mournfully.

'Then he shouldn't be marrying you,' said Victoria, as she and Lizzie exchanged an anxious glance. 'Are you really sure you're ready for this?' she continued. 'Let's face it, Kate, you hardly know the man. If your parents had any sense of responsibility they'd have tried to put you off. You can't possibly get to know a person properly during a six-week courtship.'

'That's where you're wrong,' said Kate firmly, adjusting the Edwardian-style hat on top of her blonde hair before picking up the beautiful antique parasol. 'I understand James completely. He says no one's ever understood him as well as I do. He had a rotten childhood and I'm going to make it up to him. All I want to do is make him happy.'

'You're only nineteen,' exclaimed Lizzie. 'You've got your whole life in front of you. There has to be more to it than making James "happy"!'

'You don't understand,' said Kate.

'No we don't,' agreed Victoria. 'Sure he's good-looking but what have the pair of you got in common?'

'I'm so lucky,' said Kate. 'And I wish you two would be happy for me. It's not as though he's a stranger. I mean, we've all seen him on television book shows and things haven't we?'

'I've seen all Mel Gibson's films but it doesn't mean I know him,' replied Lizzie.

'Please be happy for me,' Kate begged them. 'You're my two closest friends and with Mummy living abroad now and Daddy so busy with work you're the nearest thing to family that I've got. This is the happiest day of my life, don't spoil it.'

'I'm sorry,' said Lizzie. 'Of course we want you to enjoy your day and we both hope that you will be happy, but . . .' Her voice tailed off.

'But what?' Kate demanded.

'We don't really trust him,' confessed Victoria. 'It seems extraordinary that he wants to marry you in such a rush. You're not even having a proper honeymoon are you?'

'I just want to be with him,' said Kate firmly. 'The only reason we're not having a honeymoon is that he's anxious for me to see his house in Cornwall, the one his father left him when he died. Cornwall's a beautiful place.'

'Not for a honeymoon,' exclaimed Lizzie.

'Well I'm perfectly happy with it and I'm the one who's going,' Kate pointed out.

'But why such a quiet wedding?' queried Lizzie.

'Because he hates a fuss. While his father was alive he never had any privacy. He says that half his childhood was spoilt by the media flocking round his father.'

'I don't think that's something he has to worry about,' said Victoria acidly. 'He's never written one bestseller let alone twelve.'

'That's because his books are so different,' said Kate defensively. 'Look, I love James and he loves me. This is what I want and it's what I'm going to do, but I'd be much happier if I knew that I had your blessing.' She looked beseechingly at her two friends.

'Of course you do,' said Lizzie after a short pause and she kissed her friend gently on her cheek. 'We both hope everything works out well for you,' she assured Kate. 'If it doesn't though, you must promise to let us know and we'll rush down to Cornwall and rescue you.'

They all laughed. 'You make me sound like a heroine in some old-fashioned novel,' remarked Kate. 'I hardly think I'm in any danger. As soon as the honeymoon's over James is going to get down to work on a new book that he's had commissioned and I'm going to get the house in order. He says it desperately needs a woman's touch.'

'Won't you miss London?' asked Victoria.

Kate shook her head. 'There's nothing here for me any more. All I want now is to be with James.'

'Here's the car,' said Lizzie, who'd been looking out of the window. 'Come on. It's time we were going.'

Kate looked from Lizzie to Victoria and back to Lizzie. 'You are happy for me, aren't you?' she asked.

'Of course we are,' said Victoria, aware that Lizzie wouldn't be able to lie. 'We're probably jealous that you've snared such a handsome man while we're still waiting for Mr Right.'

Kate smiled and the three of them left the London flat where

Kate had been living for the past year and climbed into the waiting car. As they crawled through the traffic, Kate began to tremble with excitement. James, at thirty, was a well-known man of the world and yet he'd insisted that they waited until their marriage before consummating their love. At last all the frustration that she'd been feeling for the past six weeks would disappear and she simply couldn't wait for the night to come.

'I wonder if James is nervous too?' she asked Lizzie.

'Bound to be,' replied Lizzie. 'Men often get cold feet at the last minute.'

'He won't get cold feet,' laughed Kate. 'But I hope he doesn't feel as nervous as I do.'

James Lewis stretched lazily, one arm still trapped beneath Lucinda's head and then he glanced at the bedside clock. 'God, I'd better get dressed,' he said. 'It wouldn't do to be late for the wedding.'

Lucinda's dark-lashed violet eyes widened slightly as she watched her lover cross the room stark-naked. 'I expect your naive little fiancée is feeling a few nervous flutters at the moment,' she said.

'I hope so,' said James. 'That was the whole idea of making her wait.' He glanced back at the bed. 'Do you really think this is going to work?'

'Yes I do,' said Lucinda firmly. 'It has to. I've negotiated the biggest advance you've ever had yet on the basis of this book. It's up to you to make sure that it works.'

'Suppose we've misjudged Kate,' said James tentatively. 'How do we know she'll obey me?'

'She'll obey you.' Lucinda sounded very confident. 'Look, James, you're not trying to get out of this at the last moment, are you? We've spent months searching for the right girl and there's no doubt that Kate fits the bill perfectly. She's desperate for you and she'll do anything, anything at all to make you happy.'

'She might not feel the same when she finds out what does

4

make me happy,' James pointed out.

'She'll love it.'

'How do you know?' asked James.

'Because I'm good at assessing women's characters,' explained Lucinda. 'Kate's virtually alone in the world and she sees you as her knight in shining armour, someone who's tall, dark and handsome yet vulnerable too. I bet she's read nothing but romances all her life. She can't wait to make you happy after all you've told her about your miserable childhood.'

'Yes that was a neat touch of yours,' admitted James. 'It's quite an undertaking though isn't it? Absolute and total sexual obedience. I bet she hasn't even read *The Story of O*.'

'I hope she hasn't,' exclaimed Lucinda. 'We don't want her to realise that you're using her to write your latest book. She has to believe that this is the only way she can satisfy you sexually.'

'Suppose she just runs off and leaves me?'

'We won't have lost anything,' said Lucinda dismissively. 'We'll just have to find another girl. But believe me, she won't leave you.'

James disappeared into the bathroom. When he returned and started dressing, Lucinda felt her mouth go dry with desire. 'Have we got time for a quickie?'

James shook his head. 'Absolutely not. I want to get this wedding ceremony over and done with. Anyway, you've got to get yourself off to Cornwall, it wouldn't do for us to arrive there before you.'

'You're right,' said Lucinda, throwing back the covers and swinging her feet to the ground. 'Not nervous are you?'

'Of course not,' said James irritably, his eyes travelling over the curvaceous body of his mistress. She was small but full-breasted and had dark curly hair. Her curves and height were in complete contrast to Kate, who was very tall and slim with blonde, straight hair. 'God you turn me on,' he muttered thickly.

'So I can see,' laughed Lucinda, her eyes flicking lower to his erection. 'Save it for tonight, darling.'

'I don't know what time we'll get there,' said James, adjusting the double-breasted jacket of his silver-grey suit. 'We're having a meal at a hotel after the ceremony, I think she's got a couple of friends coming and I've asked Martin to come along as well. After that I'll drive us down but I won't rush.'

'Don't worry, I'll be there to greet you,' Lucinda assured him, standing up on tiptoe as he bent his head to kiss her goodbye.

'If this works it's going to be incredibly exciting, isn't it?' said James, huskily.

Lucinda's mouth curved upwards in a smile. 'It'll be fantastic,' she purred. 'I think I'm almost as excited as you are.'

'Until tonight then,' said James, and with one final urgent kiss he left her to pack and set off for the registry office.

Afterwards Kate was always to wish that she could remember the ceremony more clearly, but, due to a mixture of nerves and desire, everything rushed by so fast that she was left with nothing but a series of fleeting impressions. James looked even more handsome than usual and, although he didn't look quite as happy as she had hoped, she guessed that this was probably due to nerves. In any case James wasn't much given to laughter. His heavy-lidded eyes never gave much away, but this didn't trouble her because she found his brooding air of cynicism highly erotic. After they'd exchanged vows and placed the rings on each other's fingers, she looked at his mouth with its narrow top lip and full sensual bottom one with such a surge of desire that she was ashamed of herself.

Outside the registry office they stood on the steps for a moment while Mark took some photos. 'Smile, James,' called Mark. 'I would if I'd just married Kate.'

Kate laughed, gazing up adoringly at James who flicked his eyes down at her. 'I'm not very good at smiling,' he admitted.

'It doesn't matter,' Kate whispered reassuringly, slipping her arm through his. 'Your life's going to be completely different from now on,' she added. 'All I want to do now is make you happy.'

'Smile and look this way,' shouted Mark.

James stared thoughtfully into Kate's eyes. 'Do you really mean that?' he asked.

'Of course I do,' said Kate.

'Then I'm a very lucky man,' he murmured and Kate glowed with pleasure.

Despite her excitement and the fact that she was now officially Mrs James Lewis, Kate couldn't deny that the meal afterwards wasn't a great success. Both Lizzie and Victoria did their best, chattering away brightly and asking questions about James' house in Cornwall, while Mark told several amusing stories about events in James' life before Kate had met him. James however was like the spectre at the feast. He seemed almost distracted, as though he wished he were somewhere else, and slowly all the conversation died. It was only when Mark raised a glass of champagne and proposed a toast to the happy couple that James snapped out of his mood.

'I'm sure Kate is as grateful as I am to the three of you for coming along today,' he said smoothly. 'We both wanted a quiet wedding because we're not ostentatious people, and anyway I didn't want the media to get to hear of my wedding until it was over. There are some things in life that I think should remain private, and getting married is one of them.'

'We would have had more people if Mummy and Daddy had been able to come, wouldn't we?' asked Kate.

James looked surprised. 'Yes, yes of course,' he said hastily, but for a brief moment Kate wondered if he would even have wanted to get married had she brought all the baggage that in-laws entailed with her. She saw Victoria watching her closely and smiled brightly to hide her own discomfort.

'I probably seem a little quiet for such a lucky man,' continued James. 'The truth is I simply can't wait to get Kate to myself and, as soon as we've drunk this, we'll be on our way.'

'Can't wait huh?' asked Mark. 'You lucky sod.'

Kate felt herself blush. 'Look at that, the lovely bride's blushing,' exclaimed Mark. 'I didn't know there were any young women left who blushed.'

'That's part of her charm,' said James dryly. 'It makes such a change from most modern women.' As he spoke he looked at Victoria and Lizzie and Kate felt slightly uncomfortable.

'Because I blush it doesn't mean I'm completely naive,' she protested. 'It's just something that happens to me. I can't do anything to control it.'

'I wouldn't want you to,' James assured her, a rare smile lighting up his face. 'I find it enchanting.' He bent his head until his mouth was close to her ear. 'I can't wait to see you blushing tonight,' he whispered, and Kate's stomach tightened.

'I'm afraid I've got to be going anyway,' said Mark draining his glass. 'I could only get half a day off work.'

'That's what happens when you're tied to the tyranny of an office boss,' said James.

'Well we don't all have the luxury of an inheritance to enable us to work for ourselves,' Lizzie pointed out.

Kate felt James stiffen beside her and she quickly tried to smooth over the awkward moment. 'James didn't inherit a lot of money, did you, darling?' she said to her new husband.

'I don't see any reason to discuss my financial situation with your friends,' said James shortly.

Lizzie stood up. 'The party seems to have ended,' she remarked. 'Come on Vicky we'll let these two lovebirds set off for Cornwall. Remember, Kate, don't lose touch with us.'

'It's Cornwall not Africa,' laughed Kate.

'Just the same make sure you give us a ring. Perhaps we could come down and stay some time,' said Victoria.

'I'm afraid it will take quite a few months to get the house in order,' James replied. 'Once that's done any of Kate's friends will be more than welcome.'

'Well you can always come back to London and see us from time to time, can't you?' said Lizzie.

8

Kate nodded. 'If I want to but I've got the feeling that once I get to Cornwall I won't ever want to leave,' and she caught hold of James' arm.

'Let's hope that's true,' he said, and the tone of his voice was strange.

'Of course it will be true,' said Kate. 'We're going to be blissfully happy.'

'That's right,' murmured James. 'Blissfully happy.'

As he stood up and went to pay the bill, Lizzie and Victoria began to gather their things together. 'Look, Kate, if you're not happy you will ring us, won't you?' said Lizzie urgently. 'There's something not right about him.'

'It's just that he's different from the other men we know,' explained Kate. 'But that's why I love him so much.'

'Have a happy honeymoon,' said Victoria, and then Kate's two friends left.

'Alone at last?' asked James when he returned.

'Yes,' said Kate with a sigh of relief. 'Alone at last and for two whole weeks.'

James opened his mouth as though he were about to speak and then closed it again. 'We'd better get on our way,' he said quietly.

Once he was driving, James seemed to relax more and it was only then that Kate realised how tense he'd been throughout the whole ceremony and meal. 'It was a bit of an ordeal, wasn't it?' she murmured.

'What?' asked James.

'Getting married,' explained Kate.

'Just a bore,' said James abruptly.

'A bore?' Kate couldn't believe that she'd heard him right. 'The wedding day is the happiest day of a woman's life, or meant to be.'

James' left hand rested briefly for a moment on Kate's right knee, his fingers lightly stroking her leg. 'It won't be the happiest day of your life, I can promise you that,' he said meaningfully.

'I can't wait to get there,' admitted Kate, beginning to tremble.

'Neither can I,' said James. 'Why don't you close your eyes and sleep for a while,' he added. 'It's a long journey and you don't want to be tired for tonight.'

'I won't manage to sleep,' said Kate. 'I'm far too strung out.' Just the same she obediently put her head back against the headrest and closed her eyes and to her astonishment didn't wake up again until they reached Cornwall.

'Not long now,' said James as she stirred sleepily in her seat.

Kate glanced out of the window. 'It's beautiful,' she exclaimed.

'I must admit I'm rather fond of it,' said James laconically. 'Wait until you see the house though, that really is splendid. It's perched on the top of a cliff and the view across the sea is magnificent.'

'I can't believe I slept so long,' said Kate.

'Worn out by nerves I expect.'

'Who keeps the house clean for you?' asked Kate, suddenly wondering if she'd be expected to do all the housework and horribly aware of her lack of experience in this area.

'Mrs Duke,' replied James. 'She does the cooking and the housework with the help of a local girl. She's pretty efficient and luckily very discreet.'

'Discreet? Why does she need to be discreet?' asked Kate.

'It's always important that live-in servants are discreet,' replied James somewhat evasively.

'I suppose it is if you're famous,' agreed Kate, remembering his father.

'Or infamous,' he laughed.

'Luckily we're neither so it doesn't matter,' she said. For a time they continued in silence, Kate feasting her eyes on the rugged coastline. Suddenly James turned sharp left off the winding road that they'd been following for some time and a few minutes later Kate caught her first sight of Penrick Lodge.

Nothing that James had said had prepared her for the

splendid house. It was built out of local stone and stood on a balustraded terrace with a flight of steps leading up to the front door. The slate-covered roof looked somewhat dilapidated but Kate realised from the tiny windows set high in it that the house was three storeys high. It was comprised of one main central block and two long single-storeyed wings. She realised that by standing on the terrace you could look out across the sea and she could hardly wait to get out of the car and feel the bracing sea air and the warmth of the summer sun.

'What do you think?' asked James.

'I think I'm the luckiest girl in the world,' said Kate.

James ruffled her hair affectionately, leaving Kate feeling vaguely dissatisfied. Somehow she'd expected a more intimate or sensuous embrace, not something that a brother might do to his sister. However, once they were out of the car he came up behind her, put his arms round her waist and pulled her back against him. 'It's been a long six weeks,' he muttered. 'Do you think you can wait until after we've eaten?'

'I'm not sure,' Kate confessed.

'Well I don't want to shock Mrs Duke so I think if there's a meal ready we should try and eat it,' laughed James. Reaching out a hand he led her up the steps and rang the doorbell.

Kate was prepared to see an elderly, motherly-looking woman open it and was so astonished by the woman who finally stood framed in the doorway that for one ridiculous moment she thought she must be dreaming.

'Welcome to Penrick Lodge,' said the very attractive dark-haired young woman wearing a casual sundress slit almost to the thigh. 'You've just got time to freshen up and change before the meal's ready.'

'Great,' said James briskly and then he turned to Kate, scooped her up in his arms and carried her over the threshold. 'There, that's the way it's meant to be done, isn't it?' he remarked.

Kate stared up at him in confusion. 'Yes,' she agreed. 'Is this Mrs Duke?'

'Mrs Duke!' James shook his head, hardly able to contain his laughter. 'Of course not. This is Lucinda Finch, my agent.'

'Your agent?' queried Kate, totally bewildered.

'That's right,' said Lucinda brightly. 'Hasn't James mentioned me to you?'

Kate looked to James for guidance but he avoided her gaze and started to walk towards the splendid staircase in the middle of the hallway. 'I don't think he's ever mentioned you,' she said at last. 'Of course I know he's a writer but . . .'

'A writer.' Lucinda's eyes widened. 'He's not just a writer, he's going to be the biggest sensation since his father once his new book's completed.'

'He told me about that,' said Kate, feeling relieved that at last she was on familiar ground. 'As soon as our honeymoon's over he's going to start work.'

Lucinda smiled but there was something about the smile that made Kate uneasy. 'That's right,' she said smoothly. 'As soon as the honeymoon's over he's going to begin. That's what we planned all along, isn't it, James?'

Kate was totally baffled. She couldn't understand what this woman was doing in James' house, not now at this moment when they were just about to start their honeymoon. Neither could she understand the apparent familiarity between the two, a familiarity that seemed to go far beyond any professional relationship. Next to Lucinda Kate felt very young and rather foolish. She didn't like the sensation.

James looked back at her over his shoulder. 'Come along, you heard what Lucinda said, we'd better get changed before dinner.'

Frowning, Kate walked up the wide staircase after him. Halfway up the staircase split and James turned right. When they came to the first floor it was rather like being in a minstrels gallery and, although the wallpaper and pictures were somewhat dilapidated, Kate was still very impressed. 'You never told me how big the house was,' she whispered.

'I didn't think you'd be interested,' said James. 'I flattered

12

myself that you were more interested in me than my house.'

'Of course I am,' said Kate hastily.

Together they entered what was obviously to be their bedroom. It was a magnificent room with a giant four-poster bed in the middle providing the focal point. Feeling unexpectedly shy Kate walked over to the windows and gazed out over the sea. 'What's she doing here?' she asked.

'Who?' queried James.

'Your agent of course. Didn't she know that we were spending our honeymoon here? She isn't staying is she?'

James sighed. 'I do hope you're not going to be a nagging wife, Kate. My work's very important to me. I need to have Lucinda around.'

'But not for your honeymoon surely,' cried Kate, unable to believe her ears.

'I thought you wanted to make me happy,' said James slowly. 'If I remember rightly that's what you've been telling me for the past six weeks and it's certainly what you said immediately after we got married.'

'Of course I want to make you happy,' said Kate. 'But I didn't imagine we'd have company, not straight away.'

James unfastened his suitcase and began to unpack. 'I like company, I'm easily bored.'

Kate wondered if everyone but her was mad. 'This is our honeymoon,' she said.

'You already said that,' retorted James.

'People don't have extra people go along on their honeymoon, surely you can understand that's not right. I feel really uncomfortable,' explained Kate.

James looked thoughtfully at her. 'Has it ever occurred to you that you know very little about me, Kate?' he asked.

Kate stared back at him. 'What do you mean?'

'Perhaps I'm different from other people. Perhaps in order to make me happy you'll have to do things you hadn't expected to do.' His voice was guarded and he was watching her very closely.

Kate could feel her heart pounding behind her ribs. 'Like what?'

'You'll find out in due course,' he said casually. 'Are you going to change for dinner? You needn't, that suit looks very nice, although I'm sure what's underneath it looks even nicer.'

'Will she be eating with us?' persisted Kate.

'Yes,' said James shortly. 'Now let's get ourselves freshened up and go down shall we? I really don't want to discuss it any more.'

All at once Kate felt frightened. Here she was in North Cornwall, miles away from anyone she knew, with a man she scarcely knew either and already her world was being turned upside down. 'Lucinda's very attractive,' she said quietly.

'Gorgeous,' agreed James.

Because of the look in his eye Kate decided it would be unwise to pursue that line of conversation any further but, even after freshening herself up, she was still shaking slightly and when she and James walked into the dining room and she saw Lucinda sitting at the table her heart sank. None of it made any sense to her and she recalled Lizzie and Victoria's words of warning.

'You look pale,' said Lucinda. 'Did the journey tire you?'

'A little,' agreed Kate, taking her seat next to James.

'She slept most of the journey,' James told Lucinda. 'She shouldn't be too tired tonight.'

Kate felt herself blush. 'Don't,' she whispered to James.

He looked at her in surprise. 'Don't what?'

'Don't talk about tonight,' she whispered.

James sighed. 'You can take being coy to extremes you know,' he said shortly. 'It isn't as though Lucinda doesn't know that we've just got married.'

With her cheeks flaming Kate decided to keep silent. Throughout the whole meal she kept her eyes fixed on her plate while Lucinda and James made small talk. Kate quickly realised that the pair of them had known each other for several years and were extremely comfortable in each other's company.

She was beginning to wonder how long dinner was going to go on when, to her relief, Lucinda suddenly rose to her feet. 'Well I'm sure you two lovebirds would like to be alone for a while,' she remarked. 'See you later.'

James nodded and as soon as Lucinda was out of the room he drained his cup of coffee. 'Shall we go up?' he suggested.

Kate looked at him, her emotions mixed. There was something almost surreal about the scene that she'd just witnessed and, despite the fact that she was still desperate to finally feel James inside her, she was curiously reluctant to leave what now seemed the safety of the dining room for the bedroom.

'Not changed your mind I hope?' he asked.

Kate shook her head. 'Of course not, I just don't understand why Lucinda's here?'

'That's got nothing to do with us,' said James. 'It's my work that's all.' As he stood behind her chair he bent forward and his lips touched the soft skin at the nape of her neck. 'Let's go upstairs,' he murmured seductively. 'I don't think I can wait any longer.'

Kate felt a sudden rush of relief. She realised that she must have a very active imagination and that she'd overreacted to Lucinda's presence. After all, the other woman had gone now and at last she and James were really alone. Hand in hand they went back to the bedroom. As James closed the door behind them, Kate's knees felt weak and she sank onto the edge of the bed.

'Stand up,' said James quietly. 'I want to undress you.'

All at once Kate felt shy again. Theirs had been a strange courtship. Most of the time they'd been together James had taken her to cinemas, restaurants, theatres or art galleries. The actual amount of physical contact that they'd had had been slight and this had worried Kate but then, on the few occasions when he'd begun to make love to her, her body had responded enthusiastically. The only problem had been that James never went far enough for her to reach an orgasm. Once or twice she'd been ashamed to hear herself begging him to continue, but he'd only laughed and told her that it would be better if they waited.

Now that the moment had come, now that their sex life was to begin properly, she felt as though she was in the presence of a stranger. This would be the first time he'd seen her naked and, although she knew it was ridiculous, she felt very uneasy.

'Is this the same girl who was begging me to take her to bed?' asked James teasingly, watching as she stood in the middle of the room, her eyes wide and her body trembling slightly.

'It's because I'm excited,' murmured Kate.

'That makes two of us,' said James and then, with exquisite gentleness, he began to undress her. Once her outer clothes were removed he stepped back. Kate was pleased that she'd spent a great deal of money on her lingerie. The long-line silk camisole top with matching French knickers inset with lace was extremely feminine and flattering to her slender figure. Carefully James eased down each of her hold-up stockings in turn, peeling them off her before throwing them into the corner of the room, then he turned her round so that she could look at herself in the full-length mirror set in the wardrobe door.

'You are really beautiful,' he said appreciatively, his fingers playing with the feathered tendrils of hair at the nape of her neck. She watched the pair of them in the mirror, watched as he bent his head and nibbled lightly beneath her ears while his hands slid round her, caressing her flat stomach and the undersides of her breasts through the silk fabric. She could hear his breathing quickening and realised that her shyness had disappeared. Now she was consumed with desire for him and, turning round, she lifted her arms to clasp him round the neck. To her astonishment he grabbed her wrists in one hand and held her away from him.

'I want to do this my way,' he said quietly. Kate looked at him in puzzlement. 'You want to make me happy, don't you?'

Kate nodded, wishing that he'd continue stroking her body

as her breasts were feeling full and there was a dull ache in the pit of her stomach.

'When it comes to sex,' explained James slowly, 'I have very special needs.'

'What do you mean?' asked Kate.

'I like obedience in a woman,' he said slowly. 'In fact I'd go further than that, I'd say I need total obedience.'

'Obedience?' Kate didn't understand him.

'That's right. All you have to do is carry out my . . . ' He hesitated. 'Requests,' he added slowly.

Kate was deeply disturbed. This wasn't the way she'd imagined things going at all. On the other hand what did she know about sophisticated sex. She'd only had two sexual partners in the whole of her nineteen years and one of those had been a casual drunken coupling after an all-night party. She should have realised that sophisticated men like James expected more from sex than that.

'Is that going to be a problem for you?' queried James.

Kate shook her head. 'No of course not. I love you so much, James. All I want to do is make you happy. I keep telling you that but you don't seem to believe me.'

'Prove it to me then,' he whispered. 'Prove it to me tonight.'

'What do you want me to do?' asked Kate.

'Nothing difficult,' he assured her. 'First of all let me take these off you.' With tantalising slowness he eased the straps of the camisole top down off her shoulders, inadvertently, or so she thought, pinning her arms to her sides with them. Then he let his mouth travel across the tops of her breasts, his tongue trailing lazily over the exposed flesh. When he allowed it to swirl over the swelling tiny nipple, Kate's breath caught in her throat and she instinctively arched her upper torso towards him.

'Don't move,' he said quickly. 'Let me set the pace.'

Kate felt a flush staining her cheeks. It was as though in some way she was being too forward, trying to take control, but she knew that was ridiculous. Her reactions were normal, natural – and what most men would want on their honeymoon, but it seemed that James was different. Despite her surprise, she realised that his instructions were adding an extra erotic charge to the situation and she obediently stepped back from him, keeping her body straight while his tongue continued to roam freely across the bones at the base of her throat.

Eventually James decided to move on and, much to Kate's relief, he pulled the camisole top off over her head leaving her upper body completely naked. Next he knelt in front of her, running his hands up the insides of her thighs, his thumbs drawing tiny circles on the soft silken flesh near the top. When his fingers strayed inside the wide-cut leg of the French knickers, the ache in Kate's stomach increased and, without thinking, her hips moved forward as she desperately searched for further stimulation.

'Keep still,' James reminded her. 'Remember I'm in charge, you do what I want.'

'I'm sorry,' murmured Kate, confused as much by the sensations that were coursing through her as by James' attitude towards her. His touch remained light, arousing and yet never fulfilling, repeating the pattern that had been set during their whirlwind courtship. When he finally allowed the back of his hand to brush against her soft blonde pubic hair she shuddered, almost out of her mind with need for firmer contact there.

With a laugh James removed his hand and finally pulled on the sides of the French knickers until they were round Kate's ankles. 'Step out of them,' he ordered her.

Now she was totally naked and although her instinct told her to press herself close to James, to wind her body around his and feel the hard maleness of him, she realised that this wasn't what he wanted. He hadn't even taken off his jacket yet which made her feel disgracefully wanton. It wasn't a feeling that she liked and when she looked at James his eyes seemed to be laughing.

For several minutes they stood in silence, Kate naked and

exposed to his searching gaze, James silent and watchful, his attitude almost one of assessment. 'Wonderful,' he said at last. 'I think you're quite, quite perfect.'

Kate sighed with relief, a relief that was short-lived for, without warning, he scooped her up and put her down in the middle of the huge bed. She stared at him. 'Aren't you going to get undressed?' she asked.

James' eyes darkened. 'Don't ever question me,' he said quietly.

'I wasn't,' she protested.

'You're very young, Kate, you've got a lot to learn,' he said and immediately she felt like a schoolgirl again.

'Just lie there,' he said. 'I know what I'm doing.'

Kate realised that he did but she didn't, and now fear was beginning to creep in, fear of the unknown, fear that this tall, handsome man wasn't at all the person she'd thought him. 'Let's see just how much you really want to make me happy,' he said suddenly and before she knew what was happening her arms were being pulled above her head and fastened to the wrought-iron headrest by soft silk scarves which he deftly tied around her.

'What are you doing?' she cried.

James looked down at her. 'What's the matter? You're not afraid are you?'

Kate stared dumbly at him, mute appeal in her eyes. 'I don't like being tied up,' she explained.

James sighed. 'I'll undo you then, but it's a pity. We could have had so much fun.'

Kate gave herself a mental shake. She was being stupid she thought, James would never hurt her and she'd heard about people who enjoyed bondage games. She couldn't let him down now, not right at the beginning of their honeymoon. Perhaps his needs were unexpected, perhaps she was too young and innocent for him, but if that were so she didn't want him to realise it so early on in their marriage. She was quite determined to be the perfect wife and if this was what he wanted then she would obey. 'It's all right,' she said quickly. 'I've just never done anything like this before.'

She was rewarded by one of James' smiles and he drew a finger down between her breasts and through the centre of her belly so that her skin leapt beneath the touch. 'That's my girl,' he said, and she felt a glow of satisfaction.

At last James undressed himself and, once naked, it was clear that he was highly aroused by what was happening. Kate stared at his naked body hungrily. He was big boned, broad shouldered and well muscled and his skin was tanned, presumably from the Cornish sun. He was the most attractive man she'd ever met and she was almost overwhelmed by desire for him. She only hoped that it wouldn't be too long now before they became man and wife properly.

When James sat next to her on the bed she saw that he was holding a large white feather in his hand. Very gently he moved the feather over her body, starting at her feet and moving up her legs and her inner thighs. He stopped halfway up the sides which made her groan with despair. Ignoring this, he then proceeded to trail the feather up the right side of her body and down the left, tickling the incredibly sensitive skin beneath her outstretched arms. When he swirled the tip of the feather inside her bellybutton, her hips jerked up off the bed as what felt like currents of electricity shot through her.

All the time he was using the feather, Kate felt as though her body was swelling, filling up with hot liquid desire, and the tension was so great that she didn't think she could stand it much longer. Finally James stood up, almost absentmindedly moving the feather back and forth between her hips so that her belly was constantly stimulated and she whimpered.

'What's the matter?' he asked.

Kate didn't know what to say. Surely he knew. Surely he, with all his experience of women, must understand the effect he was having on her and yet, with what seemed almost deliberate cruelty, he was depriving her of her much needed moment of release.

'Tell me what you want,' he repeated. 'I want to hear you say it.'

Kate's head moved restlessly from side to side on the pillow. 'I need . . .' She stopped, unable to carry on.

'More of this,' he suggested helpfully, and this time the feather moved lower until it brushed against the top of her pubic hair.

'No,' she cried out. 'Not more of that. I need to come.'

'Of course you do,' said James softly. 'And you will, but not yet. I've got a surprise for you.'

'A surprise?' There was something about the expression on his face that made Kate tense with fear.

'Yes,' said James, moving over to the door. Kate turned her head to watch him and her eyes widened in disbelief as he opened it and Lucinda Finch walked in.

Chapter 2

Wearing only a patterned orange and gold silk kimono, Lucinda moved swiftly into the bedroom and stood next to where James' new young wife was lying naked and tethered to the headboard. Seeing the fear and astonishment in the young girl's eyes, Lucinda felt a surge of excitement course through her. This was it; this was the beginning – not just of James' marriage but of the book.

It had taken them a long time to find a suitable wife for James, but looking at Kate now Lucinda felt certain that she'd made the right choice. Despite the apprehension in her eyes, it was clear from Kate's erect nipples and the slight flush of sexual arousal already staining her chest and breasts that she was turned on by the situation. It was also clear that she would do anything to please James, and this was what really mattered.

The book that James was about to begin was called *Obedience* and intended to be a modern day equivalent of *The Story of O*. Lucinda felt certain that by using Kate and Kate's reactions to everything that happened to her the book would be a bestseller. This was what James needed. He needed it both for financial reasons and as a boost to his confidence. Once he'd finished the book then Lucinda had no intention of allowing Kate to stay around. James belonged to her, she was only lending him to Kate because of the book.

'Hi,' she said with a friendly smile.

Kate's blue eyes looked up at her but she didn't utter a word.

'Say hello to Lucinda,' said James, resuming his stroking of Kate's swollen flesh with the feather. 'After all she is a guest in our house.'

'I don't want her here,' hissed Kate. 'Untie me and tell her to go.'

James shook his head sadly. 'Surely you're not going to fail me already, Kate?' he asked. 'This is what I want, this is what makes me happy. You'll enjoy it too, I promise.'

Kate felt a lump in her throat. It wasn't what she wanted, it wasn't what she'd imagined would happen and yet, despite that, there was no denying the fact that she was aroused.

Lucinda watched the conflicting emotions play across Kate's face and her body tingled in response. Slowly she stretched out a hand and touched the young girl's tiny breasts. 'Her nipples are hard,' she remarked to James.

'It's the feather,' he laughed. 'It never fails.'

Lucinda gave a sigh of remembered pleasures. 'It is bliss,' she agreed, smiling down at the hapless Kate. 'The only trouble is it's never quite enough, is it, Kate?'

She could tell that Kate didn't want to reply but, after glancing up at James, she murmured a scarcely audible, 'No.'

'Never mind, there'll be plenty of other things that will let you come,' said Lucinda, her fingers toying with Kate's nipples. 'Her breasts are small but they seem very sensitive,' she commented.

'I like them,' said James. 'In fact I think she's beautiful.'

'Lovely legs,' murmured Lucinda. 'I wish I were taller.'

All the time they were talking Lucinda's hands continued to tickle and stroke Kate's nipples, while the feather in James' hand was never still, forever moving down and across Kate's body. Soon the young girl was whimpering and moaning, her hips thrusting upwards off the bed as she desperately tried to get the stimulation where she needed it.

Lucinda put a hand on Kate's stomach. 'Does this feel good?' she asked, pressing the heel of her hand down just above Kate's pubic bone. Kate gasped and Lucinda could imagine the delicious sensations that must be streaking through her. 'Good, isn't it?' she said.

'Please don't keep playing with me,' Kate begged them. 'I need to come.'

James gave a harsh laugh. 'I thought you wanted Lucinda to go,' he said dryly.

'No, no!' cried Kate. 'If this is what you want then . . .'

'What I want is your total obedience,' said James, his voice crisp. 'I want to know that no matter what I ask of you you'll do it and I'm not going to let you have an orgasm until you promise me that's what you'll do.'

Lucinda smiled to herself. James was clever, this was a good moment to make the request with Kate perched on the edge of release, her pleasure desperate to spill. Now she would probably promise anything in order to gain relief.

'Yes, yes I will,' cried Kate, confirming Lucinda's thoughts.

'Good,' said James, obviously satisfied. 'Then let's see what we can do, shall we?'

He walked to the end of the bed and spread Kate's legs apart, his hands circling each of her ankles firmly so that her body was now spread out in the shape of a cross. Lucinda followed him and she heard Kate make a small sound of protest, a protest both she and James ignored before Lucinda began to lightly pull on the girl's soft golden pubic hair. She worked slowly from the top of the labia down each side, something that she knew caused exquisite pricking sensations that would go straight to the clitoris. Sure enough, after a few seconds Kate's hips were rising and falling and she was uttering mewing sounds of pleasure, a pleasure that Lucinda could imagine only too well.

Suddenly Kate's whole body stiffened and she threw her head back. 'Stop now!' James ordered Lucinda.

The hapless girl on the bed gave a wail. 'I was about to come then,' she cried.

'I know, but it will be even better if you wait a little longer,' explained James.

Lucinda was surprised at how quickly James had entered into the spirit of the thing. She'd been afraid that at the last moment he'd lose his courage, but clearly the situation was as exciting for him as it was for her. 'I want you to promise to keep your legs apart yourself,' he said to Kate. 'If you don't then I'll leave you here for the night, do you understand?'

'Yes,' sobbed Kate, half out of her mind with sexual frustration.

'You can just watch now, Lucinda,' James told her, and reluctantly Lucinda moved away. She watched carefully as he parted his wife's sex lips and, after placing a spot of cool gel on his finger, began to circle the head of her swollen clitoris which was standing proudly erect between her sex lips.

Without realising it, Lucinda's hands moved between her own thighs, pushing aside the kimono, and she began to masturbate, following the same rhythm that James was using on Kate. First he circled the head of the clitoris at a steady pace and then, as Kate's whimpers grew more frantic and her body writhed desperately, he changed direction, making sure he kept the pace even and regular. Lucinda was gasping now, very near a climax herself, and she guessed that Kate must be only seconds away from orgasm.

'Is that nice?' James asked Kate.

'Yes, yes, but please don't stop now,' she begged him.

Despite her plea, possibly even because of it Lucinda thought, James removed his finger and once more Kate gave a cry of despair. Lucinda didn't follow suit, instead she continued masturbating herself, her body was flooded with a delicious hot sensation as her pelvic muscles contracted and the orgasm rushed through her.

'Lucky Lucinda,' James said to Kate, wiping away a tear that was rolling down her cheek. 'There's no need to cry,' he said softly. 'You're having a wonderful time.'

'But it's going on too long,' she sobbed. 'I've waited for this ever since I met you, why are you being so unkind?'

'I'm not being unkind,' explained James. 'I'm simply teaching

26

you obedience. You have your pleasure when I want you to and not before.'

'But Lucinda's already come,' Kate cried.

'Lucinda's not my wife,' he retorted. Silenced by this Kate turned her head away and Lucinda felt a moment's pity for their victim. Now James began to rub the tip of his finger incredibly lightly up and down the side of the clitoris first one side and then the other until Kate was screaming with ecstasy, her legs spread wide as he'd ordered and every muscle visibly taut as her body gathered itself for release.

Now, knowing that her climax was imminent, James changed direction again, rubbing backwards and forwards just below the clitoris until finally, as her body arched off the bed frantically, he rubbed down to the opening of the vagina and back to the clitoris again in a flicking motion that quite clearly sent Kate out of her mind.

'She's going to come now,' said Lucinda. 'Is that all right?'

'Yes,' murmured James. 'You can have your orgasm now, Kate.'

Lucinda didn't know if Kate had even heard him. Clearly every overstretched muscle and overstimulated nerve had taken over and, just as James slid a finger inside her vagina, the long delayed orgasm crashed over Kate. She screamed aloud, her body twisting and turning, her toes curling upwards as she cried, 'Yes! Yes! Yes!'

James continued to stimulate her and the orgasm seemed as though it was going on forever. Lucinda still felt hot and aching between her thighs. The sight of the young girl being pleasured so thoroughly was unbelievably arousing and when Kate's final tremors died away Lucinda grabbed hold of James.

'I need you,' she hissed at him, pressing her hips up against his as her hands moved over his torso.

'I don't know what Kate would think of that,' he said.

'But it isn't up to Kate is it?' whispered Lucinda, remembering where the power lay. 'It's up to you. Whatever you want to do Kate has to agree to, that's what obedience means.'

27

James' dark, heavy-lidded eyes sparkled and he glanced down at his wife, the blonde hair dark with sweat, her cheeks flushed and the pupils of her eyes dilated with the pleasuring she'd just received.

'I want to make love to Lucinda now,' he explained. 'I'll pull you up so that you can watch but your hands will have to stay fastened. I don't want you touching yourself while we're doing it. Do you agree?'

Lucinda wanted to laugh. She could see that at this moment Kate hated her and wanted nothing more than to see her gone. To have to agree to let her husband make love to another woman on their own wedding night must be unbearable, but that was the whole point of the exercise. If Kate refused now then there would be no book but at least they'd have found out early.

'Kate?' James was clearly pushing for an answer.

Kate looked helplessly from her new husband to the other woman and back to her husband. 'Is that really what you want?' she whispered.

'At this moment yes, but you won't be ignored,' he promised her. 'We've got the whole night ahead of us.'

'I don't think I can bear it,' whispered Kate. 'You're asking too much of me.'

'That's a pity,' said James. 'So much for all your promises.'

Lucinda wished that Kate would make up her mind one way or the other. To her surprise the younger girl suddenly nodded. 'If it's really what will make you happy,' she agreed.

James' normally severe features softened and, bending down, he kissed Kate lightly on the lips. 'You won't be sorry,' he promised her and for the first time Lucinda felt a stirring of jealousy.

Swiftly he and Lucinda pulled Kate upright, propping her up against a mountain of pillows. Then James pushed Lucinda against the bedroom wall, lifting her up so that she could wrap her legs round his waist before thrusting his erection inside her, his hips moving rapidly in and out. As Lucinda's hands clawed at his back, she felt the delicious hot glow begin deep inside her, spreading out through every centimetre of skin until her whole body seemed on fire. They were used to each other, knew each other's rhythms and needs and within a few minutes Lucinda was ready to climax. 'I'm coming,' she cried, glancing over James' shoulder to the wretched Kate.

'I know,' laughed James, thrusting even more vigorously, and now the pleasure swamped Lucinda and she felt her body tighten and then explode in an ecstatic moment of release.

She was surprised and somewhat disconcerted when James promptly withdrew. 'What about you?' she asked.

'Me? I've still got a wife to see to,' he pointed out.

Lucinda frowned. 'I thought she'd had her pleasure for tonight.'

'She's had some pleasure certainly,' agreed James. 'But we aren't yet properly man and wife. I don't want to be known as a man who didn't consummate his marriage on the wedding night. Time for you to go, Lucinda.'

'Go?' Now Lucinda was angry. 'I don't want to go, I want to watch you both.'

'But that's not what I want,' said James. 'I think you've had your fun for tonight, Lucinda. We'll see you in the morning.'

Suddenly Lucinda began to wonder if even she fully understood James. They'd discussed this night so many times in the past few weeks and at no stage had it been mentioned that she'd be asked to leave the room. She'd anticipated a whole night with him and Kate, possibly even ending in a threesome, but clearly he now had other ideas and since he was the one who'd be writing the book she was in no position to argue with him.

'As you like,' she said sulkily, picking up her kimono from the floor.

'Until the morning then,' he said. 'Say goodnight to her, Kate.'

'Goodnight, Lucinda,' whispered Kate, her eyes huge and her mouth swollen but tremulous.

'Enjoy yourself,' said Lucinda sharply. Then, feeling less than happy, she left.

Alone with her husband again, Kate waited to see what would happen next. When he looked at her his expression was grave. 'Not quite what you expected?' Kate shook her head but didn't speak. 'You did well,' James continued. 'Far better than I'd anticipated.'

While he was talking he began to roll her small pink nipples between his fingers and desire flared in Kate. Much to her astonishment she'd found that watching him thrusting in and out of Lucinda had turned her on. She could feel the telltale moisture between her thighs and even now, as she mentally replayed the scene in her mind, she trembled with need.

'Would you like me to untie you?' queried James.

'Yes please,' replied Kate, whose arms were aching from being held in the same position for so long.

Quickly he removed the scarves and then began to adjust the pillows, before pulling her down until she was lying flat on the bed with one pillow beneath her head and another under her buttocks. James lay on his side next to her, one hand roaming over her body. As it moved between her thighs, he gave a brief smile. 'So you enjoyed our little show.'

Kate was horrified. 'I didn't want to,' she explained. 'But somehow . . .'

'There's no need to apologise. I'm glad you did. It means you're ready for me.' His fingers were already sliding up and down her damp inner channel and when he inserted the tip of one finger inside her, rotating it lightly around the inner entrance, she squirmed as a deep dull ache began inside her. She longed for him to enter her properly, filling the space.

'Keep still,' he ordered her. 'I want you to learn to control your movements.'

'Not now, please,' Kate begged him, horrified that he might spoil this most precious moment.

James hesitated. 'Maybe not now,' he conceded. 'But in the

future.' His words made her tremble. Then, before she had a chance to consider what he'd said, he began kissing her, his mouth hard on hers, his tongue slipping between her teeth. She responded fervently as relief flooded through her that she was finally able to do as her instincts were bidding her. He kept kissing her while his hands moved over her breasts, ribs and stomach until she was writhing around, trying to wrap herself about him. She could feel his erection brushing against her and finally he moved on top of her, sliding his legs between hers and she felt the tip of his erection brushing between her sex lips before it slid inside her.

He was even bigger than she'd expected, stretching her to the very limit, but she welcomed him, welcomed the relief from the terrible empty aching that she'd been experiencing for hours now. As he began to move, so the sparks of pleasure started to course through her. 'Lift your left leg and put it over my shoulder,' he suggested. 'That way I can penetrate you more deeply.'

Kate couldn't believe that was possible but, as she lifted her leg and her foot rested beside his neck, she felt him thrust even further inside and gasped at the delicious sensations it engendered.

He moved slowly at first, easing in and out of her as though making sure that she was comfortable. Then, as her back arched and her hips rose up to meet him, they found their rhythm and his thrusting grew more rapid. Kate felt her muscles cramping and stirring, felt the muscles of her belly quake and coil, slithering almost in a snake-like fashion, and all the time the tension was building, building towards the wonderful moment of release.

James stared down at her, the expression in his eyes unfathomable. 'Come for me,' he urged her. 'I want you to come now.'

His words provided the final trigger and all at once she was tumbling headlong into a delicious climax, one that spread through every part of her. She knew that she was crying out, clutching convulsively at him with her arms and suddenly with a low moan he was coming too, his hips bucking furiously.

After his climax James withdrew immediately, rolling off her back to his original position next to her on the bed. Kate felt bereft, it had all happened too quickly and she wanted him back. 'There,' he said with satisfaction. 'Now we're really man and wife. Now you're really mine.'

His words, seemingly harmless, caused a frisson of fear in her. Once more she realised how little she knew about his dark enigmatic man and how little she understood his needs. Her body felt limp and sated and her eyelids began to droop.

'You can't sleep yet,' exclaimed James. 'I want to see you come again. I love the way your cheeks flush and your lips go pink.'

'I can't come again,' said Kate. 'Not straight away.'

'Not even if it's what I want?' he asked.

She stared at him. 'Why are you doing this?' she asked. 'Why do I have to keep obeying you? I thought marriage was an equal partnership.'

'Some marriages are,' he conceded. 'But it's not what I want from my wife. Perhaps we're not suited after all.'

'Of course we are,' said Kate hastily, desperate not to upset him because, however strange the night had been, she knew deep down that this was a man who could satisfy her, teach her things about herself that she had never dreamt of and she needed him.

'Then come again for me,' he repeated as he pushed her thighs apart. As his fingers began to part her sex lips Kate's body instinctively drew away. She was too tender, too sensitive to be rearoused. 'Can't you do it?' he demanded.

'I want to but I don't know how.'

'Let's try something different then,' suggested James, sliding down the bed. Now it was his tongue moving with infinite tenderness over the delicate membranes and slowly she felt the pleasure start again. It wasn't the same kind of pleasure, it was almost too much and at times she wasn't certain if it was

32

pleasure or pain but, despite this, the hot tight feelings began once more and she started to whimper as her hips moved restlessly on the bed.

James lifted his head from between her thighs. 'You taste wonderful,' he said huskily. 'Your juices are delicious.'

Kate felt embarrassed. She'd never had a man behave like this and now he was pushing aside the protective hood covering her overstimulated clitoris and as his tongue snaked across the tight bunch of nerve endings a white light seemed to explode in Kate's brain. She screamed out in a mixture of pain and ecstasy as the searing explosion tore through her and her exhausted flesh responded yet again to the stimulation.

'There's a good girl,' said James, sliding back up the bed and wrapping his arms around her. 'I knew you could do it if you tried.'

Kate could hardly catch her breath, she felt like a rag doll that someone had discarded, unable to move her limbs, but as he held her tightly, murmuring softly against her ear, pride filled her. 'Did I make you happy?' she asked.

'Very,' he confirmed.

'That's all I want to do,' she reminded him.

'And did I make you happy?' he asked. Kate hesitated. 'I want a truthful answer,' he insisted.

'Yes,' she admitted slowly. 'You did, although I feel that it was wrong.'

'Nothing's wrong if it gives pleasure,' said James, 'as you'll find out the longer we're married. Go to sleep now, you must be exhausted.'

Within a few minutes Kate was asleep.

After half an hour, James carefully disentangled himself from his new young wife, got quietly off the bed and pulled on a towelling robe before padding downstairs to his study which he always kept locked. Once inside he sat down at his desk and began to type on his computer. He began slowly but as he recalled the events of the night so his fingers moved faster and faster over the keys and two hours passed before he switched off the computer and returned to the bedroom.

He was very pleased with the way things had gone, pleased and also surprised at some of the feelings he'd experienced. He hadn't expected to feel anything for his bride. She was very attractive but he'd always preferred experienced women. He'd only married her because Lucinda had made it clear he needed this kind of a wife if the book were to work.

The heroine of *Obedience* had to be sexually naive, had to be coerced through a series of sexual games and intrigue and led along the path to a darker kind of sexuality than she would otherwise have experienced. What had surprised him was how erotic the entire evening had been and how, at odd moments, he'd felt a strange urge to protect Kate. He'd written this down, feeling that he had to be honest, that this was the only way the book would work.

As he thought about the weeks that lay ahead of them, the things that he and Lucinda had planned for Kate, his manhood stirred once more. Not only was this book going to earn him more than any other, he thought with wry amusement, it was also going to provide him with more pleasure. He wondered how Lucinda would cope. She'd been the more confident of the pair of them before tonight, but he'd been surprised by her obvious annoyance when he'd sent her from the room. He thought it would prove somewhat ironic if in the end she were the one who wasn't able to cope with the demands of the book.

Locking the study door behind him he went back to bed and slept heavily until morning.

Chapter 3

When Kate opened her eyes the next morning sunlight was streaming through the windows and she saw that James was already up. He was standing with his back to her, staring out over the garden, and her pulse quickened at the sight of his naked body. 'You should have woken me,' she said.

James turned his head. 'I thought you were probably exhausted after last night.'

It was only then that the memories flooded back and, despite herself, Kate began to blush. James watched with amusement. 'You've no idea how sweet you look when you blush.'

'I wish you wouldn't use words like sweet when you're talking about me,' protested Kate. 'It makes me feel so young and rather silly.'

'But it's your youth and freshness that attracted me,' retorted James.

Kate frowned. 'That can't have been all.'

'Of course not, you're very beautiful. I should think you've had men falling madly in love with you all the time.'

'Not really,' confessed Kate. 'I'm not outgoing enough, that's my trouble.'

'Marriage will change all that,' said James confidently.

'Are you coming back to bed?' Kate couldn't keep the longing out of her voice.

'Tempting as the offer is I think not,' he replied, much to her disappointment. 'Come on, up you get, Mrs Duke will have breakfast ready for us then I want to show you the grounds and we can take the cliff path down to the beach. You'll like it there.'

'Is it going to be hot?' queried Kate.

'An absolute scorcher by the look of it. Mind you, there's always a breeze off the sea.'

Realising that there was to be no more lovemaking for the moment, Kate got up and began rifling through the wardrobe for something suitable to wear. Eventually she chose a soft floaty print dress of scarlet and yellow flowers on a black background. It was sleeveless with a round neck that finished in a tiny V and the hem had slits all round it. As she reached for her underwear James suddenly put a hand over hers. 'Just the dress,' he said firmly. 'I want to know that you're available for me. It'll turn me on knowing you're not wearing anything underneath the dress.'

'But it's see-through,' Kate protested.

'Not completely,' he assured her. 'Anyway, Mrs Duke's not going to say anything and we are on our honeymoon.'

'What about Lucinda?'

'I don't think Lucinda will have any objections.'

Kate felt uncomfortable. 'James, about what happened last night when Lucinda was here.'

'Yes.'

'It doesn't mean that Lucinda's always going to be with us, does it?'

'Only when I want her,' he replied. 'Come on don't make a fuss, just get dressed there's a good girl.'

Kate hesitated. Part of her was excited at the prospect of being naked, of feeling the dress against her bare flesh and knowing that James could slide a hand up her skirt and caress her at any moment. Another part of her, the part that was the Kate that had existed before last night, felt uncomfortable. Somehow it didn't seem right, not when there were other people in the house. She realised that James was watching her closely and suddenly remembered what he'd said about obedience. Running her fingers through her blonde hair she decided that if it was what he wanted then she'd do it.

'I knew you wouldn't fail me,' he murmured, his hands

cupping her breasts through the flimsy material of the dress before they left the bedroom. 'I'm beginning to believe that you meant what you said about wanting to make me happy.'

'Of course I did,' said Kate. 'Surely you didn't think I was making it up.'

'Women will say anything to get married.' His voice was off-hand.

'That's a horrible thing to say,' retorted Kate. 'Besides you shouldn't make such sweeping judgements about women.'

'I think I know a great deal more about them than you do,' he replied.

Kate fell silent. She had no doubt that he did, especially where sexual matters were concerned. She was very relieved to find that Lucinda wasn't at breakfast and Mrs Duke, a short, plump, middle-aged lady with a merry smile, served them scrambled eggs, bacon and tomatoes chattering away all the time about how nice it would be to have another woman in the house.

'Doesn't Lucinda count as a woman?' enquired Kate when Mrs Duke had gone.

'I think she meant a wife,' explained James. 'Mrs Duke's too well trained to say as much but I don't think she approves of Lucinda.'

Privately nor did Kate. There was something about the other woman that made her very uneasy and she didn't feel it was simply a matter of jealousy, although that undoubtedly came into it. 'What's your new novel about?' she asked James.

To her surprise he looked startled. 'What an odd time to ask me,' he said.

'Well you've talked about it a lot but you haven't really said what the theme is,' explained Kate. 'I want to share everything with you, including your work.'

'You can't,' he said shortly. 'Writing's a very lonely occupation. I need solitude. The last thing I want is someone peering over my shoulder telling me whether my book's any good or not.'

37

'I wasn't going to do any such thing,' said Kate. 'I'm interested. I thought men liked their wives to be interested in their work.'

'Did you?' he asked. 'Well in my case that isn't true. Perhaps I should tell you at this point that I keep the study where I work locked and I don't want you going in without my permission. Is that clear?'

'Perfectly clear,' murmured Kate, wishing she'd never begun the conversation. Already she was feeling confused again. It was as though James was trying to shut her out, but if that were true she didn't understand why he'd married her. 'At least tell me what genre it is,' she said. 'I can't imagine you writing a romance.'

James' mouth turned upwards in a smile but his eyes were cold. 'No it isn't a romance,' he said flatly.

'A crime novel?'

'It's something very special. Now can we let the matter drop please.'

Kate sighed. This marriage wasn't beginning very auspiciously. She'd had such wonderful visions of coming into James' life, being loved by him, nurturing him and helping his talent to blossom. She'd pictured herself acting as hostess in the evenings when he'd been working away on his novel all day. Never in her wildest dreams had she imagined anything like what had happened last night. Nor, if she were honest, had she expected James to be so touchy. There were moments when she wasn't even certain that he liked her.

When breakfast was over he took her for a stroll in the grounds. They were vast, mostly lawn but with areas of beautiful flowers, shrubs and bushes which, although not well tended, seemed to blend in with the rugged landscape and the overall air of wildness that typified the area. After about half an hour they strolled back to the house and Kate ran up the steps to the terrace and stared out over the sea. 'When are we going for that cliff walk?' she asked.

'After coffee,' said James, who seemed to have cheered up

while they were outside. Back in the house they went into the drawing room, which again was comfortable but shabby, the furniture large and faded. James rang a bell. 'Mrs Duke will know we want coffee,' he explained. 'When the bell rings in the kitchen it lights up under the room I'm in.'

'Very useful,' said Kate.

'You were right you know,' said James suddenly. 'I *can* see through that dress. Come here a moment.' He was standing by the large fireplace holding out his arms and Kate felt a surge of pleasure as he wrapped himself around her before moving her across to one of the easy chairs. He turned her so that she was facing the back of it and then lifted her up so that she found herself kneeling with her arms along the back and her breasts rubbed against the rough fabric through the thin material of her dress.

To her astonishment James began to push the skirt of her dress upwards round her waist and she heard him unzipping his slacks. His hands were now round her waist, rubbing the undersides of her breasts, the thumbs sliding through the armholes of the dress and moving in tiny arousing circles on the flesh there. He was breathing heavily and all at once she felt his erection pushing against her buttocks and then he was lifting her hips and adjusting her as her excitement grew too.

'We can't,' she protested fearfully. 'Mrs Duke will be here in a minute.'

'Of course we can, we're on our honeymoon,' gasped James. Despite herself, Kate felt the moisture between her thighs and James eased his way up and down between her labia until the tip of his erection slipped inside her and she gasped.

'Move your hips,' he said urgently. 'I have to keep still. I'm right on the edge of the chair.'

'We shouldn't,' protested Kate, but all the time her desire was mounting and sexual tension increasing as tiny sparks of pleasure began to streak through her belly.

'Quickly,' he urged her and now she obeyed so that the glorious sensations intensified and the pair of them were gasping as they approached their climax. James thrust hard and accurately, stimulating her G-spot as he moved and within a few minutes she knew that she was about to come.

'Not yet,' James whispered in her ear. 'Wait for me.'

'I can't,' she groaned.

'You must,' he ordered her and she tried frantically to subdue her quaking flesh but it was no use. All at once the delicious tightness exploded and what felt like a hot flood of warm honey suffused her.

'Yes! Yes!' she cried and as her body thrashed around she realised that James had withdrawn. 'Why did you—' Kate stopped in horror, realising that Mrs Duke was standing in the doorway carrying a tray of coffee cups and James was once again by the fireplace with his back to the door. Mrs Duke glanced across at Kate who hurriedly tugged at her dress trying to cover the pert little cheeks of her bottom, but she knew that there was no way she could disguise what had happened.

'If you'd just put the tray down on the table, Mrs Duke,' said James calmly.

'Of course, sir,' replied the housekeeper before retreating from the room.

'What a wanton little hussy you are,' drawled James. 'For goodness' sake straighten your dress and come and have your coffee.'

Kate felt terrible. She put her hands to her hot cheeks. 'What must she have thought?' she cried.

'I don't suppose we'll ever know,' remarked James.

'I told you we shouldn't have done it,' exclaimed Kate.

James smiled. 'I wanted to see how far you were willing to go.'

'Go?' queried Kate.

'Yes, in the obedience stakes. You passed with flying colours in case you're interested.'

'Is that the only reason you did it?' asked Kate in astonishment. 'You never even came did you?'

'I didn't have time,' he said. 'You were so busy concentrating

40

on your own pleasure I didn't get a chance to have mine.'

'That's not fair,' said Kate. 'I couldn't help coming when I did.'

'You'll have to learn to come when I say and not before,' said James. 'Of course that's quite a difficult lesson to learn and you are very new to all this. Come on, it's not the end of the world. You look incredibly attractive like that.'

'I feel dreadful,' said Kate, wishing that she never had to see Mrs Duke again. 'How can I look that woman in the eyes at lunch?'

'She works for me,' said James. 'It's none of her business what you and I do. We are married.'

'But I was the one who looked . . .'

'Looked what?' he asked with amusement.

'A hussy,' she said reluctantly.

'Agreed, but then I don't think there's an equivalent for men. You enjoyed it, didn't you?'

Kate nodded. She had, but for some reason so far in their marriage every time James had given her sexual pleasure she'd felt slightly ashamed, as though what she was doing was wrong. She'd never felt like this with either of her previous lovers. It wasn't how it should be, she knew that but at the same time it was incredibly exciting. The fact that she was doing things that were different, daring, possibly even extreme, only seemed to be exciting her more. Even now, as she sat drinking her coffee, she could remember how it had felt leaning against the back of the chair with James thrusting in and out of her and her nipples rubbing against the chair fabric. Perhaps she was a hussy, she thought, perhaps she wasn't like she'd imagined. Suddenly she wondered what she was going to find out about herself during her marriage to James.

'Are we going to look at the sea now?' she asked when she'd finished coffee.

'In a minute. First I have to see Lucinda.'

'Can't Lucinda wait?' asked Kate, aware that she sounded sharp but angry that so early in the day his agent was already

41

intruding on their time together.

'No it can't,' he said evenly. 'If it could then I wouldn't have said I needed to see her, would I?'

'I'm sorry,' murmured Kate submissively, and to her surprise he reached out and caressed the side of her face.

'That's better,' he said softly. 'I think you're beginning to understand your role.'

After he'd left the room Kate tried to work out what he'd meant but without success. She sighed. Marriage was certainly much harder work than she'd anticipated and she was beginning to wish that Lizzie and Victoria were nearer. 'Don't be stupid,' she said to herself firmly. 'You're a married woman now, you've got to stand on your own two feet.' Finally, realising that James was going to be more than a couple of minutes, Kate picked up a copy of *Lady* and settled down to read it in the armchair where they'd so recently made love.

James hurried upstairs, this time turning left at the divide and along the landing of the wing where Lucinda had her bedroom. He gave a cursory tap on the door before entering without waiting for Lucinda's call. His mistress looked up at him in surprise. 'What are you doing here? I thought you'd be entertaining wifey this morning.'

'I have been entertaining my wife and I'll be entertaining her further later on but we need to talk,' snapped James.

He was pleased to see that Lucinda seemed agitated. 'You sound angry. It is with me?' she asked.

'No. It's simply that this is more difficult than I'd expected.'

'You mean she won't play the games you want her to play? You'll just have to push her harder. It'll make the book even better.'

'That's the whole point,' exploded James. 'I don't have to push her very hard. Despite her relative innocence she seems very willing to experiment.'

Lucinda shook her head. 'Don't worry, these are early days. Once we introduce something a little more dangerous she'll

42

soon start to resist and that's when the fun begins.'

'Suppose she doesn't?' asked James. 'Suppose she takes to this like a duck to water, where will I be then? No one will be interested in reading a book about someone's sexual awakening if it's simple.'

'It won't be simple,' said Lucinda. 'Okay, so it was a surprise the way she accepted things last night but you were stupid to send me away. You let her off the hook. We could have made it much more difficult for her then.'

'It didn't seem fair,' he said slowly.

'Fair?' Lucinda raised her eyebrows. 'Since when were you worried about fair? You've got a hefty advance to earn, remember?'

'It isn't only that,' confessed James. 'I hadn't expected to enjoy her quite so much.'

He watched as Lucinda's eyes narrowed. 'You mean you find her sexy?'

'Yes, very sexy. It's her combination of innocence and sensuality that's so exciting. I've never been with an innocent woman before. To be frank they've never interested me, but perhaps I was wrong.'

Lucinda shook her head in denial. 'You'll be tired of her within a month,' she said confidently.

'Maybe,' he agreed. He wasn't really bothered. He'd only started the conversation in order to agitate Lucinda, sensing that the more worried she was the more complex and difficult she'd make Kate's initiation into their games of dark eroticism. 'We're going down to the beach now,' he added. 'I thought I'd take her for a drive after lunch, show her some of the countryside.'

'Why don't I come too,' suggested Lucinda. 'Perhaps we could take a picnic. You can have all sorts of fun at a picnic.'

James nodded approvingly. 'That sounds an excellent idea. I won't mention that you're coming of course. Wait until we're actually in the car then run out to join us, all right?'

'Of course,' said Lucinda. 'Remember, James,' she added.

'You've got to go through with this. God knows you need the money.'

'I won't forget,' he promised her.

Ten minutes later he was helping Kate down the steep path to the beach. It was a private path and rarely used, which meant that it was quite difficult. When Kate stumbled and a couple of tiny rocks fell to the beach below she gave a squeal of fear and he tightened his grip around her slender wrist.

'Don't worry, I won't let you fall,' he assured her, realising that her fear was an aphrodisiac for him and feeling his manhood stir.

'You ought to have a rail put up,' said Kate.

'There's no need, like I said, it's perfectly safe.'

'I don't like heights,' Kate confessed to him.

'Then don't look down, that's always fatal.'

Finally they were on the beach. Without thinking he scooped her up in his arms to carry her over the gravel, only putting her down when they reached the soft golden sand. He watched with amusement as Kate slipped off her sandals and wriggled her bare toes sensuously in the golden grains. 'It's so peaceful here,' she said in amazement. 'Does it get crowded later in the summer when the tourists come?'

'Not here,' explained James. 'It's quite difficult to reach this cove except by the private path from our garden. It is just possible but quite dangerous because you can be cut off by the tide from the other side. I always feel it's my private beach.'

'I had no idea I was marrying a man who had his own beach,' said Kate, laughing up at him. Then she began to walk towards the water's edge. James watched her. He'd never been attracted to tall, willowy women before but now he had to admit that there was something to be said for them. He couldn't wait for the time when he would share a bed with both Kate and Lucinda because the contrast between the two of them was incredibly exciting.

'The water's cold,' Kate called to him.

'I could have told you that if you'd asked me,' he shouted,

and as she splashed around in the edge of the surf he realised that he wanted to take her again but this time he wanted an orgasm as well. He thought for a moment wondering if it would add anything to the book. 'Oh sod the book,' he said suddenly and walked down nearer the sea.

'There's a cave over here where I used to hunt for crabs when I was a boy,' he explained. 'Do you want to have a look at it?'

'Yes please,' said Kate excitedly. 'I suppose you were always on your own?'

'No I . . .' James stopped, remembering the tale of a lonely childhood that he'd spun to her. 'Sometimes my mother used to come with me before she left,' he finished lamely.

'I'll never leave you,' Kate promised him.

James looked hard at her. 'You should be very careful what you promise, Kate. You can't possibly know at this stage that you'll never leave me.'

'I do know,' she said, tucking some strands of hair behind her left ear. 'Come on, let's see that cave.'

James had never thought that he possessed a conscience and it was rather troubling to find that he did. It wasn't that he didn't want to use Kate for the book, that was very exciting, it was merely that he felt guilty for doing so without her knowledge. Also he hadn't anticipated feeling any affection for her. In general he wasn't an affectionate man, sexual yes but not affectionate. There was something about Kate that brought out new emotions in him and he found that troubling. No doubt it would pass, he thought to himself as they walked into the cave. As Lucinda had said she was bound to bore him before long.

'Isn't it dark?' said Kate, clutching hold of his hand tightly.

'Your eyes will soon adjust,' he said. 'Mind there's a pool there. Sorry, too late,' he added as she gave a squeal and he heard the water splash.

'I've soaked my dress,' cried Kate.

'Then take it off,' said James.

'I couldn't,' said Kate.

James' eyes were adjusting to the gloom now and he was able to make out her features. With one swift movement he caught hold of her dress and pulled it off over her head. 'There, now you're nice and dry.'

'Don't James,' protested Kate.

'Why not? I told you no one uses this beach. Besides, even if they did they wouldn't be likely to come in here.'

His hands were on her breasts now, massaging the small globes, feeling them swell and the nipples harden beneath his skilful touch.

'Please not here,' she protested, but more weakly.

'Here's perfect,' he said, lifting her up and sitting her on a large slate that stuck out like a ledge. Then he took off his own clothes before scrambling up to join her. He felt Kate's arms wind themselves around his neck as she pressed her slim body against his. Quickly he reached up, pulled her hands apart and then pinioned them together in his left hand, pulling them high above her head so that she was lying flat on her back and he was looking down at her as she lay almost helpless but clearly very excited.

'Tell me what you'd like me to do,' he murmured.

'Anything, anything,' she moaned, her hips thrusting up towards him.

'That's no good, I need to know the details.'

'Don't play games all the time, James,' Kate begged him. 'Just make love to me properly.'

'Tell me,' he persisted.

'I want you to touch me between my thighs,' she murmured and immediately he slid his right hand down over her pubic mound, his fingers parting her rapidly swelling sex lips until he located her clitoris which he began to massage gently until her moans grew louder and her hips moved yet more frantically.

'What do you want now?' he teased her.

'I can't say it,' whispered Kate.

'You have to or it won't happen.'

'I can't.' She was nearly sobbing with frustration as his hand continued to arouse her and he could feel her muscles tight and rippling with tension.

'It's easy. I'm your husband; you can tell me anything remember.'

'I want you inside me,' shouted Kate, and with a triumphant laugh James thrust himself into her. He knew that her back was pressed down against the hard rock but he didn't spare her. He was focused on his own pleasure, thrusting faster and faster, feeling his climax building. Then, all at once, he felt the first movement of sperm up his shaft and suddenly he was emptying himself inside her, coming and coming while she twisted and turned. She wrapped her legs around his waist and when he'd finished she was still squirming, desperately trying to wrench a final orgasm from their coupling.

Bending his head, James closed his mouth around one of her tiny pink nipples, licked it for a moment and then nipped it with his teeth. Kate gave a sharp cry of pain and then, as the cry died away, her body spasmed frantically until at last it was still.

'So you like a little pain?' he said, withdrawing and sitting on the edge of the ledge.

'No I don't. That is, I've never . . .'

It was clear she didn't know what to say but James was delighted. This opened up even greater possibilities and he knew that Lucinda would be as pleased as he was. 'I'm cold,' whispered Kate.

After pulling on his slacks James gave her back her dress. 'Here you are then, put this on. You'll be warm soon enough. It's hot outside.'

Kate was very quiet once they left the cave and James looked at her thoughtfully. 'What's the matter?'

She looked uncomfortable. 'Nothing.'

'Come on, something's the matter, where's your usual sunny smile?'

'Don't make fun of me,' said Kate sharply.

'I'm not,' he said truthfully. 'I just wondered what was the matter with you.'

'I'm beginning to think I don't know myself at all,' she confessed.

'We should have an interesting honeymoon then, shouldn't we?' said James dryly. 'You don't understand me and you don't understand yourself. At least you should get plenty of surprises.'

'I only like nice surprises,' said Kate.

'Perhaps your idea of nice will change as well,' he remarked. 'Come on, it's time to get back to the house for lunch. This afternoon we're going for a drive. I'll show you the countryside and we'll take a picnic with us.'

Kate's face lit up. 'Bliss,' she said as she started to run towards the cliff path.

James wondered if she'd still be saying that at the end of the afternoon.

'What shall I wear?' asked Kate when she and James were in the bedroom after lunch. 'It's very hot now.'

'Why not put on your black and white swimsuit with a pair of shorts,' suggested James. 'We can always stop off at a cove and you can have a swim before we eat.'

Kate nodded. She was very proud of her new black swimming costume with dramatic white lines down the sides and across the middle of the bust. It also had a detachable white halter-neck strap for sunbathing, and a pair of comfortable black shorts that, when teamed with it, made an extremely striking outfit that she knew accentuated her blonde good looks.

She could feel James' eyes on her as she changed but he didn't touch her, contenting himself with a small sound of approval when she finally slipped her feet into a pair of white strapless sandals. 'I can't wait to see the countryside,' she said with a smile.

'It should be an interesting afternoon,' James agreed.

As she slid into the passenger seat Kate felt almost bubbly

with delight. This was how she'd imagined their honeymoon being. This was what she'd looked forward to, time alone with James. Already she was in love with the Cornish coastline and she was beginning to think that her earlier fears had been silly. It was simply that she lacked experience, hadn't understood some of the more sophisticated aspects of sex, but now that she did she was certain that they'd see less of Lucinda.

'You're looking very contented,' said James.

'I feel it,' confirmed Kate. 'This is just perfect.'

James turned on the ignition but, as the car was about to start, the rear passenger door behind Kate was opened and Lucinda threw herself into the car. 'Sorry I'm late. I forgot the sun-tan cream,' she said breathlessly.

'That's all right, you didn't miss us,' said James.

Kate couldn't believe her eyes. 'You didn't say Lucinda was coming,' she cried.

'You don't mind do you?' asked James carelessly. 'She's been working hard this morning and deserves a break.'

'But . . .'

'I do hope you're not going to be a possessive wife,' said James.

Kate fell silent. She couldn't believe she'd heard him right. After all, this was their honeymoon. No woman on earth would want to share her new husband with another woman all the time. 'Is this what you want?' she asked incredulously.

'Of course.'

All Kate's pleasure had vanished now. The afternoon seemed flat, totally spoilt. Then James ran a hand up her bare leg, his fingers easing their way inside the leg of her shorts and tickling the sensitive skin there. 'We'll still have fun,' he promised her and she shivered. She was shocked to realise that even this simple caress, coupled with the knowledge that Lucinda was watching from the back seat, was enough to arouse desire in her. It seemed that whilst her mind rejected what was happening her body was accepting it with enthusiasm. 'Let's go,' he continued and they drew away from Penrick Lodge.

For half an hour James drove around the rugged coastline, occasionally stopping the car to let Kate scramble out and stand on the cliff top, a welcome breeze ruffling her blonde hair as all her senses drank in the wild beauty of the area. Every time she got out of the car she hoped that James would join her but he never did. Instead he remained behind with Lucinda and as she glanced back Kate would see them, their heads close together talking urgently. After this had happened three times she decided it was up to her to protest.

'Why is it that you won't discuss your work with me but you can't go twenty-four hours without talking to Lucinda about it?' she demanded, climbing back into the car, her cheeks flushed with a mixture of the sun, wind and temper.

'You've got a lot to learn about writers,' said Lucinda. 'They're very insecure.'

'But why won't you talk to me about the book, James?' Kate asked. 'And surely you don't have to work on your honeymoon.' A laugh escaped from Lucinda's lips which she tried to turn into a cough. 'What's so funny?' asked Kate.

'Nothing at all,' Lucinda assured her. 'The truth is writers are always working. Isn't that so, James?'

'It certainly is,' he agreed.

'I thought we were going to find a cove.' Kate knew that she sounded like a sulky child but she felt justified. She simply didn't understand what was going on.

'I don't think I like your tone of voice,' remarked James casually. 'Perhaps you'd care to apologise?'

'Why should I?'

'Because I want you to, and I like you to obey me, remember?'

'I don't see that I've got anything to apologise about.'

'It doesn't matter whether you think you have or not. It should be enough for you that I want an apology.' James sounded as though he was explaining something to a small child.

'I don't see why I should,' she repeated firmly.

James leant closer to her and she instinctively shrank away from him. 'What on earth's the matter with you?' he asked. 'You're my wife. I'm not going to hurt you.' He bent his head and began to plant tiny kisses on the satiny skin of her bare shoulders. She felt herself start to tremble. 'Apologise,' he whispered. 'You want to please me, don't you? And it gives you pleasure too, I know it does.'

As he continued to nibble and kiss at her skin and his hands tucked her hair behind her ears in a tender gesture of affection, Kate knew that he was right. She did want to obey him.

'I'm sorry,' she said in a small voice.

Immediately James moved away from her. 'Good. Let's drive on.'

Ten minutes later he pulled off the main road and followed a winding side road for about a mile and a half before turning sharp left into a small wooded copse. 'This is where we're going to have the picnic,' he explained. 'No one ever comes here and there's a path over there to the beach, so you can have your swim if you want to. Best to have it before we eat.'

Kate climbed out of the car and stretched sensuously beneath the warm rays of the sun. 'How on earth did you discover this place?' she asked.

'I discovered it when I was about your age,' explained James. 'It's where I used to bring all my girlfriends.'

'And now he's brought his wife,' said Lucinda with a smile.

'And his agent,' retorted Kate.

James laughed. 'Put like that it does sound rather odd,' he admitted. 'Are you going to swim?'

'I don't like swimming on my own,' said Kate. 'Have you brought your trunks?'

'No,' said James. 'But I'll come and watch you. What about you, Lucinda, are you going to swim?'

'I hate all sports,' said Lucinda with a delicate shudder. 'Anyway I can't swim.'

'Looks as though you're on your own then,' said James to Kate. 'Come on, I'd like to see you in the water.'

As Lucinda busied herself spreading a rug and pulling out the picnic hamper prepared by Mrs Duke, Kate took off her shorts, slipped her feet out of her sandals and followed James along the path to the beach. Just as he'd promised it was deserted. 'I suppose the water will be freezing,' she said.

'Yes, but I'll warm you up afterwards,' he promised her.

Kate stared at him. 'Why did you bring Lucinda?' she asked.

'Because it excites me to have you both here.'

Kate could see from the look in his eyes that this was true. Walking down to the water's edge she started to paddle in the shallows and gave a shriek of dismay. 'I think it's too cold to swim.'

'Nonsense. Get in quickly, that's the secret.'

'That's easy for you to say,' laughed Kate, but luckily the water soon became deep enough for her to dive in and then she was swimming parallel to the beach. Every time she turned her head to the left she could see James standing watching her. When she came out her body was tingling all over. 'That was wonderful,' she enthused.

'You're glad I persuaded you, I take it?' asked James.

'Oh yes,' said Kate fervently.

'Remember that next time you try and resist me,' he said softly and as his warm hand touched the cold skin at the nape of her neck her body started to shake violently. His words conjured up strange dark images, memories of the extraordinary events of their wedding night, and suddenly there was an erotic tension between them that almost took her breath away.

'Come on, you need to get dry,' said James sharply, taking his hand off her neck. 'I put a towel in the car.'

When they emerged back into the clearing between the trees and Kate saw Lucinda standing with a large fluffy towel in her hands, she realised that this was going to be no ordinary picnic.

'I'll dry you,' called Lucinda, and, before Kate could protest, James had pushed her gently in the middle of her back, propelling her forward. Then he was holding her while Lucinda wrapped the towel about her and began to rub her briskly.

Her skin started to tingle and glow as heat returned to it after her cold swim. 'You'd better take off that wet costume,' said Lucinda.

Kate went to turn away but James' hands gripped her shoulders. 'You can't be shy, not after last night,' he said.

'I don't want to take it off in front of Lucinda,' said Kate.

'But I want you to,' he said gently.

Kate hesitated only a moment before hooking her thumbs in the sides of the costume to peel it down. 'Let me do it,' cried Lucinda.

'Good idea,' said James, lifting Kate's arms up and away from her body so that Lucinda could grasp the costume and peel it away from his wife's skin. 'You're so slim,' Lucinda sighed, her fingers caressing the salt-flecked flesh. 'No wonder James adores you.'

Kate stiffened, willing her body not to respond to the other woman's touch, but when the swimsuit was around her ankles and Lucinda lightly tickled the creases at the top of her thighs she couldn't help herself and gave a tiny shudder of pleasure. 'I'll just finish drying her.' Lucinda continued and Kate resented the fact that she was speaking as though Kate couldn't hear.

'Fine,' agreed James. 'Stand still,' he ordered Kate. 'I'm going to let go of you but I want you to part your legs and let Lucinda dry you. Do you understand?'

Kate's mouth went dry. She felt incredibly vulnerable and exposed standing naked in this clearing in front of the pair of them. At the same time, though, she was desperately excited, her body already anticipating sexual pleasure. Lucinda was very thorough, drying carefully beneath Kate's buttocks and between her thighs, rubbing the towel backwards and forwards in a movement that was so stimulating Kate thought for one terrible moment that she was going to come there and then. She didn't think that she could have faced them if she had, she would have been so ashamed.

Lucinda laughed. 'Your Kate's becoming greedy,' she said to James.

'As long as she's obedient it doesn't matter,' he replied. 'Is she dry now?' Lucinda nodded. 'Excellent. Right, Kate, lie face down on the rug. We don't want you to get burnt. I think I'd better put some sun-tan cream on you.'

'I want to put on my shorts and the T-shirt I brought first,' protested Kate.

James' eyes were hard. 'When are you going to fully understand what this marriage is about?' he asked sternly. 'It's what I tell you to do that counts, your wishes are of no importance.'

'But you never told me about this before,' whispered Kate. 'You never mentioned obedience before we were married.'

'I wanted to surprise you,' he said dryly.

Kate knew that she didn't have to go through with this. If she refused he would drive her back to the house and nothing bad would happen to her. Nothing except the end of their marriage and already she needed him, and the strangely humiliating pleasures he was giving her, so desperately that the thought was unbearable. Strangely too she felt that she was gaining in strength every time she obeyed him, because the decision to obey was hers and by obeying she was gaining in power over him. She could see that from the way he looked at her and the fleeting admiration in his eyes.

As she obediently lay face down on the rug, feeling the wool scratch against her sensitive belly and breasts, James knelt at her head while Lucinda crouched at the side of her body. After squirting some sun-tan cream on his hands, James allowed them to glide down her body from the shoulders to the buttocks in a long slow sensuous movement. Then he slipped his hands under her hips and, to her astonishment, drew them up the underside of her body, lingering for a few tantalising seconds around her breasts as she gasped with excitement. He repeated the movement several times and she sighed with the pleasure of it all.

Now Lucinda joined in, reaching across Kate's prostrate body, slipping her fingers under it and pulling up, then releasing first on one side and then the other so that Kate's body was rocking rhythmically and her vulva was stimulated so that tendrils of pleasure snaked upwards from her lower belly to her breasts.

Lucinda and James continued to cover her body in sun-tan cream, using increasingly erotic massage strokes, turning her onto her back and lightly tracing the outline of her breasts with the cream before taking one breast each. Lucinda covered the left breast with the palm of her hand, rotating it as she rubbed in the cream. James spread it in tiny patches, moving gradually nearer and nearer the aching nipple, until finally he covered the nipple itself with the cream, sliding it delicately between his fingertips, pulling it out and releasing it so that Kate's body jerked and she felt herself teetering on the edge of a climax.

'I think she's close to coming,' remarked Lucinda.

'We'd better stop then,' said James.

Kate gave a cry of protest. 'No don't do that, not again.'

'You must learn to control your pleasure,' said James. 'It's much better that way. It means that when you do come the climax is even bigger.'

'But I want one now,' she protested.

'And I want you to stand up again with your legs apart and watch me massage Lucinda,' said James. Kate realised that she was becoming used to obeying him, that she was automatically scrambling to her feet to carry out his orders despite the fact that there was a small part of her brain that still protested.

'Very good,' he said. Now she had to watch as he stripped Lucinda and then proceeded to cover her with cream just as he had Kate, only Kate wasn't allowed to join in, which meant that Lucinda was only stimulated by one pair of hands. Nevertheless once James got as far as the breast massage, Lucinda's hips started to twitch restlessly and he slid a hand down over her belly, pressing the heel hard into the soft flesh above her pubic mound while his fingers searched between her sex lips. As Kate watched, Lucinda's body bucked in an ecstasy of pleasure as her climax spilled over.

Kate's whole body felt hot and needy. She was aching between her thighs and in her breasts and every part of her was taut and tense. She could hardly believe that James, the man she loved, was being so cruel to her. 'When is it my turn?' she whispered.

'When I say,' he said curtly. 'Does it excite you watching another woman come?' Kate nodded dumbly. 'I thought it did, why don't you bring her to orgasm?' he suggested.

Kate shook her head. 'I couldn't.'

'Of course you could. You're a woman, you know what feels good. Crouch between her legs. When you've made her come then you can have your climax.'

Her legs shaking and desperate for satisfaction, Kate decided to obey again. She sat on the ground beneath Lucinda's outspread legs and tentatively ran her fingers through the dark curly pubic hair. Lucinda's body stirred lazily and she gave a small sigh. 'Go on,' James urged Kate.

Kate was at a loss. She didn't know what to do and began to massage the whole of Lucinda's vulva with her fingers. As soon as she did this Lucinda's sex lips began to swell, parting slightly, and Kate could see the soft pink skin beneath and the tiny clitoris standing proudly erect. Hesitantly she touched the other woman and Lucinda's whole body jerked.

'You see the effect you're having on her?' said James huskily. 'How's she doing Lucinda?'

'Her touch is too light,' Lucinda complained. 'I'll never come like this.'

'Perhaps she's teasing you,' laughed James.

'I'm not,' protested Kate and she started to move her finger more firmly along the moist inner channel, accidentally brushing against the stem of the clitoris. Immediately Lucinda's head started to move from side to side and her breathing quickened. 'She likes that,' James pointed out. 'I expect you can imagine how it feels, can't you, Kate?'

Kate could. She could imagine only too well the delicious sensations that must be spreading through the other woman and her own body ached so much with need that it was a physical pain. Realising that unless she satisfied Lucinda her own pain would continue, Kate continued to lightly caress the stem of Lucinda's clitoris whilst at the same time moving her hand slowly in circular motions around the whole area.

Now she could see Lucinda's body changing, her skin was flushing, there was a sheen of perspiration across her breasts that wasn't caused by the sun and her breathing was quick and shallow. 'She's nearly there,' said James encouragingly.

To Kate's astonishment Lucinda's clitoris abruptly disappeared from sight and she stopped, completely at a loss. 'What's the matter?' asked James.

'It's gone,' said Kate in puzzlement.

James laughed. 'That always happens just before orgasm. It's one of nature's little tricks. You can either pull back the hood that's covering it or Lucinda will bear down. Bear down, Lucinda, that will show Kate how to do it when it's her turn.' Kate watched in surprise as Lucinda bore down with her pelvic muscles and the clitoris reappeared. 'Lick it,' said James.

Kate stared at him wide-eyed. 'I . . .'

'Lick it,' he repeated commandingly.

Bending her head Kate allowed the tip of her tongue to swirl over the swollen little bud, and immediately Lucinda screamed with delight as she climaxed, her arms and legs flailing wildly. Kate watched, imagining the delicious heat and the easing of tension that must be suffusing the other woman.

'You see, it wasn't difficult, was it?' asked James.

'I suppose not,' she admitted.

After a few minutes Lucinda's body was still and she pulled herself upright into a sitting position. 'It was quite erotic having such a novice work on me,' she remarked to James. 'What happens now?'

'Now you do the same for her,' said James. 'And then we can have our picnic.'

'I wanted you to bring me to orgasm,' said Kate. 'You're my husband, it's our honeymoon.'

'And I want to watch Lucinda make you come,' said James.

Kate lay on her back on the rug, her legs spread, her body rigid as she felt Lucinda's hands parting her pubic hair just as she'd parted Lucinda's a few minutes earlier. Lucinda played with her in exactly the same way as she'd been played with, touching Kate so lightly that Kate began to tremble and quake. Her climax was so near and yet so far and when the finger began to slide up and down the shaft of her clitoris Kate cried out with the pleasure. '*Her* clitoris has disappeared now,' said Lucinda.

'It's your turn to bear down, Kate,' explained James. 'You saw what Lucinda did.'

Kate was frantic for satisfaction, willing to do anything in order to gain release and, gritting her teeth, she bore down with her pelvic muscles and Lucinda's head was immediately lowered. Unlike Kate, Lucinda didn't only use her tongue, instead she closed her lips around the tiny nub of pleasure and sucked on it. Immediately, red-hot shards of delight pierced Kate's body. As the wonderful rhythmic contractions began, she screamed in wild excitement because Lucinda continued to suck even after the orgasm started to fade, rearousing Kate so that a second orgasm crashed over the first until the two were indistinguishable.

Kate no longer cared what she looked like or what was happening, all that mattered was the pleasure – the wonderful searing release of pent-up sexual tension that was coursing through her veins causing her limbs to twitch and her muscles to jump and leap. She heard herself sobbing with gratification.

'That's enough,' said James sharply. 'I don't want my wife worn out before the evening.'

Kate could tell that Lucinda was reluctant to remove her mouth but she did as James said, leaving Kate limp and exhausted on the rug.

James kissed her lightly on the lips, running his tongue around the inside of her mouth and she uttered a small sound of pleasure. 'You looked wonderful then,' he whispered. 'So shameless and abandoned. We're going to have such fun with you, Kate.'

After they'd eaten, they all got back into the car and drove back to Penrick Lodge where Lucinda immediately vanished into her room. 'Why don't you go and have a sleep,' suggested James. 'You must be tired after all that fresh air and exercise.'

'You're laughing at me,' said Kate.

'I'm not. I'm very proud of you.'

'I don't understand how I can do the things I'm doing,' said Kate, shamefaced.

'Believe me what you're doing is nothing compared to what you will do,' James promised her. 'If you continue to obey me then I'll teach you the real meaning of pleasure.'

'Do you love me?' Kate asked him.

James looked away. 'I've never known what the word meant,' he said shortly. 'I find you incredibly sexy and I want you all the time. Isn't that enough?'

For the moment Kate supposed that it had to be but it wasn't what she really wanted to hear. 'I think I will go and have a rest,' she said. 'What will you do?'

'I've got some things to see to in my study,' said James casually. 'I'll come up before dinner and we can get changed together.'

Kate watched him go into the study and heard him lock the door behind him before she walked slowly up the stairs to their bedroom, flopped down on the bed and immediately fell into a deep sleep.

Chapter 4

James was in a very good mood when he and Kate went down to dinner that evening. So far things were going better than he could ever have anticipated and he was finding that he was in a state of almost perpetual arousal, fuelled by Kate's burgeoning sensuality and Lucinda's ever-present desire for him. So far Kate had done everything he could have hoped but from tonight on it would become more difficult.

He'd been unable to resist the temptation to start the book, and simply writing about what was happening made him long to move on to the next stage. The book was good, there was no doubt about it, but the pace had to sharpen and the acts required of Kate become more complicated if it was to sustain its erotic charge.

'It's only us eating tonight,' he explained to Kate when they sat down. 'Lucinda's staying in her room.' Kate smiled, her relief obvious. 'Didn't you enjoy this afternoon?' he asked sardonically.

Kate flushed. 'You know I did, but I like it when we have time alone together.'

'I'm going to feed you your dinner,' said James.

Kate smiled at him once more. 'With a spoon?' she asked mischievously.

'Not exactly,' he replied.

Mrs Duke brought in the food and then, without even looking at Kate, left them alone again. 'I don't think she's looked at me once since that time she came in and caught us together on the chair,' said Kate awkwardly. 'Did you apologise to her?'

'Why should I apologise to my own servant?' he asked. 'Besides, she didn't see anything of me. You were the one in a state of undress. Never mind, open your mouth and eat this.' Kate's lips parted and he popped a tiny cherry tomato into her mouth. 'Bite on it,' he murmured seductively and her even white teeth closed over the delicious sweetness of the tomato. There was something very arousing about being fed, and the finger buffet had been prepared especially so that it was possible for James to do this. He fed her fingers of toast spread with caviar and topped with a squeeze of lemon. He placed thin, crisp stems of celery in her mouth and then the pair of them would nibble from each end until their mouths met and he would kiss her softly. They had small strips of smoked salmon and then he ordered her to tip her head back and slid oysters down her throat. She shivered with delight at the cool slithering sensation when she swallowed. 'An aphrodisiac,' he reminded her. James knew that Kate didn't need an aphrodisiac, that what he was doing was arousing enough. However he kept talking because he knew that his murmured words of encouragement and sexual suggestions only heightened her desire even more.

By the time he'd spoon fed her chocolate ice cream, licking the surplus from around her mouth, she was trembling all over and he stroked the sides of her face with his hands. 'You look so sexy,' he told her. 'Feel how you're affecting me.' Kate put a hand on his crotch and he moved slightly in order that she could feel the large bulge in his trousers. 'That's how much I want you,' he murmured. 'Do you want me too?'

'Of course I do,' she whispered back, her eyes bright with desire.

James cupped her breasts through her dress. 'Your nipples are hard,' he said with satisfaction, tracing the outline of one with his finger and watching as her upper torso shivered beneath the touch. 'Let's go upstairs.'

Kate's eyes lit up and James smiled to himself. This was exactly how he'd planned it. Now her obedience would really be tested and he could hardly wait.

Once in their bedroom he began to undress her, sensuously caressing every inch of her as he removed her clothes. 'I can feel how much you want me,' he laughed, sliding his hand between her parted thighs and encountering the telltale moisture. 'Tell me what you're feeling right now.'

'I ache for you,' Kate told him. 'I need you inside me, I need to feel you filling me up and your hands on my naked flesh. I want you to squeeze my breasts and lick them.'

'Do you indeed.' Briefly he allowed his hands to cup the small globes of her breasts again and then with shocking abruptness he stepped away from her. 'I'm afraid you'll have to wait until tomorrow,' he said calmly.

He watched as Kate's expression of pleasure and excitement slowly changed to one of hurt puzzlement and disbelief. 'What do you mean?' she asked.

'I mean that tonight I want you to watch me make love to Lucinda.'

'But I've done that before,' she protested.

'Not when you were feeling like this,' he said, flicking idly at her breasts and watching how her body leapt in reaction. 'You really want it, don't you? Your body's learning what pleasure means and it can't get enough.'

'That's your fault,' retorted Kate. 'It's because of the way you've been pleasuring me. Of course I respond when you touch me.'

'I'm glad you do but I think you need a rest tonight. You've had more than enough for one day. Remember, you're a new bride. I mustn't wear you out.'

'I don't care,' cried Kate. 'I want you and you're not wearing me out.'

'Stand at the end of the bed,' he instructed her. For several moments Kate sat on the bed, her body perfectly still with rebellion in her eyes. 'Remember, Kate, total obedience,' he said softly.

After what seemed to him to be an eternity, an eternity while he wondered whether the first few chapters of the book were to be wasted, she got silently to her feet and walked to the end of the bed, her eyes cast down.

'Stand there with your legs apart and your hands at your sides. I don't want you to move until I give you permission. Do you understand me?' Kate nodded and, as a single tear rolled down her cheek, James wanted to shout aloud with delight. This was what he'd wanted, this was what he needed if the book was to be a success. He had to see her subjugate her own desires to his, to learn to discipline her body's needs to his wishes. 'I'm going to fetch Lucinda now. Don't move while I'm gone. I'll know if you do,' he said.

When he returned with Lucinda, Kate was standing exactly as he'd left her and he ran a finger down her spine, ending up in the tiny dimple of flesh that he always found so exciting. 'I'm glad you obeyed, Kate,' he whispered.

Lucinda, who was fully dressed in a pale-blue thigh-length dress with stockings, suspenders and high-heeled shoes, glanced at the younger girl. 'She looks aroused already,' she remarked.

'She is,' confirmed James. 'She's had a very nice evening so far haven't you, Kate?'

'Yes,' agreed Kate submissively.

'What happens now?' asked Lucinda.

'I want her to have a rest,' said James with a wicked smile. 'The problem is I'm aroused too and I didn't think you'd mind helping me out.'

'I'd be delighted,' said Lucinda. 'Do you want me to undress?'

James shook his head. 'No time for that. I want to take you as you are,' he said roughly, and suddenly his hands were hitching her skirt up round her waist and he was pushing her over the back of one of the bedroom chairs so that her palms were flat on the seat. 'I'm glad you're not wearing any panties,' he said. 'Stockings and suspenders make things so much easier,' he added, glancing over at Kate. 'We must get you some for tomorrow, darling.'

He waited but Kate didn't reply. 'I'd like a little conversation from my wife,' he said. 'Would you like stockings and a suspender belt?'

'If it pleases you,' said Kate.

'Wonderful,' murmured James. 'Well it does please me so we'll drive into town tomorrow and see what we can find.' As he was talking he was running his hands up and down Lucinda's back as she spread her legs wide, her calf muscles stretched tightly by the position and the high-heeled shoes. James flicked a finger hard at each of the cheeks of her bottom in turn and she gave a tiny squeal. Then, still watching Kate, he unzipped his trousers and, without any more preliminaries, thrust himself inside Lucinda.

He knew that this was not Lucinda's favourite position. She couldn't move, and had to rely on him to provide her with sufficient stimulation to climax, but he didn't particularly care about Lucinda tonight. What he cared about was Kate's reaction, how she'd behave as she watched him reaching his peak of satisfaction while she was left throbbing with need, her body once more frustrated by his demands. He took his time, only just entering Lucinda and then easing himself out again, rotating his hips and teasing her with the tip of his engorged penis.

Soon Lucinda began to give tiny cries of delight as her pleasure was sparked and James managed to reach one hand beneath her to squeeze a breast tightly. His fingers clenched and unclenched and now Lucinda was breathing heavily as her pleasure was tinged with slight pain.

'Tell me when you're near to coming,' said James. 'I want us to climax together.'

He continued easing himself in and out of his mistress, gradually penetrating her more and more deeply as her cries grew louder, and then he felt her internal muscles start to contract around him and his eyes locked with Kate's. 'Are you nearly there?' he asked.

'Yes,' shouted Lucinda.

'Good, then I'll join you,' said James and now his rhythm changed and he thrust faster and faster, but all the time he kept watching his young wife whose face was scarlet. He could see how aroused she was, and watched as her hand started to stray between her thighs. When she realised his eyes were on her, she quickly removed it and stayed in the position he'd originally placed her in.

With a muffled groan Lucinda suddenly came and her internal contractions milked James, so that within seconds he threw his head back and opened his mouth in silent ecstasy as he too found release.

For a few minutes he stayed inside Lucinda, pulling her upright against him so that her back was against his chest and his hands could reach round and fondle her breasts. 'Do you want to come again?' he asked her and Lucinda nodded.

James looked at Kate. 'How do you feel now?' he asked her.

Kate didn't reply. She didn't look as though she could. Her nipples were tiny tight peaks, her breasts swollen with need and her usually flat belly seemed to be distended with desire. He smiled at her. 'You don't begrudge Lucinda another orgasm I hope, Kate?'

'Not if that's what you want,' said Kate quietly.

'She's incredibly obedient,' gasped Lucinda as James' hands moved lower down over her ribs and abdomen, stimulating her flesh and rekindling the flickering tongues of desire.

'A wonderful pupil,' James agreed. 'I want you to stay leaning against me and masturbate yourself while she watches.'

He felt Lucinda stiffen slightly and knew that this wasn't what she wanted. 'Remember the book,' he whispered softly in her ear. Immediately Lucinda moved her right hand between her thighs and began to masturbate herself. Within a few seconds she was lost in her own world of pleasure, her fingers working busily up and down between the folds of her labia, and occasionally she would slip two fingers inside herself, moving them from side to side. All the time her breathing grew heavier and more audible and Kate watched, unable to tear

66

her eyes away from what was happening.

When Lucinda finally came, her body jackknifing nearly in two with the sharp intense pleasure, Kate uttered a tiny cry of despair and James felt an incredible surge of power. 'What's the matter?' he asked. There was no reply. 'Remember, I expect answers to my questions.'

'I need to come like that,' she explained hesitantly. 'You've no idea what it feels like, being left up in the air like this. Please, James. I've done all you wanted. Let me come now.'

'I told you not until morning,' he said firmly. 'It's time for us all to get some sleep.' And he bundled a protesting Lucinda out of the room.

'I won't be able to sleep,' said Kate.

'Of course you will,' said James briskly. 'You can come and sit on the bed now.' She sat beside him, her body quivering like a racehorse before a race, and he traced the letters of her name over her belly. She began to shake and he saw her stomach literally quaking. 'You're not to come,' he reminded her.

'Then leave me alone,' she begged him.

'I suppose you're not well trained enough yet,' he agreed grudgingly, wishing that he could force her to subdue her flesh more but knowing that her pleasure would spill and the evening would be ruined. 'I'm going to tie your hands for the night,' he added. 'I don't want you pleasuring yourself while I'm asleep.'

'I won't,' she promised him. 'Please don't tie me up again.'

'I'm not going to tie you up, simply put these cuffs on you, that'll be enough.'

He clipped the softly padded leather handcuffs around her wrists and then fastened the chain around her waist so that she couldn't move her hands lower. 'There. You'll be all right if you sleep on your back and by the morning your body will be thoroughly refreshed.'

He turned his back on her, more than ready for sleep but knowing that it would be a long time before Kate's frantic body quietened enough for her to sleep as well.

★ ★ ★

67

When Kate awoke the next morning she couldn't imagine what she was doing with handcuffs on and it took several minutes before the memories of the previous night flooded back to her. All at once she realised that James was lying facing her. 'Awake at last. I'll take those cuffs off you. I didn't want to disturb you before.'

Kate realised with relief that she no longer felt aroused. Her body had come down from the peak it had reached before she was handcuffed and left so cruelly on the edge of satisfaction. She wondered what James would say but he made no reference to what had occurred.

'I thought you and I would go out in the car today,' he said. 'We'll get you those stockings and suspenders that we talked about yesterday and have a meal at my favourite fish restaurant. You get the most wonderful fish round here because it's so fresh.'

Kate was bewildered at the normality both of his tone and the things that he was saying. She wondered if she'd imagined the bizarre scene the night before, when he'd been thrusting into Lucinda and yet watching her, but she knew that she hadn't. James and his ways were a total enigma to her and she wished that he didn't have the power to arouse such passion in her.

'Come on, we mustn't waste any more of the day,' he said brightly before padding off to the adjoining bathroom to shower and get dressed.

As he'd promised the day was a normal one. They did their shopping, they ate out, they laughed and talked like any normal newlyweds and once or twice he even placed an arm around Kate's shoulders, guiding her protectively through a crowded shop or sliding his hand round her waist and squeezing softly in a possessive move.

They were out all day and never once did he ask Kate to obey him in anything. There was nothing about the day that was like the other James, the one she'd only come to know since the wedding, and she wondered what this particular night would be like. Perhaps it would be an ordinary one, she thought hopefully. Maybe tonight he'd make love to her tenderly and privately, asking not for obedience but simply for her natural responses. Even as she thought this Kate wondered whether it would be quite enough. She was shocked to realise that she was beginning to enjoy the things that were happening to her. It was as though she needed different stimulation, the added excitement of having to obey, if her body was to obtain maximum satisfaction. The realisation was sobering.

'Tonight's a very special night for you,' said James, handing her a glass of brandy.

'In what way?' she asked.

'Tonight you're going to visit the Education Room.'

'What's that?' There was something about his voice that made her stomach tense with fear.

'It's an attic room up on the third floor. It used to be my old school room, which is why it's called the Education Room.'

'But what is there for me to see?' asked Kate.

'There's not a lot for you to see,' said James quietly. 'But there's a lot for you to learn.'

'Do you mean more games?' she asked hesitantly.

'They're not games, Kate,' he explained patiently. 'I need to know how much you love me.'

'But I've married you, I want to spend my life with you, surely that shows how much I love you.'

'No it doesn't,' he said calmly. 'I need to know that you'll do anything, anything at all to make me happy just as you promised. If that's not true then how can I believe anything you've ever said?'

Kate didn't reply. She sensed that he was simply using her own words as a weapon against her when he'd had this planned all along. 'Will I enjoy it?' she asked tremulously.

'Of course you will,' his voice was reassuring now. 'After last night I wouldn't dream of not letting you have pleasure tonight, especially since we've had such a lovely day together.'

'Will Lucinda be joining us?' she asked.

James nodded. 'It will take two of us to help you learn some of the things that I want you to learn,' he explained.

Kate finished her brandy and put the glass down. 'We'd better go up then,' she said quietly.

James looked intently at her. 'Only if it's really what you want,' he said slowly. 'I want you to do it but it has to be your wish too.'

Kate looked back at him and knew that it was her wish. No matter where he was leading her she wanted to go there, because then she would be as strong and as free as he was. 'I do want to go there,' she said clearly.

'Then we'll go up,' said James. On their way to the third floor James and Kate passed Lucinda's bedroom door and James knocked on it twice before continuing to lead Kate to the Education Room.

The room itself was large, although the high ceiling tapered down almost to the floor at the far end. It was sparsely furnished but what caught Kate's eye was a high, leather couch standing almost in the centre of the room. It was a perfectly flat surface with what appeared to be a few holes cut in it. 'What on earth's that?' she asked.

'It's an old physiotherapist's couch,' explained James. 'There used to be a physiotherapist who practised just down the road from here. When he finally retired and sold off his equipment I bought that. It's proved very useful. The great thing about it is that you can change its height simply by using the foot pump underneath.'

'What do you use it for?'

'You'll see,' said James enigmatically.

At that moment Lucinda walked into the room and to Kate's astonishment she locked the door behind her then handed the key to James who pocketed it swiftly. 'This is where I really test your obedience, Kate,' he said quietly. 'Up until now everything's been fairly straightforward. Tonight is more complex. I hope you don't disappoint me.'

Looking at James and Lucinda, Kate wondered what it was

about them that frightened her. After all, James was her husband, a man who could be expected to cherish and protect her, yet she always had the feeling that he and Lucinda were aligned in some strange partnership against her. 'I hope I don't,' she said nervously.

'I'd like you to let Lucinda undress you first,' said James. 'Stand with your legs apart and your arms up, that will make it easier for her.'

Kate did hesitate for a second but no longer than that. She knew it shouldn't but somehow the way that his instructions rendered her helpless also increased her desire and her treacherous body was beginning to prickle with excitement. Lucinda took her time taking off Kate's clothes, allowing her hands to stray all over the other girl's body, tickling the undersides of her breasts and also the hollows each side of her waist. 'Your skin's so golden,' Lucinda remarked. 'Do you do a lot of sunbathing?'

Kate shook her head. 'It's my natural colouring.'

'Lucky you,' said Lucinda. 'I break all the health guidelines and lie in the sun at every possible opportunity in order to turn that colour. It's funny because blondes are usually so fair skinned.'

Kate didn't reply. She was too busy trying to conceal her rising excitement from the watching couple. When she was finally naked, Lucinda stepped away from her and James studied her critically. 'Turn around,' he said.

This simple instruction made her feel incredibly vulnerable and she moved awkwardly, hesitantly, as she obeyed, revealing every inch of herself in the process. 'If your breasts were just a little larger you'd be perfect,' he said, reaching out and tugging on one of them. At first it felt delicious but then his fingers tightened and the breast began to ache.

'Don't,' she exclaimed.

James ignored her. 'You like pain.'

'I do not.'

'You did in the cave the other afternoon,' he reminded her.

'Yes, but . . .' Kate stopped as her breath caught in her throat. He was tweaking her nipple now, twisting it so hard that it was really hurting, and yet it was a curious mixture of pain and pleasure that was spreading through the whole of her upper body and the other nipple began to harden, treacherously betraying her.

'Yes you're right,' murmured Lucinda, watching from the shadows. 'She is enjoying it.'

As the pleasure mounted and the peculiar red streaks of ecstasy began to flash to her brain, James released her. 'I mustn't get carried away,' he said regretfully. 'We've a lot to get through this evening. Do you have the blindfold, Lucinda?'

Kate looked at Lucinda's outstretched hands in dismay. 'You're not going to blindfold me?'

'I'd like to,' explained James. 'But you have to ask me to and then, when I give permission you have to put the blindfold on yourself. It's all a matter of free will, you see.'

'That's not true,' cried Kate. 'Everything I do is to satisfy your will.'

'Hopefully our desires will become one and the same,' said James. 'Now ask for the blindfold, Kate.'

Kate kept her lips firmly closed. It was bad enough that she was here, trapped in this strange room with the pair of them. The prospect of not being able to see what they were doing was terrifying. 'She isn't going to ask for it,' said Lucinda.

'Give her time,' replied James.

'There's no point, you can tell she doesn't want to.' Kate could hear that Lucinda was pleased and she thought she could guess why. If she failed then it was the end for her and James and Lucinda would take over her old role in the house. She knew that she didn't want this to happen and, anyway, if she failed to ask for the blindfold then she'd never find out what lay ahead for her tonight, and her body, having learnt its early lessons, was desperate for more satisfaction.

'Please may I be blindfolded?' she whispered submissively. James nodded. Kate waited, uncertain as to how she should proceed. James gave her no clue, his expression was unreadable. 'Please would you hand me the blindfold?' she said at last, and with a nod of satisfaction he did as she'd asked.

The blindfold was made of thick black velvet and, as Kate slipped it over her head and down over her eyes, she began to tremble. Nothing had prepared her for this moment. It was almost as though she didn't exist, she was simply a naked body desperate for pleasure and now at the mercy of James and his mistress.

'I'm going to put you on the physio couch,' said James quietly. 'Don't be afraid, there's nothing to worry about.'

'Not yet,' she heard Lucinda say.

A few moments later James had positioned her on the couch, but to her surprise she was lying face down and he had to ease her breasts through two circular openings. He then pressed down on her lower back and she felt her entire pubic area press into another hole. Even if she wanted to it would be difficult to get up because the holes were small and she only just fitted into them. Just as she was wondering what would happen next she felt something being fastened around her waist and then jumped as a cold buckle was placed on her back. 'It's simply a restraining strap,' said James calmly. 'We don't want you falling off the couch when you come.' She heard Lucinda laugh softly.

'First of all we're going to give you a couple of easy orgasms to get you warmed up,' continued James' voice as Kate lay tensely, her world one of utter blackness. From the sound of his voice she thought that he must be sitting on a chair level with her head and when his mouth suddenly touched the nape of her neck she knew that she was correct. At the same time he must have reached beneath the couch and his hand began to stimulate her right breast, stroking it very delicately and drawing tiny rings on the areolae until the nipple hardened painfully. Kate started to squirm and it was then that she realised how restricted her movements were by the strap.

James' lips continued to travel over the nape of her neck

and the top of her spine while his hands worked at the tightly enclosed breasts until she felt them start to swell and throb with delicious desire. His hands were still on her when she felt her sex lips being parted from beneath the table and she gave a sharp cry of shock.

'It's only Lucinda,' said James quietly. 'She's going to increase the pleasure. Isn't it nice to have both of us trying so hard to make you happy?'

Kate wasn't sure that it was. Admittedly she was very aroused, every centimetre of her skin seemed to be tingling and her stomach was tight, while there was a throbbing behind her clitoris that was driving her mad with need for release. Despite all this it was difficult for her to relax because she had no idea where the other two were or what they were going to do.

She felt Lucinda's fingers delicately separating her labia and then gave a cry of alarm as something cold was spread over her. 'It's to make things easier for you,' explained James. 'I don't want you to cry out any more. It distracts us.'

'I can't help it,' she explained. 'It's the shock.'

'But that's part of the pleasure,' explained James patiently. 'You will obey me on this I trust.'

'Yes,' Kate promised.

She wondered what Lucinda was going to do and for a few minutes the other woman contented herself with gently massaging the whole area, spreading the cool gel that she'd applied into every tiny crevice until Kate's clitoris felt large and hard. When the other woman's fingers slid over it, Kate automatically pressed her hips down on the couch seeking that elusive touch that would allow her pleasure to spill.

For a moment the fingers ceased moving and Kate tried to stifle a moan of frustration but then something new was happening. It felt as though a narrow plastic rod was being placed between her sex lips which were then closed around it. It felt strange but there was no stimulation and her climax began to die away. Then, totally unexpectedly, she heard a low buzzing sound and what felt like a tiny piece of sponge began to flick remorselessly back and forth with deadly accuracy, lightly tapping the clitoris and surrounding tissue in a steady rhythm.

The sensations were incredible, sending Kate nearly out of her mind with excitement, and James began to work her breasts harder, tweaking the nipples and pinching the delicate flesh between his fingers. Her whole body seemed to draw in on itself as the vibrating rod continued to stimulate her until a climax crashed over her with such force that, but for the belt and the fact that her breasts were trapped in the holes, she would have reared up off the couch.

To her horror, even while she was climaxing the wand continued to vibrate and, as the last contractions died away, she realised that she was still being stimulated. 'Please take it away,' she cried despairingly.

'Why?' asked James. 'Don't you want to learn to become multi-orgasmic?'

'Just ignore her,' Kate heard Lucinda say dismissively. 'She'll come again in a few seconds, you wait and see.'

Kate was certain the other woman was wrong. Everything felt so tender, painfully sensitive, but Lucinda must have done something to change the rhythm of the wand and the end was now rotating, causing different nerve endings to send rushes of pleasure searing through Kate's body right up to her breasts. To her astonishment she felt all the muscles bunch tightly together once more and this time as she came James squeezed both her nipples so hard that she cried out, but it was with ecstasy and she was amazed it was possible to endure such bliss.

'Better remove the wand now,' said James. 'I think she's more than ready for what we want to do.'

Kate sank down exhausted on the couch. She was used to the darkness, indeed at this moment she was grateful for it because it hid her shame, shame at the extent of her pleasure.

'Since your body's warmed up,' said James, lightly massaging between her shoulder blades with his hand, 'I'm going to introduce you to a new way of getting pleasure.'

Kate couldn't imagine what he meant. She couldn't think that there was anything better than the sensations she'd just experienced, but she lay acquiescent, obedient, waiting to see what he asked of her. 'Get the oil,' he said.

As he rubbed her back he was pressing her down against the couch, occasionally sliding a hand beneath her belly, his fingers kneading at the flesh there. When he pressed against her lower belly, she felt a slight discomfort as though she was too full and strange sensations streaked through her from her bladder. She wriggled, trying to move away from the probing hand but James held her firmly in place. 'Ah,' he said thoughtfully, 'of course you're a little full I suppose. That will only increase the pleasure.'

Kate felt slightly anxious. The feeling wasn't unpleasant but she didn't want it to intensify. 'I could probably make you come just by keeping my hand here,' he said thoughtfully, as his fingers pressed yet more firmly above the pubic bone. All the feelings were centred between Kate's thighs and in her pelvis. She felt hot, tight and heavy and her hips strained to move as he continued the pressure. 'I really think you're going to come,' he said. 'But it would be a pity to waste it. I want you to enjoy a different experience,' and the almost cruel caress stopped abruptly.

Kate exhaled and gave a sigh of relief. The relief was short-lived because as James stroked the base of her spine she felt her buttocks being parted and then a tiny drop of liquid splashed into the cleft at the top between them. This time her overstimulated body jerked and the strap bit more deeply into her waist. 'It's only oil,' said James comfortingly. 'Now that you know, I expect you to keep still until it's all been poured onto you.'

For some reason the instruction was incredibly difficult to obey and Kate knew that Lucinda was taking as long as possible to drop the oil because it seemed an eternity before the shock of each droplet and the peculiar sliding slithering sensation of the oil going between the cheeks of her bottom stopped. 'You did well,' said James.

'Does she know what we're going to do?' Kate heard Lucinda ask.

'I've no idea,' said James. 'Probably not. You're still fairly naive in sexual matters wouldn't you say, Kate?'

Kate was beginning to understand her role. 'I am naive,' she confessed.

James' mouth travelled up and down her spine licking and kissing her. 'You're being wonderfully obedient tonight,' he said softly. 'Don't spoil it now we come to the real test.'

Kate wondered what on earth the real test would be. The oil, slightly warm, was oozing down between the cheeks of her bottom and around the entrance to her vagina. It made her feel heavy and her sex lips puffy and she wriggled slightly. 'She likes that,' remarked Lucinda.

Now Kate felt the cheeks of her bottom parted and then James' fingers were moving between them, and he very gently drew one fingertip in circles around the outside of her rear entrance. Automatically Kate tensed. No one had ever touched her there and she felt that it was wrong, forbidden. Just the same the sensations were sweet and, as his finger moved insistently round and round, she felt the tension growing within her. After a time – as she began to relax in her dark world, taking pleasure from the new sensation – he suddenly slipped one oil-covered fingertip inside her anus and began to run it around the inside.

'Don't!' cried Kate, frantically trying to draw away from him.

'Keep still,' he snapped. 'I told you this would be new but you have to give it a chance. I want you to.'

'It feels funny,' she complained, wishing that he'd stop. It wasn't that it hurt but her body automatically wanted to expel the invading finger. James ignored her plea, in fact if anything the pressure of his finger increased and the highly sensitive walls of her most secret opening began to send their own messages of pleasure to her brain.

After a time Kate was relieved to find that she became used to it and indeed could understand why he'd said it would give her pleasure. 'Introduce another finger,' Lucinda urged James and immediately Kate's body went rigid.

'For goodness' sake relax,' James commanded her. 'Breathe through your mouth or something, your muscles need to be loose.'

'Please don't do this to me,' Kate begged him.

'If you tell me to stop I will,' James promised her, and a heavy silence fell on the room.

Kate didn't know what to say. Her body, unused to this new form of stimulation, was nevertheless aroused. She could tell that a climax was building within her, a climax that she needed because her well-trained flesh was now used to dark satisfaction. If she told him to stop he would but she'd be left stranded, her pleasure not allowed to spill, and suddenly she knew that she had to go forward with him. 'I don't want you to stop,' she whispered.

'Say it more loudly,' commanded James.

Kate swallowed hard. She wished that he wouldn't do this to her, wouldn't keep humiliating her, but it seemed that no matter what she did he was determined to push her further. 'I want you to carry on,' she said clearly.

As soon as she'd finished speaking, James removed his finger and then reinserted it with another by its side, moving the two around the tight little entrance. Now she felt overstretched, but the discomfort was accompanied by a delicious hot pleasure, a totally new kind of pleasure that had her toes curling.

'She'll need to be bigger than that if she's going to take you,' said Lucinda.

Kate couldn't believe her ears. The thought of James actually penetrating her was incredible, terrifying, but somehow she knew that this was what they were aiming for, this was what her education was to be about.

'Pass me the anal butt,' said James and now something smooth and cold took the place of his fingers. It was thick, stretching the walls of her anus wider and she was unable to suppress a tiny whimper, but all the time her flesh was swelling and the insistent pulse beating deep between her thighs was almost driving her out of her mind. 'I think she's nearly ready,' said James after a few minutes. Two small cushions were placed beneath her belly, lifting her bottom higher into the air, and she heard James climb onto the table and felt his legs splayed outside hers as he knelt up.

'You'd better play with her clitoris while I enter her,' he said to Lucinda. 'It will distract her.'

Kate didn't believe that anything could distract her, not as she felt his swollen glans pushing its way inside her and this time she did cry out in protest. 'I asked you before to be quiet,' he said shortly. 'If you can't obey then perhaps we'd better end this session.'

'Say sorry,' Lucinda whispered to Kate and Kate was astonished to hear herself apologising despite the fact that she was terrified. It was a strange kind of fear, a fear that was acting like an aphrodisiac on her. When Lucinda began to stroke softly around her clitoris, rubbing the side of the shaft in the way that Kate loved best, Kate knew that she was willing to do anything to experience this new kind of pleasure.

As Lucinda worked on Kate's vulva, expertly bringing her time and again to the edge of orgasm before stopping her manipulations, so James eased himself gently further and further inside Kate's second opening until finally he was as deep as he could go. His hands gripped Kate's slim hips and he began to move slowly in and out.

Lucinda, clearly well versed in her lover's ways, immediately started to slide two fingers in and out of Kate's vagina in a matching rhythm, while at the same time she continued to manipulate the highly sensitive clitoris. Kate, her eyes covered, was lost in a dark world of incredible sensations. Streaks of pain mingled with the most incredible piercing shards of pleasure. Her nerve endings seemed to be stimulated beyond bearing and her whole body was swollen with passion. She was desperate to climax, to feel that final cataclysmic explosion, and began to gasp as deep within her the first contraction began.

'Any minute now,' Lucinda called and immediately James' thrusting became less gentle. Kate's head was turning helplessly from side to side. Incredibly she wished that there was someone else there, someone who could massage her breasts and lick her aching nipples. Almost as though she was psychic Lucinda withdrew her fingers from inside Kate and moved that hand to her breasts, squeezing lightly on the swollen nipples while at the same time continuing to rub around the clitoris.

'Oh God, I can't bear it,' screamed Kate as the pinpoint of white-hot heat seemed to draw nearer and nearer. 'Hurry! Hurry!'

James' hand slid from her hips to her belly and, just as she thought that it was impossible for the sensations to increase, he let his fingers dig deep into the soft flesh above the pubic mound. Now her full bladder was stimulated as well and the heavy pressure from that combined with all the other stimulation tipped her over the edge and wave after wave of pleasure coursed through her.

She could hear herself moaning, half laughing, half crying and almost unconscious with the intensity of the pleasure. It was like nothing she'd ever experienced before. Both Lucinda and James continued stimulating her until they'd extracted every last ripple of pleasure. Only then did they leave her shattered body alone, leave her shamed and sated on the leather couch.

She was vaguely aware that the strap was being removed from around her waist and that James and Lucinda were easing her breasts out of the confining openings before pulling her off the table and onto her feet once more. 'Stand up straight,' said James abruptly. Kate could hardly obey him. Her limbs felt limp and she didn't know if she had the strength to stand upright. 'Ask my permission to remove the blindfold.'

Even these simple words were enough to start fresh tingles of excitement within Kate's body. 'Please may I remove my blindfold?' she asked obediently.

'Of course,' he said smoothly.

It was almost with regret that she obeyed him because now she had to face them, see their expressions after her display of total abandonment to what was, she knew, a forbidden pleasure. James was looking at her with interest, his head slightly to one side and he seemed pleased. Lucinda, on the other hand, was clearly not pleased. 'That was a revelation,' she remarked.

On an impulse Kate walked towards James, laid her blindfold in his hands and then knelt submissively before him, running her hands down the outside of his trousers. She stayed in that position for several minutes and the atmosphere in the room became electric.

Just as she was about to get to her feet she felt James' hands on her shoulders as he pulled her upright. 'You did so well there's something I want you to wear,' he said huskily, and from his pocket he withdrew a tiny leather choker which he fastened around her neck. 'From now on I want you to wear this,' he said.

Kate welcomed what she knew was a collar of servitude. She was proud of herself, proud of the way her body was learning to take pleasure and of her blossoming sexuality. Above all she was proud of the fact that she hadn't failed when Lucinda had expected her to. 'May I leave the room now?' she asked.

'Yes, but I want you to walk to our bedroom wearing only that,' said James.

Kate knew that only a few days earlier such a thing would have been impossible for her but now she didn't care. She didn't even mind if she saw Mrs Duke on the way. She was lost in this strange new world that James was showing her, enjoying every moment of it. She wanted to be tested further so that she could show him that she would obey, that she would do anything he asked with unquestioning obedience. With her head held high and without a backward glance she left the room, closing the door quietly behind her.

Once in the safety of the bedroom she looked at herself in their mirror. Her hair was tousled, her cheeks flushed, her eyes large and luminous but she knew that she'd never looked more beautiful or felt more fulfilled. All at once she was overwhelmed with exhaustion and slid beneath the duvet cover, wearing only the collar so recently placed on her. Her last thought before she fell asleep was of James and the look on his face when she'd removed her blindfold.

'Mrs Duke seems rather busy this morning,' remarked Kate to James over breakfast. 'She's got some help too. There's a young girl working in Lucinda's half of the house who I've never seen before.'

'She comes from the village,' explained James. 'Mrs Duke will need some help over the next few days.'

'Why?' asked Kate.

James glanced at her in apparent surprise. 'Didn't I tell you? We've got visitors coming.'

Kate couldn't have been more surprised if he'd told her the Martians had landed. 'Visitors? Isn't it enough that Lucinda's here with us? This is still meant to be our honeymoon, James. I thought things were going really well between us.'

'Allan's an old friend of mine,' said James. 'He rang to let me know he's over from America for a few days. We always meet up when we can, so naturally I invited him down.'

'Didn't you explain that you'd only just got married?' asked Kate. 'I'm sure he wouldn't have expected to see you if you'd told him that.'

'I did tell him,' James assured her. 'He's looking forward to meeting you.'

'You said visitors, plural. Who's coming with him?'

'His latest girlfriend I imagine. Their names change but they usually look the same.'

'How old is this Allan?'

James frowned. 'I'm not sure. A few years older than me, about thirty-three or thirty-four I suppose. He's great fun. I know you'll like him.'

Kate wasn't so sure. She was beginning to think that she and James didn't share the same tastes when it came to friends. 'How do you usually entertain him when he comes to stay?'

'Don't worry about that, he's a very easy guest,' replied James. 'He'll go along with anything I suggest. I thought it would be nice for you to meet some friends of mine. We can't live in total isolation.'

Kate shook her head. 'Sometimes I don't think I know you at all,' she said slowly. 'Of course I don't expect us to spend our lives in isolation but I did expect our honeymoon to be spent alone.'

'Well, I want Allan and his partner to come and stay and that's the end of it,' said James firmly. 'They'll be arriving for lunch, in case you're interested.'

'Should I wear something special?'

James flicked his dark eyes over her. 'That dress is fine,' he said at last. 'It clings to your body very nicely. Allan will like it.'

'I'm not interested in what Allan will think of it,' snapped Kate. 'I dress to please you or myself, not some stranger.'

James put his elbows on the table and rested his chin on his clasped hands. 'There's something you ought to understand, Kate. I want you to be nice to Allan. I want him to like you. I always like his girlfriends so it's important that he likes my wife.'

Kate felt the muscles of her stomach flutter. 'You can't force people to like each other,' she said weakly.

'That's not what I mean,' said James. 'So far you've done very well when it comes to obeying me but over the last couple of days I've been rather lax. I think it's time I tested you further and I shall use Allan's visit as an opportunity to do just that.'

Kate's mouth went dry. 'I hope you don't mean what I think you mean.'

'I mean precisely what I say. Once Allan is here I want you

to please him. Right now I've no idea what that will involve. It might be anything from taking him down to the beach and showing him our cave to showing him a great deal more. What's important is that you don't make a fuss in front of him.'

'Does he know about this obedience game?' Kate asked.

'I didn't tell him about it over the phone if that's what you mean but no doubt he'll work it out for himself. Despite his surface appearance Allan is a very shrewd man.'

Kate got up from the table. 'I'm going to check that Mrs Duke's getting on all right,' she muttered before fleeing the room.

Once upstairs she went into one of the spare bedrooms and sat in the bay window, her hot cheek pressed against the window pane. She did understand James very well and the realisation that she was now going to be expected to demonstrate her sensuality in front of his friend was terrifying. She wondered what the man was like, what kind of a man he could be. She wished that she had the courage to walk away, or at least pick up the phone and ask Vicky to come and collect her. But it wasn't just a question of courage she realised. The truth was, James held her in his dark sexual spell. She, or perhaps more accurately her body, was obsessed with him. The incredible pleasure, the heights of ecstasy that he brought her to, were addictive and at this very moment she was becoming aroused by the prospect of further erotic discoveries. 'Don't be a hypocrite,' she muttered to herself. 'No one's making you do this, you're choosing to.'

It was true, but a lot of it was because of her love for James and her desire to show him that she really had meant what she said and that her one aim in life was to make him happy. She knew he needed that reassurance, that his lack of belief in himself both as a writer and a person was something that she could cure. If she managed that then he would be free to write the book of his dreams and together they'd form a wonderful partnership.

'I'm sorry,' exclaimed Mrs Duke, coming into the room. 'I

have to make the bed up in here.'

Kate turned her head. 'That's all right, Mrs Duke. I was just leaving. Tell me,' she added as she walked past the housekeeper, 'what's this Allan like?'

'Very American,' said Mrs Duke.

'Meaning what?'

Mrs Duke shrugged. 'There's nothing more to say, Mrs Lewis. When you meet him you'll know what I mean.'

'At least I haven't long to wait,' said Kate.

'No indeed,' said Mrs Duke, bustling around the room. 'He and Mr Lewis go back a long way.'

'What about my husband and Lucinda?' asked Kate tentatively.

Mrs Duke gave her a swift glance and then looked away again. 'I'm sure your husband can tell you much more about that than I can,' she said.

'Of course,' agreed Kate, feeling slightly ashamed that she'd tried to gain information from a loyal retainer.

The next few hours seemed interminable. James had vanished into his study locking the door behind him and Lucinda was nowhere to be found, which meant that Kate had nothing to do to take her mind off the forthcoming visit. In the end, taking her courage in both hands, she made her way down the tricky cliff path and onto the beach. She always felt soothed by the sound of the surf breaking on the sand and for a long time she walked up and down the beach trying to compose herself. She even went into the cave where she and James had coupled so swiftly and urgently and ran her hand over the out-hanging slate that they'd used as a makeshift bed. She smiled to herself at the memories but the smile faded when she remembered the visitors.

Finally she glanced at her watch and saw it was one o'clock. Either Allan would have arrived by now or he should be there within the next half hour. Knowing that James would expect her to be at his side to greet his friend, she almost ran back up the path, skidding on the loose stones, and then rushed across

85

the front lawn. James was standing by the front door, one hand above his eyes, shading them from the glare of the sun as he watched her approach. 'Where on earth have you been?' he asked irritably.

'Down on the beach. I knew you'd be working for some time and I love it there.'

'It's lucky you came up when you did,' he said shortly. 'I can see Allan's car now.'

Kate waited next to her husband as a low-slung red sports car was driven at high speed through the gates of Penrick Lodge and up the drive before screeching to a halt just in front of them. 'Who does he think he is, Damon Hill?' she asked.

James smiled. 'Allan does everything at high speed.'

Despite her reservations about what was going to happen, Kate realised that she was interested in getting her first glimpse of the American. The driver's door was flung open and a pair of tanned leather ankle-length boots appeared, swiftly followed by one of the biggest men she'd ever seen. He was tall, taller even than James, but what made him look so big was the huge breadth of shoulder. He looked, she thought, like an American footballer and she was very aware of a pair of piercing blue eyes gazing at her with interest.

'Hi, you must be Kate,' he said, stretching out an enormous hand and almost crushing hers in a handshake. 'Nice to see James went for class in the end.'

Kate heard a sharp intake of breath and realised that Lucinda was standing with them. She wanted to giggle because clearly Lucinda took this as an insult to herself. 'You're still here then, Lucinda?' Allan continued, running his fingers through his thick but short-cut blond hair. 'Great, I hoped you would be because I know you and Pam will get on just fine. Pammie come and meet my friend James and his beautiful young wife.'

The girl who got out of the passenger side of the car was as tiny as Allan was large. She was blonde too, with long sun-bleached hair but she only seemed to come up to Allan's waist. When she smiled it was obvious that she was an American.

Kate wondered why it was that Americans had so many perfect teeth.

'Real pleased to meet you,' said Pam enthusiastically. 'Allan's been telling me so much about you, James,' she continued, fixing James with her china-blue eyes.

'All good things I hope,' said James with a smile.

'Sure, great things.'

Allan gave a knowing smile before flinging his arms round Lucinda in what looked like a bone-crushing bear hug. Kate was grateful that he hadn't done the same to her.

'Cute as ever, Lucinda,' he said. 'So what are you going to do with yourself now James here has gotten married?'

'He still needs an agent,' pointed out Lucinda briskly.

'Yeah, but I don't suppose you have to carry out quite so many services for him?' Then, with a loud laugh, Allan Harkness strolled into the house leaving Kate feeling tired already.

'What do you think?' James asked her.

'He's certainly friendly,' said Kate.

James nodded. 'Indeed he is. He's a great guy. We get on really well together. I want you to like him, Kate.'

'Is there any reason why I shouldn't?' murmured Kate.

James shook his head. 'None at all. All the ladies love Allan.'

'Lucinda didn't seem bowled over.'

James shrugged. 'Lucinda doesn't think Allan likes her. She's always on the defensive when he's around.'

'Is she right?'

'No. At least, if she is Allan's never said anything about it to me. She's probably not his type but he gets on with everyone.'

Lunch was a boisterous affair with James and Allan discussing people and places that Kate knew nothing about. Occasionally Lucinda would join in but Pam seemed quite content to eat her food and laugh at the odd joke. Kate wondered why it was that she felt so excluded. She supposed it was because she was meant to be on her honeymoon and now this large boisterous American had arrived and was taking all James' attention away from her.

In the afternoon Allan pleaded jet lag and whisked Pam up to their bedroom, although from the look in his eye Kate didn't feel that the pair of them were going to sleep very much. She and James went down to the beach for a swim while Lucinda sunbathed in the back garden. At six o'clock James and Kate went to their bedroom to get washed and dressed for dinner. 'I don't know what to wear,' complained Kate, searching through the dresses hanging in the wardrobe.

'I've bought something for you especially for tonight,' said James.

Kate was astonished. It wasn't the sort of thing James ever did. 'When did you get it? What's it like?' she asked excitedly.

'Here, open the box and see,' said James with a smile, handing her a square cardboard box.

Opening it, Kate carefully parted the layers of tissue paper but when she withdrew the cream satin creation she stared at it in surprise. 'It's not a dress, it's a slip,' she protested.

'Nonsense, it's a beautiful satin dress and I want you to wear it.'

'I can't go to dinner dressed like this,' exclaimed Kate. 'They'll think I'm wearing my slip.'

'They won't think anything of the sort. I'm sure Allan will think it's beautiful,' said James. 'Come along, Kate, it's time to make me happy again.'

Kate slipped the cream satin chemise over her head. The material was soft and velvety against her skin, sumptuously finished with a plunging lace breast panel and she realised that it made her look very sexy. 'Do you really want me to go down and eat dinner wearing only this?' she asked weakly.

'Not exactly,' said James. 'But I do want you to wear it. Do your hair and face and then stand in the corner until I'm ready to go down with you.'

For the first time in several days Kate experienced the strange erotic charge that obeying James now brought her eager body. She tried to imagine the expression on Allan's face when he saw her and how the other two women would react, but it was impossible. Why, she wondered, was she going through with this? Why didn't she simply refuse to obey? The truth was, she couldn't. She needed to know what was going to happen and she wanted pleasuring again, the kind of pleasuring that she'd had during the first days of her marriage.

She and James were the first to arrive in the dining room where the table was beautifully set with a white Damask tablecloth, the best crystal glasses and silver cutlery. There was a beautiful floral arrangement in the middle of the table and bright-red napkins in the shape of fans were standing in the wine glasses.

'Mrs Duke's done a good job,' said James. 'I want you to stand over there, Kate.' He pointed to the far end of the table and Kate, who at the last minute had been ordered to slip on a pair of high-heeled cream shoes, walked self-consciously in the direction he'd indicated. 'A little further back,' he continued. 'Not quite up to the wall, about a foot away from it. Yes that's perfect.'

Kate stared at him. She felt ridiculous standing in his elegant dining room wearing what amounted to nothing more than a cream shift and high-heeled shoes, but before she could say anything the door opened and Lucinda came in. 'Is she to stand there all through the meal?' she asked.

'Until I decide she can join us,' said James.

'But I'm hungry,' said Kate.

'I don't remember asking you to speak,' snapped James.

Kate hung her head in shame. It was surprising how much she'd forgotten in the past two days. Just as she raised her head, Allan and Pam joined them, Allan resplendent in a dinner jacket and bow tie, Pam in an elegant ankle-length dress.

'Do sit down,' said James. 'Allan, I thought you might like to get to know Kate better before we eat.'

Kate knew, without being told, that she had to keep her head erect and her eyes remained fixed on the large American as he advanced towards her. At first sight she'd thought his piercing blue eyes were cold, but now she realised that there was both warmth and humour in them, and also admiration. 'I love blondes,' he said with a smile, his large hands slipping the straps off her shoulders and down towards her elbows. 'English blondes are the best. You look so cool and remote it makes the passion all the more exciting.'

Kate didn't reply. She didn't dare say anything because James was watching her narrowly. 'Go ahead, examine her,' he said.

Allan's hands were now peeling the plunging top of the chemise away from Kate's small rounded breasts and while he continued to look into her eyes his fingers began to move in circles around each of her breasts.

She was so tense, so embarrassed by what was happening that at first her body failed to respond, but as he continued with the same rhythm, neither fast nor slow but steady and delicate, she felt the first ripples of pleasure begin. Her nipples turned pink and hardened until she longed for them to be touched, but Allan merely continued circling her breasts and now she could feel the ripples of pleasure between her thighs as well. It was as though his hands were there, gently circling her clitoris at the same time.

Without realising it her hips moved slightly and Allan gave a low laugh. 'You're responsive. I like that, honey.'

Kate still didn't reply. 'You should answer Allan when he speaks to you,' said James, sounding cross.

'I guess she didn't know what to say,' remarked Allan. 'But you do like it, don't you, Kate?'

'It feels good,' Kate admitted quietly.

Everyone else was seated at the table and to Kate's horror, at that moment, Mrs Duke and the village girl came into the room. Allan simply made sure that he was standing in front of her, protecting her from their gaze, his hands slipping to her shoulders for a moment as though the pair of them were engaged in conversation. As soon as the pair had left the room his fingers resumed their tantalising arousal of her burgeoning flesh and she whimpered softly with growing need.

'Do you think you can come just through this?' he asked her.

Kate shook her head. 'No,' she said miserably. 'I need more.'

'Pity,' he said with a charming smile and then he turned away from her and sat down at the table. Kate was forced to remain where she was, waiting for some instruction from James before she moved, but it seemed that she'd become invisible. The other four ate their melon and talked of everyday things while she remained semi-naked, her breasts exposed to their view and her belly beginning to cramp with desire.

When the second course was served, Allan again stood in front of her and she wondered what on earth Mrs Duke must think was going on, but then she guessed that Mrs Duke made it her business not to get involved and assumed that the village girl was also used to James' ways.

'I think you ought to have a little treat as you're not eating yet,' said Allan, gently cupping her right breast. As his finger touched the rigid point of her nipple, flashes of pleasure streaked through her and she gasped. 'Almost there now,' he said encouragingly and she knew that he was right. Every nerve ending was screaming for release, all it needed was some tiny trigger, some direct stimulation on her nipple or between her thighs and then her pleasure would spill.

'Keep looking into my eyes,' said the American and she did, almost hypnotised by them. 'Great,' he murmured, his voice deep and dark, and immediately his fingers pinched the skin to the side of her nipple, tugging at it so that the whole area was moved while his spare hand gripped her other breast and squeezed rhythmically, almost as though it were an exercise ball.

The extraordinary combination of sensations in the two breasts was enough. Kate felt her belly swell and tighten and then the delicious heat rushed through her and she gasped, her eyes widening and colour flaming in her upper throat and cheeks. 'Interesting,' said Allan thoughtfully. 'I can think of some nice games to play with you, honey.'

With that he returned to the table and began to eat his main course. Kate couldn't believe that she was still going to have to stand there but James never even glanced in her direction. It wasn't until the whole meal was over that he finally turned his head and spoke to her.

'You can eat later,' he explained. 'Right now I'm giving you to Allan as an after-dinner treat.'

Kate's eyes filled with tears. She couldn't believe he was going to do this to her, to simply hand her over to another man as though she didn't matter to him in the least. 'Don't you see, it's because you're special to me,' he said gently. 'Allan's my friend, I want him to share you, perhaps I even want to make him jealous.'

'I'm jealous already,' said Allan with a smile. 'Don't look so miserable, Kate, we're gonna have a great time. You're my kind of girl.'

'Off you go then,' said James briskly. 'Allan will bring you back to me when he's finished, won't you, Allan?'

'Sure,' said the American easily and then he was putting one powerful arm around Kate and ushering her out of the room. He guided her up the stairs, stopping at one stage to wipe a tear from her face. 'Hey, don't cry, that's not much of a compliment. Like I said you're going to have a good time. James is a lucky guy to have found a wife who shares his enthusiasm for this kind of thing. I sure wish I could.'

Kate wanted to tell him that she hadn't known, that nothing had been explained to her, but she didn't. She didn't partly because she didn't want to let James down and partly because, surprisingly, she wanted the American to believe that she was like the rest of them. It was peculiar, but in those few intimate moments together in the dining room she'd felt more genuine warmth from him than she'd felt from James in all the weeks she'd known him and this confused her.

'Here we are,' said Allan, pushing open his bedroom door. 'The first thing we're going to do is take a hot tub together.'

Chapter 5

Allan Harkness was intrigued. When he and Pam had been invited to Penrick Lodge he'd assumed that it was to celebrate James' marriage. In a way he'd been disappointed because he, Lucinda, James and various other women had had some very exciting times over the past three years. Mostly they'd met up in London for weekend parties where complex sexual games had been played out, games which Allan had greatly enjoyed. He'd been surprised to hear James describe him as a close friend in the dining room earlier that evening because that wasn't the way Allan considered himself. He was a friend certainly, but not a close one. In some ways the two men were totally different. Allan liked women, whereas he suspected that James – like many Englishmen – did not.

The one thing Allan hadn't expected during this visit was to be offered James' new wife on the first evening. Not that he was objecting, she was incredibly attractive and far classier than most of James' girlfriends had been, but it still seemed extraordinary. He knew that if he was married to her he wouldn't spend his honeymoon sharing her around among friends. Also, it was clear there was a hidden agenda here. Kate wasn't like the other women who Allan had met through James. It didn't seem to him that she was used to this kind of thing and he wondered exactly what was going on.

Even now she was standing with childlike docility in the middle of the bedroom, clearly awaiting some command or other. He moved closer to her, his large hands stroking the tops of her arms. 'What's that round your neck?' he asked curiously.

Kate looked even more uncomfortable. 'James put it on me,' she explained.

'I see,' said Allan thoughtfully and he did. He wondered if Kate was a natural submissive, if so then that explained everything but his intuition told him that wasn't the truth. Certainly she was playing the game well, but not like someone well versed in the practise. The strange thing was that James had never before shown a desire to have a totally submissive woman. They'd enjoyed all manner of sexual games during their meetings but it had never seemed to him that James was obsessed with dominating women.

'I don't think you have to wear it when you're with me,' he remarked, putting a hand behind her slim neck and unfastening it.

'It's not meant to come off,' exclaimed Kate.

'When you're with me it comes off,' he said firmly. 'You're pretty new to all this, aren't you?' he added.

Kate stared at him. 'We've only been married just over a week.'

Allan shook his head. 'That's not what I meant and you know it, honey.'

She opened her mouth as though to speak and then closed it again. Allan frowned. There was something much deeper going on here than he'd imagined and before he left he was determined to get to the bottom of it. Vastly experienced in the ways of women, he could tell a sexually sophisticated one when he met her and Kate wasn't such a girl. Nevertheless, she was extremely sensual and since James wanted Allan to enjoy her then he intended to make the most of the invitation.

'Let's get that hot tub run,' he remarked, striding through the bedroom and down the two steps that led to the luxurious en-suite bathroom, aware that Kate was following obediently behind him.

The bath was large and sunken, it took some time for it to fill and while the water was running Allan carefully eased the satin chemise over Kate's head. When he touched her breasts he heard her catch her breath and smiled. 'Kind of sensitive there, aren't you?'

Kate nodded. 'I liked what you did downstairs tonight,' she said hesitantly.

'Good,' said Allan, who enjoyed giving women pleasure. Once more he began to circle her breasts with his fingers, watching them react, the veins showing more prominently and the nipples hardening. Pausing only to turn off the taps, he then sucked lightly on each peak in turn, drawing them tenderly into his mouth and caressing them with the tip of his tongue. As he aroused her she began to tremble and he put his hands on each side of her waist, his fingers splayed out, enjoying the feel of her soft skin. He fully expected her to climax quickly and was surprised when she didn't. Pausing for a moment he looked thoughtfully at her. 'Is there something else you'd like me to do?' he asked.

Kate looked astonished. Obviously she wasn't used to such a question. 'No,' she said quickly.

'But you didn't come.'

'I didn't know if I was allowed to,' she whispered.

Allan raised his eyebrows. 'You have to have permission, huh? I guess I'm not up on the rules of this game. James must have changed since our last meeting. This is how you get your kicks too, is it, Kate?'

'He's my husband,' explained Kate. 'I want to make him happy.'

Allan mentally filed her answer away. Plainly it wasn't the way she got her pleasure but it was the way she was being taught to, which was an entirely different matter. 'When you're with me you can come as often as you like,' he assured her, his fingers resuming their caress. As his mouth fastened round her nipples once more, he felt the muscles of her belly tighten and then she trembled violently as a climax seized her.

'There, that was easy, wasn't it? Let's have some fun in the bath now.' He was intrigued that Kate didn't attempt to climb into the bath herself but instead waited docilely for him either to issue an instruction or put her in himself. Despite her height she weighed very little and it was easy for a man of his size to scoop her up and place her in the tub. He'd poured in bubble bath mixture before turning on the taps and the suds came up to the tops of her breasts, so that when he slid his hands beneath the water he was able to slide them easily over her slippery flesh.

Taking a large natural sponge from the side, he proceeded to wash every inch of her carefully and saw how her skin turned a delicate shade of pink as he worked his way upwards from her feet. When he washed the backs of her knees and slid the sponge high up her inner thighs she wriggled sensuously but then looked anxiously at him, clearly feeling guilty at her response.

'Relax and enjoy it, that's why you're here,' he reminded her. 'I expect James has other things planned for later on but right now just make the most of it all.'

He was pleased that she seemed to trust him because soon her body was relaxed. When he unhooked the shower head from the wall and allowed the spray to play on her upper body, her head fell back and her eyes closed as she wallowed in the sensations. Putting a hand beneath her, he lifted her upwards until the flesh of her belly was exposed and he then played the spray over that, watching her flesh leap and jerk. Instinctively she parted her thighs, allowing him access to her most vulnerable part so that now he could let the spray play there.

'Open yourself up for me,' he urged her. 'I don't have a free hand.'

He was pleased that she obeyed with alacrity, and it was obvious from the way her body was twisting and turning in the water that another climax was near. Despite her need, her fingers were hesitant and he felt a surge of tenderness towards her as she awkwardly opened herself up for him until he could see the tiny swelling that was so vital to giving her the ultimate pleasure.

'Let it come now,' he urged her, moving the head of the

spray close to her vulva. As the spray fell on the exposed nub of pleasure, Kate moaned and then cried out as her whole body spasmed with the delicious sweetness of fulfilment.

By now Allan was very aroused. Gently easing Kate back into the water, he stripped off his clothes, tearing off his black jacket and crisp white shirt with a total disregard to the popping buttons, until finally he stood naked beside her. He saw her eyes move to his erection and heard her gasp, it was a reaction he was used to but which still gave him pleasure. 'Mind if I join you?' he asked with a laugh.

For the first time since he'd met her Kate gave a genuine smile. 'I'd like that,' she said shyly.

It was lucky, thought Allan, that the tub was large enough to take them both. Even so, it was quite difficult for him to get her positioned so that he could actually penetrate her, and at first he contented himself with pulling her between his legs so that her back rested against his broad chest while his hands continually stroked and caressed her. He knew that she must be able to feel his erection pressing hard between her buttocks and once or twice she wriggled slightly, which only increased his desire.

'I can't wait any longer,' he confessed at last. 'Do you think you can rest your arms against the far end of the bath and kneel up for me?'

Kate swiftly readjusted her position and then it was easy for him to kneel between her calves, his hands reaching round beneath the water to fondle and stroke her belly and pubic mound as his penis thrust between her buttocks, searching blindly for the elusive opening that he needed so desperately. Much to his delight Kate suddenly reached between her legs and with her fingernails she lightly teased the tip of his glans so that for one moment he was afraid he was going to come without actually entering her.

'Guide me in, honey,' he urged her and she needed no second bidding. All at once he felt himself enveloped by the soft velvet warmth of her. Once he was inside he was amazed at how tight and virginal she felt, and he knew that he wasn't going to last very long.

Quickly his fingers located her clitoris, still slippery from the bubbles in the bath and, using the pad of one finger, he tapped very softly around the area surrounding it. Her whole body stiffened and immediately he thrust hard, ramming so deeply into her that he felt himself brush against her cervix and now Kate was frantic with excitement too, begging him not to stop.

Allan wanted it to last forever, to remain enclosed in that tight comforting warmth and to hear her cries of delight and excitement, but despite his years of practise this was one time when self-control proved elusive. The moment Kate's body spasmed, he felt her pelvic muscles tighten around him and with a cry of dismay he spilled himself into her.

When the last blissful tingles of his climax had died away, Allan wrapped his arms around the still kneeling kate, pulling her hard against him and nibbling the side of her neck. 'You're fantastic,' he said. 'James must be mad to lend you out. Was it good for you too?'

Kate nodded. 'It's never been . . .' She stopped and Allan guessed that she was afraid of letting James down. 'It was incredible,' she admitted.

Realising that the water was growing cold, Allan reluctantly climbed out of the bath and then lifted Kate onto the floor next to him, wrapping them both in the large soft towels hanging on the rail. 'Tell me about yourself' he urged her. 'How did you come to meet James?'

'We met in a nightclub,' said a voice from the bathroom doorway.

Turning his head Allan saw James standing there. 'I don't remember inviting you in,' he said.

'But Kate's my wife and this is my house. Anyway, you didn't lock the door.'

'I didn't think I needed to,' said Allan, hearing the edge to his voice but unable to hide it.

'Did you have a nice bath, Kate?' James asked his wife.

Kate's face was expressionless now. 'Very nice thank you,' she said flatly.

'Good. Then you'll be nice and clean for us all, won't you?'

'What do you mean?' asked Kate nervously, while Allan watched the pair of them with interest.

'Pam wants to come to bed now,' explained James. 'So we're going to have to take you away from Allan just for the moment. Don't worry though, Lucinda and I are both very anxious for your company.'

'You mean you're having a threesome without letting me watch?' asked Allan.

'I didn't think you'd be interested,' said James.

'Yeah I'm interested,' said Allan laconically. 'The night's young. If Pam really does want to sleep then she can, if not she and I can both watch, can't we?'

He was pleased to see that James looked annoyed. 'You're the guest,' he said at last. 'But I'm not sure that Kate . . .'

'Does what Kate wants count for anything?' asked Allan. 'Surely you're in charge?'

He'd said the right thing and he knew it. James nodded. 'Of course I'm in charge. If that's what you want then that's what will happen.'

'Not straight away,' whispered Kate.

'Don't tell me Allan's worn you out in that short time,' snapped James.

'It's the thought of so many people being around,' said Kate.

'You'll soon forget we're there,' Allan assured her, putting a comforting hand in the middle of her back. 'I'm interested in seeing what James is like as a married man, that's all.'

'We'll expect you and Pam in our room in about half an hour then,' said James. He glanced at his wife. 'Hurry up and get dry. I want you in our room as soon as possible.'

Once James had gone Allan felt a sense of deep satisfaction. This would give him a chance to see what was really happening, what kind of game James was playing and why. 'I take it

99

Lucinda's been here for most of your honeymoon?' he asked Kate.

'She was here from the first night,' she confessed.

'Were you expecting that?'

'Of course not!'

'You didn't know James that well, did you?' he persisted.

'Clearly not as well as you know him,' said Kate.

Allan laughed. 'You're right there. Nothing James does surprises me, except getting married that is. He's the last man on earth I expected to do that. Now me, I make a habit of it. Admittedly it never lasts but I enjoy having a wife. James has never wanted one, in fact he always said that if he ever talked about getting married we were to do our best to dissuade him. Obviously there's something very special about you that made him change his mind.'

'Yes,' murmured Kate.

'So he's madly in love with you, is he?' persisted Allan.

'Of course,' said Kate weakly, but Allan knew that she didn't even expect him to believe it.

He patted her on the bottom. 'Off you go, honey. Your husband and his mistress await you. Don't be shy about what happens,' he added. 'Whatever it is, it's not going to shock me.'

'When will he be happy?' she asked suddenly. 'When's it going to end?'

'If you don't like it, leave him,' suggested Allan.

'That's the trouble,' she admitted quietly. 'I like it too much.'

When Kate joined James in their own bedroom she felt thoroughly confused. She couldn't understand why it was that sex with a virtual stranger, Allan Harkness, had seemed to be more genuine and caring than sex with her own husband. She was also alarmed to realise that she liked the American. Despite his rather overpowering size and personality there was a warmth and genuineness about him that was totally lacking in her husband. It wasn't that she loved him, she knew that, but he'd made her feel good about herself, something that James never did. Also, her climaxes with him had been good, deeply satisfying, and it had shown her that she didn't necessarily need the darker eroticism that James provided.

Nevertheless, she enjoyed it and her heartbeat quickened when she found James waiting for her. The realisation that she would again be tested, expected to obey, was rearousing her and she wondered why she'd never known before her marriage what a deeply sensual person she really was.

'You're looking rather pleased with yourself,' said James.

Kate tried to keep her expression neutral. 'I don't feel pleased with myself' she said quietly.

'What was Allan like as a lover?' he asked curiously. 'Most women seem to like him.'

'He was all right,' said Kate circumspectly.

'All right? Talk about damning him with faint praise. He did manage to make you come did he?'

Kate nodded. 'Yes.'

'So tell me what he did to you.'

'Nothing very special. We had a bath together and he used the shower head to bring me to orgasm before actually having sex with me.'

'I agree that doesn't sound very thrilling,' said James. 'I'm sure you'll enjoy the rest of the night better.'

Kate realised that despite his words he was still anxious, still suspicious that she'd enjoyed Allan too much. 'He has loads of women you know,' James continued. 'He makes them all feel special but he discards them very quickly. He's got through four wives already.'

'I didn't know that,' said Kate quietly. 'But it really doesn't interest me.'

'Good,' said James. 'Now take off that chemise. I want to see if he marked you at all.'

'Marked me?'

'Yes, with his mouth or his fingers. After all, he's a big man.'

Kate stood silently, naked once more as James examined

her from head to toe. 'There's a small bruise here,' he said at last, his fingertips touching the underside of one breast. 'I don't like having my wife marked by another man.' With that he bent his head and his teeth nipped sharply on the exact spot where the bruise was. Kate squealed in protest. 'Now my mark's over his,' said James with satisfaction. 'Stand there a moment, Lucinda should be here any second.'

No sooner had he spoken than Lucinda tapped on the door and entered. 'Have you told her what we're going to do?' she asked.

'Not yet,' admitted James and Kate glanced fearfully at him and his mistress. 'Allan's coming to watch us,' he explained to Lucinda. 'I don't know if Pam's coming with him or not.'

'He'll probably make sure she comes with him,' laughed Lucinda. 'I seem to remember he's very good at simultaneous orgasms. Did he manage it with you, Kate?'

'Tell the truth Kate,' James ordered her.

She didn't want to. She knew that James would resent it but it was impossible to disobey. 'Yes,' she muttered.

'Speak up,' said James.

'Yes,' she said raising her voice.

'He's a very good lover,' mused Lucinda. 'I was talking to Pam downstairs and she says he wears her out. I don't know where he gets his energy from. You'd think it would take him all his time to run his business empire. Did you know he was a millionaire, Kate?'

Kate shook her head. 'Money doesn't interest me.'

'It would do if you'd ever been short of it,' said James.

'I suppose so,' admitted Kate, wondering how he knew.

'Tell her about the game,' Lucinda reminded him.

'Ah yes, the game. Lucinda and I are going to make love to you for the next half hour, Kate. We've decided that in that time you can have two orgasms. You can have them whenever you like, one early on and one at the end, one in the middle and one at the end or save them both for the end but what you mustn't do is exceed the total.'

'What happens if I do?' she asked anxiously.

'Then I'm afraid you'll have to be punished,' said James. 'You haven't been punished yet but Lucinda's very good at administering discipline.'

Kate imagined that she was. She also knew that Lucinda would like nothing better than an opportunity to punish her. 'I don't know how I'm going to stop myself from coming more than twice,' she said plaintively. 'You're both so clever, you know how to arouse me, what am I meant to do?'

'I thought you'd learnt enough self-discipline for this now,' said James curtly. 'It will be exciting for you to have Allan watching, won't it? It should add a little frisson of extra eroticism to the whole thing.'

Kate was horrified. She realised that it was true, that the knowledge that she was being watched might make her more likely to come and, as Lucinda led her to the bed and James refastened the collar of servitude around her throat, she heard the door open and saw both Allan and Pam come into the room. 'Since we're all here we may as well begin,' said James, taking off his clothes. He explained the rules of the game to Allan who gave a deep laugh.

'I'll time you,' he said.

'Thanks and give us five minutes warning before the half hour's up will you?' James asked. 'That way Kate will know she hasn't got to hold on very long or, if she's still got a climax in hand, she'll know she can come.'

'I shouldn't think she'll have one to spare,' said Allan. 'She certainly wouldn't have if I was on the bed with her.'

Kate saw James dart a swift look of what was almost dislike at his supposed friend and then her body was sandwiched between him and Lucinda and the half hour began.

Kate was vaguely aware that the bedside table was cluttered with bottles and objects that she hadn't seen there before, but she didn't have time to work out what they were before her back was pulled against James' chest and he hooked his feet around her ankles while his arms imprisoned her across the hips. This meant that Lucinda was free to work on Kate's upper body and, taking a tube from the bedside table, she started to spread lotion over Kate's highly sensitive breasts.

Kate's first surprise was that the lotion didn't feel cold, in fact it felt slightly warm. Then, as Lucinda massaged it firmly over the whole area of the breasts before spreading it across the areolae and nipples, it became even warmer. The feeling was sensuous, delightful, and Kate wriggled with pleasure.

'Blow on it,' James told Lucinda, his hands beginning to massage Kate's stomach, now and again moving to the thin skin over her hips which he tickled with the lightest of touches, sending spirals of excitement through her. Lucinda did as he said and the gentle warmth became a heat, a strange deep throbbing heat that sent pulses of pleasure right through the centre of Kate's breasts, down between her ribcage and into the belly being so insidiously massaged by her husband.

She could feel a pulse beating between her thighs and knew that a climax was starting to build. Frantically she tried to subdue it, to think of other things and not concentrate on the pleasure that was being administered. 'Give some to me,' said James. 'I'll spread it over her belly as well.'

'No please don't,' protested Kate. 'It's too good.'

'But we want to give you pleasure,' said James. 'That's why we're here.'

'Not yet, I mustn't come yet,' she cried.

'You can if you like,' said James. 'It simply means you'll have to wait a long time before the next climax. Besides, your body must be feeling very ready now. I can tell your pleasure's about to spill.'

She wished that he wouldn't talk to her like that, wouldn't arouse her with his words as well as his hands. When he started to spread the lotion across her already tight belly she groaned with despair as the incredible warmth suffused her lower body as well. Now the tingles were spreading between her thighs and her body started to wriggle, the cheeks of her bottom rubbing against James' hip bones.

To her surprise Lucinda slid down the bed and then, realising with horror what was about to happen, Kate cried out once more. 'Don't do that, not yet,' she whimpered. As she cried out she saw Allan standing at the foot of the bed, watching her intently, his piercing blue eyes assessing every movement of her frantic body.

The heat seemed to be everywhere. Deep within her pelvis, spreading through all the tissue, making her breasts swell and glow. When Lucinda parted her sex lips and almost lazily touched the hard straining clitoris with the tip of her tongue Kate's body exploded and she was forced to give herself up to the sharp contractions of her first climax.

'How long did that take?' James asked, as her body continued to twist and turn against him.

'Eight minutes,' said Allan.

'You'll certainly need your self-control now,' James continued. 'We'd better wash this off you.' Lucinda hastily fetched a damp sponge and wiped Kate's body clean, but even this innocent caress started to arouse her nerve endings again and she looked down to the end of the bed where the American was standing. Her eyes locked with his and she knew, from the expression on his face, that he understood how despairing she felt and how ashamed she was of the easy way her body succumbed to pleasure.

James propped himself into a semi-upright position with his legs parted and his feet flat on the bed. He was very aroused and, as Lucinda pulled Kate up the bed and forced her to kneel up above the purple glans, Kate realised that she actually wanted James. She wanted to feel him inside her, sliding in and out, filling the aching void that, despite her climax, was still torturing her.

'Lower yourself onto him and then lift yourself up and down,' Lucinda ordered her. 'Move slowly at first and then more quickly, I'll tell you when you can stop.'

Once more Kate obeyed. As she lowered herself onto her husband's shaft she realised that the angle he was at meant that every time she rose and fell he was stimulating her G-spot, which triggered a sweet pleasure that grew and grew with every movement she made.

For what seemed endless minutes Kate obediently rose and fell to the rhythm dictated by Lucinda, and all the time her breathing grew more and more rapid and perspiration beaded her upper lip and breasts. 'You want to come, don't you?' whispered Lucinda. 'Why don't you let yourself? Give yourself over to the pleasure.'

'Don't listen to her,' said James. 'I want to see how well you can control yourself. However good it feels you mustn't come again so quickly.'

Kate knew that he was right, knew that if she did there was no way she'd manage to last the rest of the half hour without a third climax, but she was finding it impossible to stop the wicked pressure from building. She started to moan and increase the speed herself without any urging from Lucinda.

She was lost now, lost in the world of blissful sensuality, every muscle tensed, poised ready for the moment of relief and just as her head went back and her neck arched Allan spoke. 'You've still got fifteen minutes to go, honey,' he said loudly.

His voice broke the spell and for a moment she lost her rhythm. It was enough to bring her back to her senses. With a gasp of gratitude she wrestled to subdue her frantic flesh and slowly, relaxing and forcing the tense muscles to lose some of their tension, the build-up towards climax started to fade.

James stared at her and she couldn't tell whether he was pleased or not. 'Get off me now,' he said curtly. As soon as she did so, Lucinda pushed Kate up the bed, spreading her legs wide. To Kate's horror, the long feather that had been used on the first night of her honeymoon was produced again. 'I'm sure you remember this,' said Lucinda with a smile.

'She loves it,' James told the watching Allan.

'I'm sure she does,' said the American, his voice thick with desire. James fastened her hands to the headrest and spread her ankles apart so that Lucinda could start the light caress of

106

the feather, Kate saw Allan begin to make love to Pam.

The blonde responded swiftly, eagerly wrapping her arms around the American's neck as he removed her clothes and nuzzled between her breasts, his mouth moving hungrily from one nipple to the other. This only added to Kate's excitement and, as the feather delicately swirled and twirled over her silken skin, she could hear Pam's pleasure mounting, hear her giving low moans of excitement which made Kate's torment all the greater.

This time it was James who moved between Kate's legs and once he started to use his mouth on her she knew that she was lost. He licked and sucked at every part of her, his tongue darting in and out of her vagina, moving upwards to encircle the throbbing clitoris and then back down again, even travelling across the thin membrane of skin between her front and rear entrances in a tantalising caress that caused her to go rigid.

'Suck hard on her clitoris,' Lucinda urged James, as she swirled the feather round and round Kate's straining breasts. 'She'll come then, won't you, Kate?'

Kate couldn't reply. She didn't know what to do. Pam was clearly about to have an orgasm and she could hear the American urging her on. Her own body, having been thwarted once, was determined to gain satisfaction this time and she knew that Lucinda was right. If James should close his mouth around her desperate clitoris then there was no way on earth that she'd be able to control herself. Already she could anticipate the searing pleasure, the wonderful release from the terrible tension they were causing her.

'Here we go then,' said James, and suddenly he was sucking hard on the centre of all her pleasure. Just as Pam screamed with excitement, Kate cried aloud in a mixture of relief and despair as wave after wave of blissful hot pleasure coursed through her veins.

'That's two,' said James, kneeling upright. 'How long is there left, Allan?'

It was a few minutes before Allan could disentangle himself

from his frantic girlfriend long enough to look at his watch. 'Five minutes,' he muttered, pushing Pam to the ground and lowering himself on top of her.

'Do you think you can last another five minutes, Kate?' asked James. 'I do hope so. Remember if you don't you'll be punished.' Kate stared at him silently, knowing that it all depended on what he and Lucinda chose to do to her.

James got off the bed and walked across the bedroom floor to the large padded dressing table stool. When he sat on it, his legs firmly apart, Kate could see how his erection, still hard and inviting, was straining upwards towards his belly. 'Bring her over here,' he said to Lucinda.

Lucinda unfastened Kate, hooked one finger inside her leather collar and led her over to James. Once more she was forced to lower herself onto him, but this time he held her in place by grasping her tender breasts in his hands.

Kate realised that in this position he couldn't move very much and it would be up to her to provide stimulation. If she was careful, she thought with relief then she should be able to prevent herself from coming.

James' eyes were on her and it was as though he could see the hope and relief in her face. 'Do what you were doing before,' he said. 'But only slowly.' Obediently she allowed the full length of him to slide inside her before raising herself up until the tip of his glans was once more at the entrance to her vagina. To her surprise these slow, leisurely strokes were just as arousing as quicker ones and because his hands were so firm on her breasts, rearousing the already excited tissue, her excitement grew and her pleasure mounted.

'Now use the anal vibrator,' James said to Lucinda, moving his hands to Kate's shoulders and pushing her abruptly down on him so that she was sitting on his knees. Even as she gasped at the swift movement and the highly erotic sparks of pleasure that it had caused, Lucinda parted the cheeks of Kate's bottom and she felt the smooth latex head of a vibrator being eased into her rectum.

Immediately her body, remembering past pleasures, tightened in anticipation of release and she had to choke down a cry of despair. The vibrator had a T-shaped bar at the bottom which meant that once it was inserted and with Kate angled forward slightly towards James' shoulders, it remained firmly inside her while Lucinda operated the speed of its vibrations from a hand-held remote control.

They'd never done this to Kate before and when it first started to move, its thick-set sides rubbing against the incredibly sensitive nerve endings of the thin membranes around it, Kate's whole body cramped in a spasm that held both pain and pleasure. James was inside her, filling every inch of her. The vibrator was moving remorselessly inside her rectum and, as every screaming nerve end yearned for release and Kate gritted her teeth in a frantic last-ditch effort to prevent her pleasure from spilling, James reached between her outspread thighs and flicked with unerring precision at the underside of her clitoris.

With an agonised scream of despair Kate came. All her muscles were cramping, coiling, tightening and then releasing while the delicious heat rushed through her veins and her body arched forward so that James was forced to catch hold of her breasts in both hands tugging her back towards him. The movement only engendered further streaks of dark pleasure-pain and now she was sobbing despairingly as her body was racked by one final explosion.

'Was the half hour up?' Lucinda asked Allan.

For a few minutes he didn't answer and Kate realised that he and Pam were still pleasuring each other. When he did it was impossible to tell what his feelings were. 'It looks like she failed,' he said.

'What a pity,' said James in mock sympathy. 'Then I shall have to let Lucinda punish you.'

To Kate's bewilderment James didn't even seem interested in coming himself any more, because he lifted her off him and pushed her onto her knees on the floor as she stood over her. 'Tell her what's going to happen, Lucinda,' he said.

'Yeah, I'd sure like to know as well,' said the American.

'You have to make him come with your mouth,' said Lucinda to the trembling Kate, 'and while you're working on him I shall use this latex crop on you. It doesn't really hurt, it just stings a little.'

'That depends on whether you're the one using it or feeling the blows I imagine,' said Allan. 'Have you done this kind of thing before, Kate?'

Kate glanced at James, uncertain as to whether or not she should answer. 'Tell him,' said James. 'Let him know what a naive little thing you are.'

'No I haven't,' said Kate, feeling ridiculously ashamed.

'Well it can be an acquired taste,' he murmured. 'Anyway, by the look of your husband it shouldn't take you long.'

'I'm good at self-control,' said James and, glancing up at his face, Kate realised that there was no pity there. He was going to last as long as he could and make her endure the latex crop.

As she closed her mouth about her husband's straining organ, she tasted her own juices, the sweet honeyed scent of herself, and licked at it. She moved tentatively, slowly at first because she was unused to this, but then her whole body jerked in astonishment as Lucinda allowed the latex crop to fall across Kate's unprotected back and a sharp stinging sensation like nothing she'd ever experienced before shot through her, to be followed a few seconds later by a strange and not uncomfortable heat.

'Mind you don't bite me,' said James irritably. 'You're not meant to jump around like that.'

'I'm sorry,' she apologised, but now she was working more quickly, her tongue and lips sucking hungrily at him. She couldn't believe that he had such self-control. He was so tight, his testicles drawn up to the base of his shaft, and she could taste the saltiness of the first drops of pre-ejaculatory fluid, yet still he managed not to come and she had to endure blow after blow from the latex crop.

Within a few seconds she could feel the skin of her back

burning and pricking but was astonished to realise that her nipples were once more hard and between her thighs she was damp. Just the same she wanted it to end, not least because of the tall powerful American standing watching her, his blue eyes assessing every nuance of expression that crossed her face.

Finally she saw James' belly twitch and she ran the tip of her tongue around the ridge beneath the glans before sucking hard. Now he lost control and suddenly he was pumping his hips, spilling himself into her mouth and the blows of the crop ceased.

When it was over Kate sank to the floor. She felt strange, aroused, despite all that had happened to her, and also powerful because she knew that she'd forced James to come before he'd wanted to. At last she understood why he liked to control her pleasure, why he liked her to come only when he wanted, because her control of him made her feel good.

'An interesting evening,' said Allan Harkness, his arm round Pam. 'I guess we've all learnt a lot about each other tonight.'

'I haven't learnt anything about you that I didn't know before,' giggled Pam, gazing adoringly at Allan.

'Well, there's a limit to what *you* can understand about anything,' he remarked, patting her affectionately on the bottom. 'Just as long as you had a good time.'

Pam giggled but Kate saw that Allan wasn't looking at his girlfriend, instead he was staring at her and then, realising that she was aware of it, he looked away. 'Time for bed,' he said with a yawn. 'See you all at breakfast.'

'Can I sleep here for the night?' Lucinda asked James.

James looked down at Kate. 'What do you think, Kate?' he asked.

Kate was astonished he should even bother to ask her. She thought for a moment. 'I really don't mind,' she said at last, realising that this was the truth.

Clearly James realised it too. 'In that case there's no point in you staying,' he said to Lucinda. 'Besides, I need some sleep. No doubt we'll all be busy tomorrow.'

'But I want to stay,' said Lucinda pouting.

'Good night,' said James firmly. Kate felt yet another moment of triumph as his mistress had to leave them alone for the night.

Chapter 6

As usual Allan woke early the next morning. He needed very little sleep, which was something he always quoted when interviewed in American magazines. He felt, rightly or wrongly, this was one of the attributes that had helped him become such a success. His business interests were many and varied and only he knew the exact extent of his wealth and power. He enjoyed life, especially if there was a challenge to be faced, whether it was business or sexual. His first thought on this particular morning was that somehow he was going to get to the bottom of the mystery of Penrick Lodge.

He knew beyond any shadow of doubt that there was something strange going on. Last night, watching Kate spasming in helpless ecstasy as she'd climaxed for the third forbidden time and then seeing her punished by Lucinda as she tried desperately to bring James to a climax with her mouth, he'd known that there was a sub-text to everything that was happening.

He'd been excited, as any man would have been, and he was enjoying his stay, but he didn't like mysteries. This was definitely not one of James and Lucinda's usual erotic weekends and he decided that now was as good a time as any to start trying to discover the truth that lay behind his invitation.

When he got downstairs James, much to Allan's surprise, was coming out of his study. 'You're not usually an early bird,' Allan remarked.

James looked slightly awkward. 'Couldn't sleep,' he said abruptly.

'Strange, in your place I'd have been exhausted.'

'Perhaps I was overstimulated,' said James, trying to smile.

'Working on a book at the moment?' asked Allan. He wasn't particularly interested but he knew how much James' work mattered to him.

'No. Well, that is, yes but of course I'm not really working on it until the honeymoon's over,' said James.

Hearing the other man's awkward words Allan knew that he was on to something. It seemed that asking about James' work had been the right thing to do. 'Your usual sort of novel?' He tried to keep his voice casual, anxious not to reveal his sudden keen interest.

'Not exactly,' confessed James.

'Going more commercial are you?' Allan asked.

'Why do you ask that?' snapped James.

Allan held up his hands palms forward. 'Hey, I didn't mean to offend you. It seems a sensible move to make. I remember last time we met you said that you needed some money to do this place up. Writing a more commercial book seems a sensible way of getting a big advance. Have you managed that?'

'I really don't want to discuss it,' said James stiffly.

'Okay, fine,' said Allan easily. 'Remember though, I've got plenty of contacts in the publishing world in the States if you do come up with the goods.'

'You have?' Now it was James' turn to be interested. 'The thing is,' he said lowering his voice, 'Lucinda doesn't want me discussing this new book with anyone at all until it's finished.'

'But she's your agent, surely she wants to get the best deal possible for you?' said Allan.

'Of course, only it's a little controversial.'

'Hey, that sounds interesting. Not another book about your Royal family I hope.'

This time James' laugh was genuine. 'Quite the opposite.'

'Are we going to fence around like this forever or are you going to tell me something concrete about it?' asked Allan, half-turning away in an attempt to provoke James into what would clearly be an indiscretion.

'It's an erotic novel,' said James quietly.

'Nothing new about that,' said Allan. 'Everyone's doing it these days.'

'Yes, but not like this,' said James. 'You see, my book's more of a diary.'

Allan nodded. Now it was beginning to make sense. 'I see. You mean this weekend, my visit, it's all going to form part of the book, is it?'

'Yes.'

'Perhaps I don't like that,' said Allan.

'Well I'll change the names naturally,' said James swiftly. 'Anyway, you'd only be a bit-part player.'

'Gee thanks,' laughed Allan. 'I hope that's now how Pam thinks of me.'

'You know what I mean,' said James.

'So the book's about you, is it?' persisted Allan.

James glanced up and down the hallway, obviously worried that they might be overheard. 'Not really,' he confessed. 'It's about Kate.'

'Your wife?' Allan was stunned. 'Does she know?' he asked after a moment's pause.

'Of course not,' said James, clearly shocked at the idea. 'It wouldn't work if she knew.'

'When are you going to tell her?' asked Allan.

'I'm not sure,' muttered James. 'I wasn't going to tell her at all but . . .'

'I don't see how you can avoid it,' remarked Allan. 'Once she reads it she'll know.'

'Yes, but by that time we may not be together,' confessed James.

Allan nodded. 'I see. So that's why you got married. I must admit I couldn't understand it, not after all your outbursts against the married state. So you married Kate because she was the perfect heroine for your novel, is that it?'

'For God's sake keep your voice down,' hissed James. 'And

please don't tell Lucinda I've told you. She'd be furious. It's just that, between you and me, I think Lucinda's beginning to resent Kate rather and I'm not sure she's going to push things the way we'd intended. If you feel that you can get me an American publisher or something then obviously I'll carry on whatever Lucinda says.'

The two men strolled outside. 'So how's it going wrong?' asked Allan. 'Isn't Kate coming up to the mark?'

'Kate's perfect,' said James, and he sounded so enthusiastic that Allan guessed immediately what the problem was. Presumably Lucinda hadn't expected James to feel anything for his wife, but by the sound of it she'd aroused some complex emotions in him, emotions that would disturb any mistress.

'Why did you choose Kate?' he asked curiously.

'It wasn't easy to find someone suitable,' confessed James. 'Young girls these days just aren't inexperienced enough. You see, the whole point of the book is that the heroine has to be relatively naive at the start. Then, driven by love for her husband, she's drawn into an exciting new world of complex sexuality. This is only brought about by the fact that she has to obey her husband, carry out his every command, even if it isn't always what she herself would want.'

'I hope she's got a get-out clause,' said Allan.

'In the book or really?'

'In real life,' said Allan, startled to realise that James was finding it difficult to differentiate between the two.

'Well of course she doesn't have to obey me. I don't tie her up and keep her a prisoner in the house. She's free to go any time she chooses.'

'I suppose she loves you,' said Allan slowly.

'I should damn well hope so after all the work I put in to courting her,' said James. 'Actually, she's a nice girl and I find her sexier than I'd expected, even though she isn't really my type. One other problem that's arisen, quite apart from Lucinda's objections, is that Kate hasn't opposed me so much as we expected.'

'She didn't seem very happy last night,' said Allan.

James frowned. 'We wanted a deeper reaction than that. She never pleads or begs for long enough. Just the same the book's good, only different from the way I'd imagined it.'

Allan said nothing. It took a lot to shock him but he realised to his surprise that he was slightly shocked by what he was hearing. It wasn't the idea behind the book so much as the way it had been carried out. Getting someone to fall in love with him, even going to the extreme of marrying her when all the time he felt nothing for his wife seemed morally wrong, but then Allan realised that he was really in no position to judge. Many of his business deals would be considered immoral by other men. In the end it was up to each person's conscience to do what they believed right. In any case, as James had made clear, Kate was always free to go.

Presumably, despite what had happened, she still wasn't disillusioned by James and remained in love with him. He was surprised by this and thought that James may have grown falsely confident. Last night, when Kate had looked at him, Allan had seen a look of appeal in her eyes and he knew that her reactions to him in the bath had been genuine. In other words, she was still capable of finding other men attractive, arousing and satisfying.

'I agree with you on one point,' he said at last.

'What's that?' James was obviously curious.

'Kate's a very sexy, desirable young woman.'

James nodded. 'Lucky me, eh?'

'Yeah, but I don't think she's quite so fortunate.'

'The exciting thing about this,' James confided, 'is that neither Lucinda nor I know the ending to the book.'

'I can see that would be intriguing,' said Allan, his mind going through endless possible permutations. 'You'll just have to wait and see, won't you?'

'I'll let you know when the book's done,' James promised him. 'What do you reckon the end will be?'

Allan thought for a moment, his body quickening as he

remembered the way Kate's body had responded to his touch when he'd made love to her in the bath. 'I wouldn't like to guess,' he said truthfully.

'Fair enough,' said James. Glancing at his watch, he turned back towards the house. 'Mrs Duke should have breakfast ready by now. Let's go and eat.'

Kate overslept that morning and it was gone ten o'clock before she came down to the dining room for breakfast. Allan was still sitting at the table reading the newspapers and drinking coffee. There was no sign of anyone else.

'Where's James?' she asked, hoping desperately that he hadn't gone somewhere with Lucinda.

'In his study,' said Allan, smiling at her. 'This new novel of his is quite an obsession, isn't it?'

Kate frowned. 'Not really. He says he isn't going to start working on it properly until our honeymoon's over.'

'Is that a fact? Guess I misunderstood him then,' said the American.

'What about Lucinda and Pam?' continued Kate.

Allan folded his newspaper and put it on a spare chair. 'Pam never gets up before midday, she says it's bad for her complexion! As for Lucinda, she's sunbathing in the back garden. Do you like sunbathing?'

Kate shook her head. 'I'm lucky, my skin's quite golden and . . .'

'That's right, I've noticed,' he said slowly.

Kate felt suddenly awkward. Hastily she started to butter a piece of toast. 'Do you like swimming?' she asked, trying to fill the awkward silence that had arisen.

'Only in a heated Californian pool. Tell me, Kate, did you enjoy yourself with me last night?'

Kate wished that he hadn't asked her. She'd imagined that what had occurred between them was such a common thing for a man like him that it would hold no significance. She certainly didn't want to discuss her feelings about it, particularly as she didn't understand them herself. 'Of course I did,' she said shyly. 'It was very satisfying.'

'But not as satisfying as what came later?' he asked, watching her intently.

Now Kate felt really uncomfortable. She couldn't bear to think about what had gone on between her, James and Lucinda while Allan and Pam had watched. It had been so humiliating, and also exciting in a way that she felt it shouldn't have been. 'That was different,' she said at last.

'It sure was. Have you done that kind of thing before?'

'No!' She realised that she was protesting too vehemently. 'That is, not exactly that sort of thing but of course . . .'

'Do you really like where he's leading you, Kate?' asked Allan curiously.

Kate nodded. 'Yes,' she admitted.

He smiled at her. 'Then that's okay. No harm done. I think it's great when women start to learn about their own sexuality. As James said he and I go back quite a way but I think you ought to remember one thing.'

'What's that?'

'That in the end you've got to take responsibility for your own actions.'

'I can't,' she said, for some reason desperate that Allan should understand the situation properly. 'I love James and I want to make him happy. He's only happy when he's making me obey him, making me do things that I wouldn't do on my own initiative. That's how he gets his satisfaction and in the end it's how I get mine.'

'But you can still take responsibility for what you're doing,' said Allan sharply.

Kate wished that he wouldn't talk to her as though she were doing something wrong. 'If I take responsibility for it then it isn't a game of obedience any more. Besides, I don't know why you're trying to make it sound as though I'm doing something wrong. You didn't have to stay and watch and it certainly turned you on. I could hear you and Pam having a great time.'

He grinned lazily at her. 'I don't think you're doing anything wrong and it sure did turn me on. I just wondered if you'd really thought about what was happening?'

'My relationship with my husband's private,' protested Kate.

'I hardly think you can call it private when he gets his visitors to join in,' said Allan.

Kate felt confused. She was certain that Allan liked her and knew that he found her desirable. He was also a friend of James and Lucinda. It didn't make sense that he should be talking to her like this, almost seeming to be warning her about something. 'Is there something I'm missing here?' she asked.

'How do you mean?'

'Are you trying to tell me something that I don't know?'

He shrugged. 'Nope. I guess you know all you need to know. Anyway, I'm pretty much a hedonist. I've been invited here for a weekend of sexual pleasure and I'd be pretty stupid to try and spoil it. You're just very young.'

'I hate it when people say things like that to me,' exploded Kate. 'I'm not a child. I like what's happening to me. This may seem odd to you but I feel more confident now than when I got married. I understand myself and my body and I'm beginning to learn what I really need rather than what society has always dedicated I should need.'

'I'll get you a soap box and put it out on the lawn,' drawled Allan.

'Why are you being so horrible to me?' she asked in surprise.

Allan shook his head. 'That wasn't my intention. I'm sorry if I've offended you. I guess I got carried away because . . .' His voice tailed off and he picked up his newspaper again.

Kate wished that he'd finished his sentence. She wanted to know why he'd got carried away. Even now she sensed that there was something between them, the same sexual pull that she'd felt in his bedroom the night before and she wondered how this was possible when she was so much in love with James. As soon as that thought had crossed her mind a more disturbing one followed it. She realised that her feelings for James had changed a little.

As she nibbled on her toast she tried to work out when it had happened. She realised quickly that it had been last night, as she'd knelt before him with Lucinda striking her in front of Allan and Pam. At that moment, for a few fleeting seconds, she'd resented James and his power over her and now it seemed that that resentment had changed the intensity of her feelings for her husband.

'It's very quiet in here,' said Lucinda, breezing into the room. 'I thought you'd be down on the beach showing Allan your favourite cave, Kate.' And she laughed.

'I've only just got up,' said Kate calmly.

'I'm sure Allan would like to see the cave, wouldn't you, Allan?' continued Lucinda.

'If that's the case then he's perfectly capable of walking down the cliff path and seeing it for himself,' retorted Kate.

She saw Allan lower his paper in surprise while Lucinda stared at her. 'I don't think James would like to hear you take that tone with me, Kate.'

'Really?' asked Kate. 'Since he isn't here, I don't see how you can know. You're not my husband, Lucinda, you're just his agent. Now I'm going up to get dressed and then I'm going to take a book out to the summer house.'

As she left the room she felt good. It was the first time she'd had the courage to stand up to Lucinda and if she was honest she knew it was only because she'd had Allan in the room when she spoke. It was strange that the sheer bulk of his physical presence was comforting even without his surprisingly gentle personality.

Although it was called the summer house it wasn't Kate's idea of a typical summer house. It was really a pavilion, the stones matching the house, and the balustraded terrace of the main house was also repeated. The windows were large to allow warmth and light in and the floor was marble in a geometric design. Kate wondered if it had been modelled on someone's idea of a Roman bath because the seating consisted of long narrow benches running round three sides and she felt that there should be a sauna or steam bath in the room.

The walls were decorated with erotic paintings of a style more usually seen in the Far East. When Kate had questioned James about these he'd explained that he'd had a friend do them as soon as his father died. They certainly didn't match with the interior of the main house, but Kate liked the summer house and was especially glad to retreat there now. After about half an hour she was joined by all the others. 'What are you reading?' asked James.

Kate held up her book. 'It's a biography of the Brontë sisters.'

'Boring,' said Lucinda with an exaggerated yawn.

'I'm enjoying it,' retorted Kate.

'Didn't one of them write *Vanity Fair*?' asked Pam innocently.

Allan shook his head. 'That was Jane Austen, honey. Anyway how would you know? You never read anything more taxing than the fashion magazines.'

'But they were repressed or something, weren't they?' persisted Pam. 'Aren't their books seething with sex?'

Now it was Kate's turn to laugh. 'A very repressed kind of sex.'

'The kind of sex Kate knew about before she married me,' interjected James.

Annoyed, Kate stared hard at her husband. 'You didn't complain before we got married,' she said.

'How could he? He didn't try the merchandise,' said Lucinda, sitting herself down at the far end of the room from Kate.

Kate was suddenly embarrassed. She looked down at the floor unable to meet anyone's eye. 'More fool him,' said Allan. 'If you ask me he was very lucky.'

'We didn't ask you,' said Lucinda, an edge to her voice.

Allan smiled and Kate could tell that he was pleased to have annoyed her. 'Neither did you,' he agreed. Kate was pleased when he came and sat down next to her. 'You prefer this sort of thing to fiction?' he enquired.

'Not really. I read almost anything,' confessed Kate.

'You must ask James to show you his new book then,' said Allan.

'I told you he hasn't begun it yet,' explained Kate. 'Have you James?'

'I had to do a synopsis for the publisher,' said James. 'But no, I haven't begun the manuscript.'

'You haven't done a single page?' asked Allan, slipping his arm around Kate's waist.

'Maybe one or two,' conceded James, clearly irritated by the questioning. 'What are we all going to do today?' he added.

'I'm happy to sit here with Kate,' said Allan. 'This place really catches the sun.'

'That's precisely why it was put here,' said Lucinda.

'You don't say.' Again Allan's eyes gleamed with pleasure and Kate smiled.

'Well I'm bored,' Lucinda declared. 'I suppose nothing really exciting's going to happen until tonight.'

'We're on holiday,' said Pam. 'You're not meant to be busy all the time when you're on holiday.'

'Or when you're on your honeymoon,' said Allan.

To Kate's surprise Lucinda peeled off her summer dress. Beneath it she was wearing only a black G-string and, without a word to anyone, she stretched herself down on the marble floor where the rays of the sun came through a small glass pane in the roof, so that her body seemed to be lit up. 'Mmm. This is nice,' she murmured.

Kate looked over at James. For a moment it looked as though he was about to take off his clothes as well but then, seeing how Allan was sitting with his arm around Kate, he clearly changed his mind and came and sat on the other side of her, putting one hand possessively on her knee.

'It's lovely here, isn't anyone going to join me?' asked Lucinda.

'I'd quite like to,' said Pam suddenly. She glanced at Allan as she spoke and he shrugged. 'If that's what you want.'

Now the atmosphere in the summer house changed and Kate realised that Pam wasn't simply going to lie down next to Lucinda and sunbathe. Clearly she was aiming for something far more exciting than that because the moment her clothes were off and she was lying on the floor, she put her head on Lucinda's stomach. 'This is the life,' she said.

'Carry on and enjoy yourself,' urged Allan. 'I'm sure no one here will mind.'

Kate and the men watched the two women lying in the centre of the summer house floor. For a few minutes nothing much happened as Pam continued to rest her head on Lucinda's stomach while Lucinda's hands played lazily with her own breasts. Then Pam became restless and, getting up, she knelt over Lucinda's body, cupping her breasts in her hands and teasing her large nipples until they were erect. Lucinda lifted her head to watch what was happening and, encouraged by this, Pam let her fingers trail down over her ribs and belly before starting to tease at her own pubic hair.

Pam's body was voluptuous, her breasts large with unusually dark areolae, and Kate found the scene surprisingly arousing. It was evident that Lucinda did too because her legs started to move restlessly and her hips arched off the floor a little.

'Rub yourself on me, Pam,' she urged the American girl.

'In a minute,' said Pam, her fingers busy between her thighs, and all at once her body shook violently as she brought herself to a speedy climax.

Kate was surprised at how erotic the scene was and felt herself beginning to ache deep in her belly. As Pam lowered herself onto the desperately gyrating Lucinda, both Allan and James slid a hand on Kate's knee and she felt their fingers moving up her thighs. It was an extraordinary sensation because their touch was so different. Allan's fingers were stronger, firmer and yet his movements were more delicate and tantalising than James'. James' caresses were firmer and when he reached the top of the inside of her thigh he nipped at the tender flesh there. Startled, Kate jumped but despite the discomfort her desire flared and she gave a sigh of frustration.

The two women were now rolling around on the floor, arms and legs entwined, taking it in turns to fasten their mouths around each other's pubic mounds and occasionally rubbing their pubic bones together, crying out sharply with excitement every time they climaxed.

'I think your little lady would like some satisfaction,' murmured Allan, as his fingers strayed into Kate's fine blonde pubic hair. She drew in her breath sharply as she felt James part her sex lips for his friend, allowing Allan to run his fingers up and down the aching flesh, teasing at her clitoris while all the time the pressure built. Soon she was gasping as loudly as the other two women.

'You're not to come yet,' said James abruptly.

To her shame Kate wailed in dismay. 'Oh just this once,' she begged him. 'I only want—'

'You're really into this obedience thing, aren't you?' remarked Allan idly, his fingers still doing magical things between her thighs so that the tight forbidden pleasure threatened to spill over.

'Yes,' admitted James. 'It's a great turn on.'

With his free hand Allan massaged the back of Kate's neck, his hand moving in a slow steady rhythm. 'Yeah, I can understand that,' he agreed. 'But it's pretty hard on your wife.'

'She enjoys it, don't you, Kate?' asked James.

At that moment Kate wasn't enjoying it. She was having to bite on her lip in order to subdue her treacherous body, to distract herself from the hot flooding pleasure that was threatening to engulf her, and, when James thrust two fingers inside her while Allan continued to massage the stem of her clitoris, she thought she'd go mad and wriggled frantically against their teasing touch.

'Better not do that, you'll come even quicker,' Allan cautioned her.

'You're not meant to give her advice,' exclaimed James. 'She has to work this out for herself.'

'Gee, you're a hard taskmaster,' said Allan.

It seemed to Kate that he felt some sympathy for her, but not enough to stop arousing her. His fingers were so knowing that he was driving her out of her mind and soon she was on the very edge of a climax. As her clitoris retracted she breathed a sigh of relief but, knowing what would be happening, James started to massage the top of her pubic mound in circles so that the protective hood was moved.

As soon as the sensitive nerve endings were revealed again, Kate felt the pad of one of Allan's fingers touch it with the lightest of strokes and she began to sob with dismay as her body became caught up in the rhythm of her impending climax. The realisation that two men were playing with her, had their hands between her thighs and were working in unison to force her to orgasm, was so exciting that she found it impossible to control herself. She'd never imagined such a thing happening, never realised how arousing it would be, and she heard Pam give a cry of joy as she orgasmed even more intensely.

This cry of abandonment combined with everything that was happening to Kate meant that she could no longer control herself. Instead, regardless of the consequences, she simply gave herself over to everything that was happening, allowing herself to wallow in the pleasure of the two men's fingers, of their quickened breathing and excitement and the messages that her own body was giving her. 'I'm coming,' she screamed and the two men doubled their efforts so that when the orgasm finally crashed over her it was so intense she nearly fainted with the pleasure of it.

Her body jerked forward, her thighs clenched themselves tightly around the two men's hands and she twisted from side to side, moaning and gasping as the final pulsations of pleasure swept through her body. 'Since she's disobeyed she may as well have another,' she heard James say. Before she could protest, their hands resumed their skilful ministrations and her hungry body, now more accustomed to rearousal, immediately began an assent towards another climax.

At some point the men lifted her off the bench and laid her on the floor, parting her legs. 'We're going to watch you come,' said James and she trembled with excitement.

'She looks good enough to eat,' remarked Allan.

'Go ahead,' said James.

Kate knew that she'd go out of her mind if Allan's tongue was half as skilled as his fingers, and it was. He seemed to know exactly what to do, precisely how hard to press and where but he also succeeded in keeping her on the edge so that she heard herself crying out, begging for that final touch.

'You'll have to move your head or we won't be able to see her,' James remarked.

As the delicious lapping warmth of Allan's tongue was removed Kate gave a cry of protest, but now both men began to use their fingers on her again, filling her and remorselessly stimulating her swollen clitoris until at last she was allowed to come once more.

'I want to put my fingers inside her as she comes,' said Allan and, just as her contractions of release began, she felt his fingers inside her and her muscles tightened convulsively around them. She didn't care that they were watching her, that the other two women had now stopped and were also standing around, all she cared about were the delicious sensations and the indescribable ecstasy of the moment.

Only when it was over, and she was lying with legs sprawled and hair clinging damply to her forehead, did Kate start to feel self-conscious. 'You're a disgrace,' said James, his voice hard. 'For goodness' sake get up. That's hardly the way a man expects his wife to behave.'

Kate knew how she was expected to respond to this and quickly she got to her feet, pulling her dress down over her thighs. 'I'm so sorry,' she said. 'I know I've let you down.'

'That's an understatement,' said James. 'I should think you've shocked our guests.'

For a moment Kate wondered if Allan was going to play the same game, but that idea quickly vanished when he spoke. 'Hell, nothing shocks me,' he said with a smile. 'I like to see a woman enjoying herself. In fact I liked watching all the women enjoy themselves.'

'But Kate wasn't meant to,' said Lucinda sharply. 'It seems she finds discipline difficult still, James.'

James gave a mock sigh. 'It's a shame but I think Lucinda's right,' he said, reaching out and touching Kate gently on the face. She stared at him, longing for a tender word, a look of complicity in his eyes to show her that it was only a game, but his expression remained detached. It was as though she was nothing to him, nothing but a sex toy designed to excite him with this wonderful game of obedience, and for the first time she felt a surge of resentment. 'You tried so hard too,' he continued, pushing her hair behind her ears. 'Well, tonight there won't be any problems about you coming. In fact, the more you come the better.'

'Why? What's happening tonight?' she asked.

'We're having a beach party,' explained James. 'It's fancy dress.'

'Fancy dress on the beach?' asked Pam. 'Is it your own private beach?'

'Pretty much,' said James. 'I've checked the tides and no one will be able to get on the sand tonight except us. We'll be perfectly safe and free to do what we like.'

'And what's that?' asked Allan with interest.

'I thought we'd have a medieval banquet,' said James. 'We can set a barbecue up, roast half a pig or something and the women will enjoy dressing up. Lucinda's got some clothes in that will be suitable.'

'What role do you have in mind for Kate?' asked Allan with interest.

For the first time James' eyes were animated. 'I've got a very special role in mind for Kate,' he said. 'She's going to be the slave girl.'

'Whose slave?' asked Pam.

'Why everyone's of course,' said James with a laugh. 'That way you can all get to enjoy Kate and she can enjoy herself as well.'

'I don't want to do that,' said Kate quietly. 'I don't want to be everyone's, I'm yours.'

'But I want you to be everyone's,' said James.

Kate realised that Allan was watching her thoughtfully. 'If you don't want to be a slave, be a queen,' suggested the American.

Kate was tempted for a moment but then, looking at her husband's dark saturnine face, she felt once more the huge surge of sexual attraction that he'd aroused in her at their first meeting and remembered why it was that she'd wanted to marry him so badly. 'If James wants me to be a slave then that's what I'll be,' she said quietly.

Allan shrugged. 'Suit yourself, but you may regret it. Come to that,' he added thoughtfully, 'you may regret it one day, James.'

'How's that?' asked James curiously.

'If she's everyone's slave she might choose a new master. I presume that's allowed?'

Suddenly there was total silence in the summer house. James' eyes narrowed and he looked from Allan to his wife and then across at Lucinda. 'What's the matter?' said Allan. 'Afraid I'm right?'

'Of course not,' blustered James.

'That's okay then, let's make it part of the deal.'

'I don't know,' said James. 'Lucinda, what do you think?'

'Hell, what kind of a husband are you?' asked the American. 'How come you have to ask your agent whether or not it's all right to give your wife the freedom to go off with another guy?'

'Because—' James stopped abruptly.

'Because what?' asked Kate, feeling that this was important, that James had very nearly said something vital.

'I don't need to,' he said quickly. 'Sure, she can do what she

129

likes. I've always said that. Anyway, Pam's more than enough for you, isn't she?'

Pam giggled. 'He could manage two of me,' she said. 'It's okay, I'm just having fun. We're not a serious item.'

'Pity,' muttered James beneath his breath and Kate realised that for the first time James was genuinely apprehensive. Suddenly the idea of the beach party was more attractive.

Chapter 7

Lucinda looked at James, sitting disconsolately by his word processor, and she felt a moment's irritation. She couldn't imagine what was the matter with him. It was all going so well. Allan had entered into the spirit of things far better than she could ever have hoped and Pammie was the perfect companion for him. Tonight was obviously going to test Kate to the limit. Already she seemed somewhat bewildered by the way things were turning out although, to give her credit, she'd coped far better than anyone could have anticipated. Despite all this, and the fact that James was getting everything he could need for his book, it was plain that he wasn't happy.

'What's the matter?' she asked, trying to keep the irritation out of her voice.

'It's all going wrong,' he complained bitterly.

Lucinda sighed. 'No it isn't, it's all going right. This was what we planned, remember? What did you think was going to happen?'

'I don't know but it wasn't this.'

'What do you mean?' She genuinely didn't understand him.

'Surely you can see what's happening?' he asked, his voice full of anguish.

'Yes, we're taking Kate further and further along the path of sexual discovery, which is what the book's all about.'

'I wish you'd shut up about the bloody book,' snapped James.

Lucinda was astonished. 'That's what this is all about. That's where our money's coming from. I hope you haven't forgotten that.'

'It's difficult with you forever at my elbow reminding me,' he remarked.

Lucinda realised that she was going to have to be more tactful. Gently she put an arm round James' shoulders. 'Tell me what's worrying you,' she said gently.

'It's Kate,' he exclaimed. 'She's beginning to fall for Allan.'

Lucinda's eyes widened in surprise. 'Are you sure that's true? I haven't noticed anything.'

'That's because you don't care whether she does or not.'

Privately Lucinda knew that this was true. Actually, if it were, it was the best thing that could possibly happen. She certainly didn't want Kate hanging around messing up their lives once the book was complete. 'All women like Allan,' she explained. 'There's something about him. He manages to make them feel special but they aren't. Look at the number of wives he's had.'

'That's not the point,' groaned James. 'She's falling in love with him.'

'Don't be ridiculous,' said Lucinda wearily. 'She's utterly besotted with you.'

'Oh she was,' agreed James, 'but she isn't any more. Because of all the things I've made her do she's beginning to question whether I love her or not. That's why she's turning to Allan.'

'Since you don't love her I fail to see why that matters,' said Lucinda crisply. 'The main problem about this plan has always been what we did with Kate when the experiment was over. If she falls out of love with you, so much the better.'

'But I don't want her to fall out of love with me,' cried James. 'I'm starting to realise how much she matters to me.'

Lucinda withdrew her arm. She felt like slapping him. This was never the intention. She and James had been lovers for over two years now and she'd invested everything in him emotionally and financially. She couldn't believe that he was telling her he was falling for another woman. 'I think you're confusing pity with love,' she said.

James looked up at her. 'I think I understand my own feelings better than you do.'

'Look, James,' she said placatingly. 'This is a difficult time for all of us. Obviously you were bound to become emotionally involved with her, but we discussed that risk before we began. She isn't your type. For a start she's far too pliable and too young. Come to that she's too young for Allan as well. What does it matter if she thinks she's falling in love with him? Surely that makes it all the more interesting?'

'Not for me it doesn't,' he snarled. 'She's my wife. Am I meant to just stand by like a fool while another man whisks her away from me?'

Lucinda sat down on the opposite side of the desk from him. 'I think you ought to be more sensible about this, James. Firstly, Kate isn't falling in love with Allan. Maybe she is a tiny bit disillusioned with you but that's only natural. It will make the book more interesting and it also leaves it up to you to rekindle her old feelings for you. Secondly, there is no way that a man like Allan Harkness is going to want someone like Kate as his mistress. You know Allan. He likes carefree, open, happy-go-lucky girls who treat sex like a sport. Kate isn't like that. She's full of emotions and very intense.'

'She's also very sexy,' muttered James.

Lucinda felt as though he'd hit her in the stomach. 'Is that how you see her?' she demanded.

James had the grace to look a little abashed. 'Sometimes,' he admitted. 'She's such a strange combination of innocence and sexuality.'

'The way things are going she won't be innocent much longer,' retorted Lucinda. 'Look, James, you signed the book deal and you want the money. You can't back out now, nor can you start changing the plot. You have to go on the way we intended.'

'I don't see why,' he said irritably. 'Haven't we done enough? God knows we've opened her eyes to a few things. I'm not sure that this barbecue tonight is a good idea.'

'Why not?' asked Lucinda challengingly. 'You're not afraid of the competition, are you?'

'Perhaps I am,' admitted James. 'You're deliberately closing your eyes to what's happening, Lucinda. If Kate falls out of love with me then the plot's ruined. The whole point is that the heroine does everything her lover demands of her because she's so besotted with him. She's not going to do that if she doesn't love me any more is she?'

'She's your wife,' Lucinda reminded him. 'Also, with any encouragement from you, she'll be madly in love with you again. This is only a temporary hiccup, even supposing that you're right. Personally I haven't seen any sign that she's fallen for Allan and gone off you.'

James' lips were set in a tight line. 'You're bound to see it differently,' he said at last. 'You're jealous of her and you have been from the start.'

'That's ridiculous,' retorted Lucinda. 'I helped you choose her. This whole book was my idea and I negotiated the deal. Why should I be jealous of her? She's pathetic.'

'No she isn't,' said James. 'She's incredibly sensual and when I see her struggling to control herself, literally writhing around trying to obey me when she's desperate to come and I won't let her, I get this incredible urge to just pick her up and ram into her, making her come and come until she can't come any more. I feel so possessive of her that I don't even want Allan around, let alone touching her and making love to her.'

Now Lucinda was truly shocked. She could cope with James complaining but not with this. 'Are you saying you've fallen in love with her?' she asked slowly.

James hesitated, his eyes evasive. 'I'm not sure.'

'Well you damn well better be sure,' she said. 'Listen carefully, James. I'm not the one who owes thousands of pounds and who's inherited a house that needs a fortune spent on it. I'm not the one who's living on credit and doesn't know where to turn in order to repay my debtors. You are. You're the one in that situation and you're the one who stands to earn a fortune if you do this book properly.

'For years now you've been complaining about the fact that nobody takes you seriously, that they only remember your father and that you're nothing but second best. This is your chance to be your own person, to establish yourself in an entirely different genre from him and make a fortune at the same time. Sex makes money, that's an undeniable fact and you're going to benefit from it. If you foul up now, if you mess it all up because of some pathetic adolescent puppy love then don't expect me to stand by you and pick up the pieces.'

She fully expected James to start shouting at her, to tell her that she had no right to talk to him like that and reassert his authority over her but to her astonishment he didn't. 'I know you're right,' he said quietly. 'But I can't help myself.'

Lucinda was devastated. This was a nightmare situation and she couldn't think what to do to retrieve it. 'Listen,' she said after a moment's thought. 'If you're really bothered and you genuinely believe that you might have some kind of feelings for Kate then tonight's your chance to show it. If you set your mind to charming Kate, Allan doesn't offer any competition. He's always got the pick of loads of women. Men with money like that have, even without Allan's charm and sexual ability. Use the barbecue as an opportunity to win Kate back if you truly believe that you're losing her.'

'And what about you?' he asked. 'Where does that leave our relationship?'

Lucinda knew that she had to feign indifference, had to pretend that it didn't matter. She'd deal with Kate later. Right now what mattered was the book. 'If, at the end of the day, you're in love with Kate then obviously I'll go,' she said lightly, amazed to hear how genuine her voice sounded. 'We've had a good couple of years together but neither of us have ever pretended it was love. Actually, I didn't think you knew the meaning of the word.'

'I'm not sure I do,' he said gloomily. 'What I am sure of is that Kate's my only chance of finding out.'

'Fine, then find out,' said Lucinda crisply. 'There's nothing worse than a man sitting around moaning and being miserable. Clearly if she likes Allan she likes successful dynamic men. You'd better try imitating one.'

'There's no need to be like that,' he said angrily.

'I'm just trying to get some reaction from you,' explained Lucinda. 'This book matters to me as well you know. I am your agent as well as your mistress.'

James nodded. 'I know you're right. Honestly, Lu, I never meant this to happen. I still can't believe it has, but I've got to find out if I am in love with Kate and if I am then I have to win her back.'

'As I've already said you haven't lost her,' repeated Lucinda.

'No, but I'm beginning to.'

'Fine, then the book's going to be different but we can still have the barbecue, only at the end, after all her ordeals, you can sweep the heroine up in your arms and rush her off to the bedroom.'

'Sarcasm really doesn't suit you,' he said coldly.

'Love doesn't suit you,' she retorted, unable to control her anger any longer, and with that she slammed out of the room.

Once up in her bedroom she stood looking out of the window, her jaw tight with fury. She couldn't understand how this had happened, how someone like Kate, whom she'd picked so carefully, could ever have come to mean anything to a man like James. She'd seemed so innocuous, so insipid and naive that it had never for one moment crossed Lucinda's mind that James could fall for her. There'd been other girls, just as promising in some ways, whom she'd sensed might present a danger, but not Kate.

Unfortunately for Lucinda, Kate's sensuality and spirit had proved stronger than she'd anticipated. She only hoped that once the barbecue got under way James would revert to his more normal self. Either that or Kate would do something to show James how ill-suited the pair of them were.

* * *

'How do you feel about tonight?' James asked Kate as she stood naked and passive in front of him, waiting to see what she'd be wearing.

'I'm nervous,' admitted Kate.

'But excited too?'

She nodded. 'A little. James, how much more are you going to ask of me?'

'I'm not sure.'

'It's just that . . .' She hesitated for a moment.

'What?'

'You're changing things,' she admitted reluctantly.

It was obvious that her remark worried him. 'I'm changing you, but not our marriage,' he said quickly.

'I meant your changing me, but perhaps not in the way you intended.'

'In what way then?' he asked anxiously.

Kate didn't know whether to tell him or not. It was strange but the closer they got to the barbecue the more excited she became at the prospect of being Allan's slave, rather than at the prospect of having James in control of her. She realised that this was something she couldn't tell her husband, and, despite everything, she half hoped that once they were all on the beach and the evening's entertainment began she'd feel differently. 'It doesn't matter,' she said slowly.

'Of course it does. Look, Kate, after tonight there won't be very much more, but you have to do everything I tell you once we're on the beach. You do understand that?'

'Yes.'

He smiled and kissed her softly on the lips. 'There's a good girl. Right, now it's time for me to give the orders again.'

'You mean we're back in the game?'

'It isn't a game, it's a way of living.'

'For you, yes,' she agreed.

'For both of us. You can't deny that you enjoy it. You get enough pleasure from everything we do.'

'I know,' said Kate.

'Right, then let's begin,' he said briskly. 'I've got a white mini kimono here. It's mid-thigh length, fastening with a loose tie. That's all you'll wear apart from the collar of servitude and a small gold chain lead which will be used to pass you from one guest to another. You'll look fantastically sexy.'

Kate glanced at the tiny garment. It would hardly cover anything and meant that people could slip their hands in to fondle her breasts or touch her between her thighs without even having to unfasten it. 'Surely I could wear more than that?'

James nodded. 'These too,' he said, producing a pair of silver sandals with laces that would crisscross around her legs and tie just below the knee. 'Perfection!' he said with obvious pride. 'I think your skin needs to be shinier though. Lie face down on the bed and I'll start oiling you.'

Obediently Kate settled herself as instructed and James knelt beside her, pouring sandalwood-scented oil into his cupped palm before rubbing his hands together and then placing them across the backs of the calves of her legs just above her ankles. One hand was then above the other with the fingertips pointing in opposite directions and slowly he slid them up her leg, spreading the scented oil right to the top of the thigh and over her buttock, occasionally kneading gently and then finishing off with long sweeping strokes. He did the same with the other leg and she murmured with pleasure. Next he oiled her back, arms and hands, massaging the fleshy area of her palm and the base of her thumb. It was astonishingly sexy and when his fingers glided over the inside of her elbow, spreading the oil in slow circles, she closed her eyes at the sheer pleasure.

'Stand up so that I can do your front,' he said sharply, his voice breaking into her daydream. She wished that he seemed to be enjoying it more but, as his hands moved upwards from her ankles over the knees, between her thighs and then across her belly until finally he reached her aching breasts, there was no sign of anything but professional interest in his eyes. As he worked the oil into her breasts she gave another soft moan of delight.

'Be quiet,' he ordered her. 'This isn't meant to arouse you.'

'I can't help it,' she protested.

With casual indifference James flicked each of her protruding oiled nipples with a finger and the stinging pain broke the spell of pleasure. 'Perhaps that will help you control yourself,' he said.

There was an ache in Kate's throat as he stood back and surveyed her nude shining body. She didn't understand why he hadn't taken pleasure in touching her in the same way as she'd taken pleasure from his touch. Even if he was looking forward to the evening, even if he wanted to see her debased and humiliated, taking and giving pleasure to others, surely he should still enjoy caressing her.

'Put on the kimono,' he said, handing her the tiny garment, and she slipped her arms into it before fastening the sash. Then she sat on the bed so that he could put on the sandals, crisscrossing the long straps over her gleaming golden legs. 'Absolutely perfect,' he said at last. 'Take a look in the mirror, Kate,' and he pushed her over to the looking glass.

She stared at herself. Her cheeks were flushed with the massage, her nipples showing clearly through the silk of the tiny kimono and every bare inch of flesh was gleaming from the oil. It was obvious even to her that she looked incredibly sexy and her flesh was throbbing with desire, a desire aroused by the massage.

'Now for the finishing touch,' murmured James and for the first time she felt a moment's disquiet as he clipped the gold chain lead onto her collar, holding the end in his hand and pulling her tightly up against him so that she could see his reflection in the mirror as well. 'My beautiful obedient slave,' he whispered. 'I can't wait to see you carry out my orders tonight.'

For a moment their eyes locked in the mirror but Kate felt that the excitement she could see on James' face was because of what was going to happen and not because of her, her body or his feelings for her. He tugged sharply on the chain and her head snapped back. 'Excellent,' he said to himself and then he led her from the room.

It was nine-thirty and the light was fading as he led her down the cliff-top path. For Kate this was a dreadful ordeal. The sandals provided no firm grip on the shifting surface and because of the chain she was forced to go at a pace dictated by James, a far quicker pace than was usual, and time and again she half stumbled. Each time this happened he would jerk sharply and the collar bit into her throat causing her to cough. 'Don't look down,' he reminded her, as she glanced apprehensively at the beach below.

'Don't do this to me,' she whimpered. 'I don't like the lead.'

'You're not meant to like it,' he said shortly.

Kate fell silent. When they finally reached the beach she gave a sigh of relief. A little way away the barbecue had been set up and she could smell the roasting meat. Pam and Lucinda were wearing long velvet dresses but the design was hardly medieval since both dresses had plunging necklines and long zips down the back. Pam's blonde curly hair had been piled up on top of her head, making her look almost regal, and Lucinda was displaying her cleavage to its best advantage, spilling out of the dress. Both women turned to stare at Kate as James led her towards them.

Neither James nor Allan had attempted to dress up. They were both wearing Chinos and short-sleeved linen shirts, but for some reason this didn't seem incongruous. It was clear that it was the women who were the main players in the game, the men were there to enjoy themselves.

The smell of the food cooking made Kate hungry. She realised that she hadn't eaten since lunch and saw that Lucinda was nibbling on a slice of crisp roast pork. Her mouth watered and she started to move towards the barbecue but James jerked on the lead pulling her away. 'Slaves don't eat with their masters,' he reminded her.

140

She stood mutely beside him, anxious not to feel the pressure of the collar around her neck again, and then listened to the sound of the surf breaking on the beach. It was such a normal sound, something she'd grown to love since coming to Penrick Lodge, and she thought how bizarre it was that the sea and the sand were the same while she was forced to play out this strange game to satisfy her husband's desires.

Allan wandered over the sand towards them, a large pewter jug in one hand and a goblet in the other. 'I think our slave's entitled to some wine,' he remarked, pouring the dark red liquid from the jug. 'Here, get this down you.'

'Put your hands behind your back,' James ordered her. 'Allan can give you the drink.'

As she carried out his order, clasping her fingers together, Kate realised that everyone's eyes were on her. Allan put the edge of the goblet between her lips, tipping it gently, and she swallowed, but he tipped it at a sharper angle and she had to move her head back so that every time she swallowed they could all see the muscles of her throat moving. Some of the wine spilt out of her mouth and trickled down her throat and between her breasts.

'Mustn't waste any,' chuckled Allan, licking the outer edges of her lips, and then his tongue moved lower, lapping at her throat, and his large hands parted her kimono so that he could catch the sweet sticky liquid that was there.

Kate's flesh trembled beneath his tongue and when he started to give her more wine she was longing for drops to spill so that she could feel the rough moist flesh against her once more. For several minutes he continued to give her sips of wine whilst lapping at the spillage until she felt herself start to tremble and pleasure began to rise in her.

'That's enough,' said James. 'We don't want her drunk.'

'No that's not at all appropriate for a slave,' agreed Lucinda. 'What are we going to do with her?'

James looked at everyone. 'Here, Pam,' he said, handing her the lead. 'She can be yours first.'

Pam gave her by now familiar giggle. 'I never thought I'd have my own slave! Can I get her to do anything I like?'

'Absolutely anything,' James confirmed.

Pam looked straight at Kate and for the first time Kate realised that the American girl didn't like her very much. Behind her laughing exterior there was a hardness in her eyes that boded ill for Kate. 'First you can feed me the rest of my meal,' she said. 'Then undress me and bring me to a climax but don't take longer than five minutes.'

Her mouth literally watering with hunger, Kate carefully fed the other blonde girl tiny morsels of meat until her plate was empty and then, watched by the others, she unzipped the back of Pam's dress and eased it off her body before folding it carefully. She padded up to the stones at the top of the beach so that she could place it somewhere dry where the sand wouldn't get into it. When she returned Pam was watching her thoughtfully. 'Remember, five minutes,' she reminded her.

'Don't worry,' said Allan reassuringly. 'Knowing Pam it shouldn't take you five seconds,' and he laughed.

'Maybe she's not as skilled as you,' said Lucinda.

'She certainly doesn't have his equipment,' laughed Pam.

Kate began to tentatively fondle the other woman's breasts but she soon realised that it wasn't having any effect. Pam merely looked bored. Hastily Kate fell to her knees and, remembering what had happened to her earlier, began to massage the other girl's parted legs in the same way as James had massaged hers. Pam's breathing became more rapid and shallow and when Kate touched her between her thighs she could feel telltale beads of moisture.

'Two minutes have gone,' said James.

Kate continued to move her hands up and down Pam's legs, at the same time burying her face in her pubic mound. She felt the other girl's sex lips swell and part as her excitement grew.

Pam's legs were shaking and there was tension in every muscle. Kate swirled her tongue around the entrance to Pam's vagina, then up and down the slick inner channel, around the

142

clitoris and back to the vagina. She pushed it in and out of the hot entrance and Pam moaned with delight.

'One and a half minutes to go,' called James.

Kate could tell that Pam was fighting her own arousal, that she was determined Kate should fail. Kate was equally determined to succeed and suddenly she stopped massaging Pam's right leg and slid that hand across the other girl's belly, pressing down hard above the pubic bone, knowing full well that this would increase the delicious sparks of heavy pleasure. At the same time she clamped her mouth firmly around the swollen clitoris and sucked on it. With a scream of delight Pam came, her muscles spasming and her juices flowing, juices which Kate licked away, a move that ensured Pam's climax continued for several seconds.

'Well done, Kate,' called Allan. 'You did a great job.'

Pam jerked on the leash, pulling Kate upright. 'Don't think you're anything special to him,' she muttered. 'The only thing that's different about you is that you're British.'

Kate was startled. Obviously Pam was jealous and yet she'd never seemed the possessive type. In fact Kate had thought, right from the start, that both Allan and Pam had made a point of telling everyone that their relationship was a casual one. 'I guess he's the first millionaire you've ever got near,' continued Pam quietly, as Kate stood silent keeping her face carefully blank. 'He's my first too and I'm not going to give him up easily. You might think we're not an item but I don't see it that way. You keep your hands off him, you're a married woman.'

Surprisingly her words made Kate feel good. She was pleased that Pam should see her as a sexual threat, and pleased too at the power she'd had over the other woman, forcing her to come when she hadn't wanted to.

Despite the indignity of being a slave she was starting to enjoy the night. It was rapidly becoming dark and she saw that someone had put lanterns on sticks around the beach and the lights glowed eerily in the twilight.

'Give the lead to me,' said Lucinda. 'You're hungry, aren't you?' she asked Kate.

Kate nodded. 'A little.'

'I'd say a lot from the look on your face. Here, have this,' and she fed Kate a raw baby carrot from between her fingers. 'Nice?'

'Yes.'

'I've got some larger ones here, you'll probably like them too,' said Lucinda with a smile. 'Lie down on this blanket and we'll see.'

As soon as Kate was on the blanket Lucinda pushed her legs apart and knelt between them while Pam knelt above Kate's face. 'Look, there's this carrot or this courgette,' said Lucinda, showing the long smooth vegetables to her slave. 'Which would you prefer?'

'I like both,' said Kate.

Lucinda laughed. 'I'm not going to feed them to you, silly! I'm going to pleasure you with them. Now, which would you prefer?'

Kate couldn't imagine having either of them inside her. 'The courgette I suppose.'

'They go in more easily,' agreed Lucinda. 'But don't worry, we'll get you thoroughly excited first. While I'm working on you, you can give Pammie another orgasm. She seemed to enjoy the first one. Be careful though, we don't want you nipping her in your excitement.'

Kate's whole body tensed as she waited for Lucinda to start touching her. At first Lucinda's hands strayed up and down her legs, but then she untied the kimono, pulling it off and lifting Kate's arms out so that she was entirely naked. Next her hands massaged the already oiled breasts. 'Mmm, lovely and smooth,' she remarked. 'Did James do this for you?' Kate nodded. 'How thoughtful of him, it makes massage much easier.'

Now the hands were moving all over her body, teasing the breasts and then leaving them as Kate's pleasure began, wandering down over the hip bones, fingers fluttering there lightly before descending to the creases between the thighs and again the fingertips danced in a tantalising way over the tightly stretched flesh.

Kate's nipples were rigid with desire, her breasts aching to be cupped and massaged, but they were ignored. Suddenly Pam lowered herself onto Kate's face, parting her own sex lips so that she was totally exposed. 'Lick me, suck me the way you did before,' she ordered her.

'You girls certainly know how to have a good time,' said Allan, standing to one side of them.

'It almost makes me feel redundant,' said James.

'I can't wait for my turn.' There was no mistaking the excitement in Allan's voice.

'I'm sure you can't,' said James and Kate could tell that the prospect didn't delight him as much as it did Allan.

'Look at those breasts,' enthused Allan. 'The skin's wonderful, tight and smooth just the way I like it, and those poor little nipples. They look desperate.'

She wanted to scream at him that they were, to beg him to touch them, suck and lick them, but she knew it was forbidden. She was their slave, their sexual plaything, and her pleasure could only be delivered if they wished it.

'Use your tongue more,' said Pam crossly. 'You're not concentrating.'

'Naughty,' reproved Lucinda and her finger and thumb pinched on the stem of Kate's clitoris causing a sudden flush of pain to travel through her belly. She cried out and started to lick feverishly between Pam's sex lips, trying to remember what she'd done to the blonde girl before.

'That's better,' murmured Pam approvingly and soon she was moaning with delight.

'She's very damp between her thighs,' Lucinda told the men, as her fingers continued to work busily on the frantic Kate. 'I think she's ready for the courgette now.'

Kate felt the rounded top of the smooth-sided vegetable

being eased inside her opening and, as it was pushed into her, she gasped with gratitude at the silken fullness as the aching need dissipated, but she was still a long way from climaxing and longed for further stimulation.

'Have you come yet, Pam?' called Lucinda.

'No.'

'Kate, you can't have an orgasm until Pam's had one,' Lucinda explained and Kate redoubled her efforts. When she managed to find the tiny button and suck on it, Pam's thighs gripped Kate's face tightly and Kate felt Pam's whole body shake.

'She came then,' said Allan.

'I don't think they need you to tell them,' exclaimed James.

'Then I'd better let Kate come,' said Lucinda. She moved the courgette around a little, while her free hand rotated the whole of Kate's pubic mound. She felt a throbbing begin deep inside her, beating insistently, driving her almost out of her mind with need as her excitement grew. To her astonishment she felt Lucinda's mouth moving near the opening to her vagina and heard a strange crunching sound. It was then she realised that Lucinda was nibbling at the protruding end of the courgette.

'In a minute I'll reach you,' murmured Lucinda. 'When I do I'm going to lick your little clitoris until you come, and when you're coming I shall go on licking it until you beg me to stop.'

Kate heard herself uttering a tiny mewing sound of desperation. The words alone were an aphrodisiac, arousing her to new heights, while above her Pam continued to press downwards, her ever-hungry flesh demanding yet more pleasure.

At last Lucinda's lips brushed against Kate's silky pubic hair and now the moment she'd promised had come. Kate braced herself as the other woman's tongue moved upwards, delicately tracing a circle around the centre of Kate's pleasure.

'Yes! Yes!' Kate screamed, lifting her hips off the rug as

Lucinda's mouth fastened around the frantic nerve endings and she began to suck. Almost instantly the muscles tightened and then the slow rippling sensation began. The throbbing increased along with the strange sharp yet sweet tendrils of pleasure, and the pressure behind her clitoris grew.

'One last suck,' murmured Lucinda, tightening her mouth around Kate's centre of pleasure. Suddenly, with searing intensity, the tension exploded and she writhed helplessly as the climax consumed her. She was crying out, her voice muffled between Pam's thighs, and as her body began to relax, to recover from the shattering explosion, Lucinda resumed sucking fiercely whilst at the same time she tapped lightly on the end of the courgette, causing vibrations to travel through Kate's vagina.

'Stop, please stop,' Kate begged her.

Lucinda ignored her pleas. 'You're my slave, I can do what I like with you,' she reminded her.

With a groan Kate thrust her tongue into Pam's soaking entrance and heard the other woman's exclamation of pleasure. As Pam climaxed for the second time, so Kate's body was forced by Lucinda's almost cruel ministrations to endure yet another cataclysmic explosion of ecstasy that stretched every muscle to its limit. She flung her arms and legs wildly around, unable to control her jerking limbs.

Pam hastily lifted herself off Kate as the young girl's head started to roll from side to side. She was sobbing with the almost painful pleasure of it all, her cries echoing across the empty cove and out over the water, seeming to carry far into the night.

'Gee, that sounded good,' said Allan.

'I think she needs one more,' said Lucinda, her nimble fingers extracting the courgette which she now replaced with a vibrator turned on to full power. Kate felt that she couldn't endure it, that such pleasure was not to be borne, but as a slave she had to. To her astonishment her flesh quickly began to tingle with rearousal, every aching muscle gathering itself together for yet another tearing explosion. Inside her vagina it felt as though

147

every nerve ending was going mad, sending pulsing messages to her brain. 'I can't bear it, I can't bear it,' she gasped.

'Of course you can,' said Lucinda. 'You're a very lucky girl.' She began to massage Kate's swollen belly firmly, pressing down into the spasming muscles until it felt as though every part of Kate's lower body was being tormented and stimulated and with another ear-splitting scream she came again. This time, when the last contractions were over, she lay exhausted, arms and legs flung wide in limp abandonment, and closed her eyes.

'I wish I'd brought my video recorder,' said Allan.

'I don't imagine you'll forget it,' retorted James.

'I sure as hell won't,' said the American.

Kate could hear them, could hear their voices, but it meant nothing because all she wanted was peace and quiet and a chance for her shattered, abused flesh to recover from the surfeit of pleasure that Lucinda had inflicted on her.

'Before I have my turn I think she could do with cooling down,' said Allan, crouching on the sand and taking the end of the leash. He put his arms beneath her prostrate body and lifted her up as easily as though she were a doll. Then, followed by the others, he walked down to the water's edge and laid her on the sand her feet pointing towards the sea, parting her legs wide. 'You'll enjoy this,' he assured her, stroking her damp hair back off her forehead.

She hardly knew what was happening, but was aware that she was near the sea and then suddenly a wave broke between her ankles and the water rushed up over her, the cold, salty water cooling her hot flesh but stinging slightly at the entrance to her vagina.

Instinctively she started to struggle into a sitting position but Allan pushed her back against the sand. 'I want you to stay here a few minutes,' he said. And now, every time she heard the surf breaking or a wave approaching she tensed in anticipation of the sudden rush of cold water covering her entire body. It felt delightful, especially over her swollen breasts, but caused her nipples to harden even more and she wished that

148

someone would touch her there.

Allan made her remain still for about five minutes until all her flesh had cooled and then, just as she started to feel chilled, he lifted her up and took her back to the barbecue, standing her up on her feet and rubbing her briskly with a towel.

'There, that should feel better,' he said. 'I imagine you're hungry too. Have some meat.' He fed her tiny strips of the delicious roast pork which she ate so quickly that she accidentally nipped one of his fingers.

'I'm sorry,' she said hastily.

Allan laughed. 'Don't apologise. It's not often my cooking's that appreciated.'

After a few minutes he stopped feeding her and ran his hand thoughtfully down her flanks. 'So now you're my slave,' he said looking into her eyes. 'There's so much I'd like to do with you that the night isn't long enough.'

Kate felt a strange sinking sensation in her stomach and realised that it wasn't fear but desire. Horrified by this betrayal of James she averted her gaze from the piercing blue eyes of the American. 'I guess you don't know what to say,' he continued. 'Okay then, here's what we're going to do. James and I are both gonna make love to you at the same time. How does that suit you?'

It suited Kate very well. In fact, she couldn't think of anything she'd like more, especially when she saw the look of envy on Pam and Lucinda's faces. 'If that's what you want,' she murmured submissively.

Allan laughed, putting his fingers beneath her chin and tilting her head upwards so that she was forced to look at him. 'Don't pretend it doesn't suit you too,' he said. 'I think I'm getting to know you pretty well.'

'What's happening?' asked James. 'I missed that.'

'You and I are going to share her,' said Allan. 'She'll be the filling in the sandwich.'

Kate could see that James wasn't sure whether he wanted to do this or not. 'But it's your turn,' he protested.

'Yeah, and this is what I want to do. Don't I get my wish? After all, she is my slave to do with as I want.'

'Yes, but I'm not,' said James.

'What's the matter, afraid of the competition?' asked Allan.

'Of course not,' laughed James. 'It just wasn't something I'd thought of.'

'And you a writer too! You should have plenty of imagination. Come on, let's get to work.'

Allan and James stripped off their clothes and then James sat on the rug, pulling Kate down until she was sitting between his outspread thighs. He put his arms around her and rubbed the palms of his hands over her throbbing nipples until she started to moan with pleasure.

Allan, who was standing in front of her, reached down and removed James' hands. 'That'll do for now. Kate, kneel up and let me see you masturbating.'

Kate's heart began to pound. Despite the fact that it was her husband sitting behind her, her husband whose hands had started to ease the terrible ache in her breasts, there was no use denying the fact that it was Allan who really interested her. Obediently kneeling up she let the fingers of her right hand play between her thighs, tickling and teasing herself in the way that she loved best, until her hips began to jerk and she felt the hot pressure heavy inside her. While she was playing with herself she watched Allan's erection grow and saw him swell to his full impressive size, the purple glans seeming to strain, the skin stretched painfully tight.

She was rapidly reaching the point of no return and kept her eyes on Allan's. 'Stroke her buttocks,' Allan said to James and she felt her husband's hands caressing the rounded globes. Almost as soon as he touched her she climaxed and Allan quickly stepped forward, burying his hands in her hair and pulling her head towards him.

She opened her mouth, anxious to start working on him, her tongue dipping into the tiny slit at the head of his cock. She heard him give a quiet moan of delight and promptly swirled her tongue around the underside of the glans, making him groan as he started to thrust himself backwards and forwards inside her mouth.

'That's enough,' he cried. 'I don't want to come yet.' She released him, but reluctantly. She'd loved the taste of him, the salty musky odour of his manhood and wanted to devour him. Kneeling down opposite her, Allan licked the tip of one finger and then, reaching slowly forward, he circled each of her rigid nipples in turn. 'This is what you wanted, isn't it?' he asked.

'Yes,' she moaned, feeling her breasts swelling as the flesh expanded with excitement.

'Such lovely pink nipples,' mused Allan. Kate could hardly breathe. Everything he did was so slow, so calculated, and she could feel James' hardness thrusting against the base of her spine as he waited for Allan's orders. Now Allan was rolling her nipples between his fingers, occasionally squeezing them before pulling them towards him and then releasing them. It all felt delicious, and the sight of his naked body in the strange light of the lanterns made her desperate to be possessed by him, impaled on his massive rod.

'James, lie back,' said Allan. 'Then Kate can lie with her back on your chest.' As James slid down onto the rug he put his arms about Kate and pulled her down on top of him, his hands cupping her breasts where Allan's fingers had been only moments earlier. 'Is she used to anal sex?' Allan queried.

'Sure,' said James.

'Great, then you penetrate her there and I'll take her from the front.'

Kate tensed. She didn't know if she could take both of them, especially that way. Nevertheless, the idea was exciting. She could picture how it would be with each of them deep inside her, filling her as she'd never been filled before, and if she was clever she could bring them both to a climax using her internal muscles as both a weapon and a caress.

'Better use some oil,' Allan suggested and he passed James a small bottle. She felt her husband's fingers moving around her rear entrance, spreading the oil around the outer rim before moving two fingers inside her. For a moment her internal muscles tightened, attempting to expel him, but then she remembered to breathe through her mouth and the dreadful full feeling eased. James continued to move his fingers slowly back and forth until the muscles of her rectum relaxed and stretched. 'Is she ready yet?' asked Allan.

'I think so.'

'Lift yourself up, Kate,' said Allan. 'Then he can ease you down on top of him.'

She did as she was told and felt James' hands firm on her hips, pulling her half-reluctant body down until she felt the tip of him moving against the tight sphincter muscles. Again she forced herself to breathe slowly through her mouth, attempting to ease the cramping spasms that he was causing, and finally he was able to enter her. Using his hands he moved her down a fraction and then up then down a little further, sliding deeper and deeper, and the delicious, almost forgotten dark pleasure started to fill her.

Allan was kneeling between her thighs, his hands tickling the soft curve of her waist, and he watched her face carefully, studying every emotion that passed over it. 'I guess you feel pretty full, huh?'

'It's too much,' she gasped.

'It's just right,' he assured her quietly. At the sound of his voice her body relaxed more and then his fingers were spreading her sex lips and she felt him start to ease his massive erection inside her. Again she realised how large he was, so large that she wondered if she'd be able to take him, but this time he was quicker, thrusting fiercely inside her. It seemed to Kate that the amount of skin separating the men from each other was tiny, that they must almost be touching each other as Allan moved back and forth in an ever-quickening rhythm.

'Squeeze yourself around James,' he ordered her. 'Use those muscles to make him come. I want us both to spill ourselves inside you at the same time.'

Kate wanted that too, she wanted to feel them come in unison, to know that they both wanted her. She tightened her sphincter muscles and this time it was James' turn to moan. 'I can't hold out much longer,' he gasped.

'Sure you can,' said Allan, still moving smoothly and swiftly, one hand massaging Kate's left breast and the other keeping his weight off her. 'Touch yourself now,' he gasped, just as she could tell he was nearing his climax. 'Stroke yourself, touch the side in the way you like best.'

Kate couldn't believe this was happening to her. She was dimly aware that the other two women were watching, whispering to each other, and guessed that they were probably pleasuring each other too. She didn't care, all she cared about was the incredible sensation of fullness, the fact that both the men were trapped inside her, their pleasure dependent on her and all at once she understood that she was free. She wasn't anyone's slave, she was in control because she'd chosen this and it was bringing her more pleasure than she could ever have had in any other way.

'I'm coming,' cried James, and she felt him bucking beneath her and Allan. Wickedly she continued to tighten her sphincter muscles about him even after he'd finished and she heard him begging her to stop but she didn't because every time those muscles contracted so did the ones around Allan and his pleasure was increased.

'Nearly there?' Allan asked her, gazing down at her face.

'Yes,' she gasped as her fingers danced lightly along the stem of her clitoris. 'Great 'cos I'm coming now,' shouted Allan and immediately she felt him shuddering as he spilt his seed inside her, his hand gripping convulsively at her breast.

The elusive tingle between her thighs changed to a hot throbbing pleasure and only a few seconds after Allan, Kate came too, her body trapped between the two men, unable to move, but still the pleasure tore through her and she sobbed with gratitude.

Allan rolled over wrapping one arm round Kate so that she

was pulled off James and on top of Allan instead. For a moment she was disorientated, then, as she lay against Allan's chest, her breast squashed against his muscular torso, she realised that she still wasn't satisfied. Without thinking she began to grind her pelvis against his body.

'Go ahead, honey,' he whispered. 'Take your pleasure any way you want it.'

She doubted if she could have stopped whatever he said because she needed to come again, needed to writhe lasciviously against the huge American who'd come into her life and totally disrupted it. She wanted pleasure from him, pleasure given freely and willingly, and not controlled simply by his desires.

'She's your slave,' said James from where he was lying beside them. 'You can't let her take control.'

'I can do what I like,' Allan reminded him. 'When she's yours you call the shots, right now she's mine.'

Kate knew that she should be shocked at her own abandonment but she wasn't, she gloried in it. When Allan moved a hand across and reached between her buttocks, round to the front of her so that he was able to touch her between her thighs, she gave a sigh of relief, relief that he understood her so well.

'You're nearly there now,' he said encouragingly and his words tipped her over the edge as she bore down against him more fiercely. At last her pleasure spilled one final time and then she collapsed against him, her head resting just beneath his chin, every muscle relaxed and sated.

'It's time to give me the lead,' said James, his voice petulant in the darkness.

'Sure,' drawled Allan, easing Kate carefully off him and handing James the small chain. As James pulled her upright she felt Allan draw his fingers down the backs of her legs and smiled to herself. She was surprised when James put an arm round her waist, forcing her body against his. 'Let's go to the cave,' he said huskily. 'It's our special place. I want to take you there, away from the others.'

'Whatever you wish,' she said demurely.

'That's right,' he said quickly, and before anyone else could speak he was leading her up the beach and into the cave. Once inside his fingers started fumbling at the clasp of the collar and for the first time in many days it was removed. 'Kate, I love you,' he blurted out.

Kate said nothing. She was stunned. These were the words that she'd waited to hear ever since she'd first met him. She'd dreamt about them, longed for them during the first perverse days of their honeymoon and yet now, when he finally was saying them, they had no effect on her. 'Did you hear what I said?'

'Yes.'

'Haven't you got anything to say?'

'No,' she said softly.

'But you must have! I've never told anyone I love them before.' He sounded thoroughly bewildered.

'I suppose that's because you never have loved anyone before.'

'I suppose it is,' he admitted.

'Not even me,' she pointed out.

'What do you mean?'

'I mean that you didn't love me when you married me, did you?'

'No, but I do now. Come on, Kate, there's our ledge over there.'

'Do I have a choice in this?' asked Kate.

'Yes, yes.'

'I'm really tired,' she said slowly. 'I don't think I want to make love any more tonight. Perhaps another day.'

'What's happened to you?' asked James in confusion. 'You're always asking me if I love you and now that I say I do you're not interested.'

'Maybe you've left it too late,' she said quietly.

'Don't say that!'

'I want to go back to the house,' said Kate firmly.

'If that's what you want then of course.' He sounded utterly miserable and Kate could understand that, but she couldn't help herself. Things had changed and she needed time to work out exactly what she was going to do. 'You do believe me, don't you?' persisted James, kissing her on the forehead.

'Yes,' she assured him. 'I believe you.'

'Well that's something,' he said with relief and, taking her hand, he led her out of the cave and up the cliff path, leaving the others behind on the beach.

Once back in their bedroom Kate had a shower and then slipped between the sheets, turning her back on her husband and closing her eyes. She didn't want to talk and she didn't want him touching her. It could wait until morning. Hopefully, by then, she would know better what she really wanted.

Chapter 8

After James and Kate left the beach, Lucinda, Pam and Allan were left behind. Lucinda, who was not at all pleased at the way things had gone, turned to the other couple. 'Do you want to stay on down here or go back to the house?' she asked.

Allan looked unusually thoughtful. 'Guess we might as well go back up.'

'I'm not ready for bed yet,' complained Pam. 'Let's have some more fun.'

Lucinda could see that Allan wasn't in the mood for more fun and neither was she, but at the same time she didn't see why Kate should ruin the evening for all of them. 'I'm quite happy to carry on,' she said. 'Why don't we have a midnight swim?'

'I've already told you I prefer swimming in warm water,' said the American.

'You might enjoy it,' said Lucinda, 'especially if Pam and I go in with you.'

Now he looked a little more interested. 'Yeah, maybe you're right,' he conceded 'Come on then, let's try some skinny-dipping.'

'Skinny-dipping doesn't seem the right word for you,' giggled Pam, looking at her lover's massive frame.

'When you come up with a better one, let me know,' he suggested. 'Let's have one last glass of wine each and then I'll race you girls in.'

Lucinda filled up the goblets one more time and quickly drained her glass. Inside she was fuming, desperate to know what was happening up at the house. The night had gone so well and she'd enjoyed watching Kate sandwiched between the two men, her body climaxing helplessly as they thrust in and out of her. It would all be ruined if James gave it a sloppy romantic ending, she thought to herself. It just wouldn't fit, but there was nothing she could do about it right now. As the wine coursed through her veins her spirits lifted a little. 'Come on then,' she called to the other two, and began running naked across the sand.

Allan and Pam followed closely on her heels and the three of them tumbled into the surf, both girls shrieking as the cold water covered their warm bodies. 'It really is freezing,' screamed Pam, her teeth beginning to chatter.

Laughing, Allan disappeared under the water then suddenly popped up with his head between Pam's legs, lifting her high on his shoulders as he waded through the waves. She clung to his head still screaming in mock terror and, as Lucinda watched, Allan forced her legs apart and then tossed her away from him back into the sea. For a moment Pam disappeared beneath the surface and when she emerged, choking and spluttering, she was obviously angry.

'What the hell did you do that for?' she asked.

'Because I felt like it. Let's swim.' With that he started to move through the water using a powerful crawl. Both Lucinda and Pam swam around as well but in a more desultory fashion and they were both relieved when Allan returned to them. He stood up, shaking the water out of his eyes, and his hands gripped Lucinda's shoulders as he positioned himself in front of her, waist deep in water. 'Just wrap your legs around my waist, why don't you?' he suggested.

As soon as her feet were behind his back he put his hands under her shoulder blades and carefully lowered her upper body onto the surface of the sea. 'Let go with you legs,' he said, still keeping one hand in the small of her back. Now she was floating, her body rising and falling with the swell of the waves. Allan's hands caught hold of her each side of her waist and, without any preliminaries, he suddenly pulled her hard against him and she felt him thrust himself inside her. She'd forgotten how large he was and welcomed him with a cry of shocked pleasure. 'Pammie, move round and work on her tits,' he called to his girlfriend.

'I'm cold,' she whined.

'Don't be a spoilsport. It'll be your turn next.'

Lucinda closed her eyes as Pam began to massage her breasts while Allan continued thrusting roughly in and out of her. As her climax approached, Lucinda reached up and grabbed hold of Pam's long blonde hair, pulling the girl's head down so that she fastened her mouth around Lucinda's left breast. 'Bliss,' murmured Lucinda.

'No wonder you suggested a swim,' gasped Allan, and she could tell that he was very near to coming. 'You nearly there?' he asked her.

'Almost,' gasped Lucinda. 'Pammie, suck harder on my nipple.'

Pam obeyed and, within seconds, with the water lapping around her and moonlight streaming down on her, Lucinda shouted her pleasure aloud to the night sky as Allan continued to ram mercilessly in and out of her.

Only a few seconds later he came as well, but silently, not uttering a sound, his relief only betrayed by the urgent jerking of his hips and then the complete cessation of movement.

For several minutes he remained inside Lucinda and she floated limply on the water, feeling languorous and content. Briefly James and Kate had been banished from her mind and she realised that she'd forgotten how much she enjoyed the swift urgent couplings that she and Allan had had over the past few years.

'That sounded good,' he remarked when he finally disengaged himself from her. She put her feet down onto the soft sand beneath the sea and he wrapped his arms around her, giving her a brief hug before moving away. 'I'm afraid you'll have to give me a few minutes before I can do the same for you, Pam,' he said with a laugh.

'I'm not waiting around here for a second longer, never mind a few minutes,' retorted his girlfriend. 'This was a silly idea.'

Lucinda watched the voluptuous blonde walk angrily to the shore and she glanced at Allan. 'I think you've upset her.'

'She'll get over it,' he said casually. 'I don't know what's the matter with her. She's usually loads of fun.'

'Californian girls never like the cold,' said Lucinda.

'Guess you're right.'

Lucinda nodded but she didn't really think that was the reason for Pam's loss of good humour. She suspected that Pam was just as fed up with the way the evening had gone as she was. It must have been plain to her that Allan was taking a more than active interest in Kate. She'd have had to be an absolute fool not to realise he was fascinated by James' wife, and, although she might seem dizzy, Pam was no fool. If she had been Allan wouldn't have bothered with her.

As the three of them packed up the barbecue and made their way up the path to the cliff top, Lucinda managed to have a private word with the American girl. 'I'm sorry about tonight, it didn't quite go the way I'd intended,' she said.

'Not your fault,' said Pam.

'It's no good coming to England for warmth I'm afraid,' continued Lucinda chattily.

'It's not the warmth that bothers me,' snapped Pam.

'What's the trouble?' asked Lucinda, feigning ignorance.

Pam glanced over her shoulder but Allan was a long way behind. 'It's Allan,' she admitted. 'I think he's falling for Kate.'

'Really,' Lucinda tried to look surprised. 'Are you sure?'

'He's pretty interested and he was really enjoying making love to her.'

'I've known him some time,' said Lucinda. 'And I have to admit he does seem fascinated.'

Pam's eyes glinted. 'She's got a husband, and she's not having Allan.'

'But you said you and he weren't an item,' Lucinda reminded her.

'We're not, yet,' said Pam, her voice taking on a hard edge. 'We will be though, if I have my way.'

'He's not exactly ideal marriage material,' whispered Lucinda. 'He gets through wives like I get through hairdressers. He's forever changing style!'

'That's okay. As long as we actually get married I'd get a share of his money when we divorced.'

Lucinda was surprised. 'You're a pretty shrewd little operator aren't you?'

'It's the only way to get on,' said Pam. 'I'm playing it cute and girlie because that's how he wants me.'

'Difficult to keep up though if he married you.'

'I wouldn't bother then,' said Pam. 'Besides, he doesn't suit my sexual tastes that well.'

'I'm surprised about that.' This time Lucinda's astonishment was genuine. 'I've never heard any other woman complain and he always satisfies me.'

'I think I prefer women,' said Pam. 'They're so much more sensitive.'

'I see,' said Lucinda slowly. 'Well, I'll bear that in mind. I certainly enjoyed myself in the summer house.'

Pam smiled at her. 'So did I. If Allan and I do get married you'll have to be my maid of honour.' Both of them exploded with laughter.

'What's the joke, girls?' asked Allan, catching up with them.

'We're just being silly,' called Pam.

'So what's new?' muttered Allan, but when he and Pam went off to their bedroom Lucinda realised that the American girl had given her something else to think about as well. It was fascinating how the equation was changing all the time, and she decided that she'd have to tell James about the conversation.

After a hot bath Allan padded naked from the bathroom back to the bedroom rubbing vigorously at his short blond hair with a small towel. Pam was lying on top of the bed wearing, for the first time that he could remember, an ankle-length nightdress.

'What the hell's the matter with you?' he asked.

'Nothing.'

He couldn't help smiling. 'Then why are you covering yourself up like a Muslim wife?'

'Maybe I'm tired of being treated as some kind of sex object and then ignored when another woman takes your fancy.'

Allan continued drying his hair. He wasn't surprised, Pam hadn't exactly hidden her displeasure while they'd been on the beach, but he felt she was being unreasonable. The pair of them hadn't been together that long. They'd met at a friend's party. She'd been there with her fiancé but had left with Allan. He'd made it plain from the start that he was only looking for fun and Pam had agreed. They'd had fun as well, but now he had the suspicion that the fun was coming to an end. As far as he was concerned the timing was quite good, especially in view of what had happened since coming to England.

He was quite willing to admit that he liked Kate, in fact he was more than a little in love with her. If he'd felt that James genuinely loved her himself, and that the marriage was founded on truth, then he'd have walked away. He wasn't the kind of man who went round splitting up newlyweds, but clearly that wasn't the case here. James' casual admission of why he'd got married and how he intended to use Kate to make a fortune had, Allan felt, taken away any right James might previously have thought he had to sole possession.

If Kate should tire of James, and Allan thought that she was already disillusioned, then he would be ready to step in. She was a classy broad, the kind of woman he needed at this point in his life. An attractive blonde English wife would do nothing but enhance his reputation, but it wasn't only her looks that he admired. He liked her honesty, her obvious sensuality and the friendly personality that he could tell was there, hidden by the strange games James was making her play.

'I take it you want to sleep then?' he asked Pam.

'What are you smiling about?' She was clearly aggrieved.

'I'm just not used to seeing you dressed at bedtime!'

'I was freezing in that water,' she said suddenly. 'You know how I hate getting cold.'

'Gee you're not gonna go on about that again?' he asked wearily. 'What do you want me to do about it? Heat up the ocean?'

He sat down on the side of the bed, throwing the towel across the room and running his fingers through his hair because he couldn't be bothered to find himself a comb. 'You go to sleep then,' he said evenly. 'Maybe you'll be in a better mood in the morning.'

Pam scrambled to her knees and leant against his broad back. 'Don't you love me any more?' she asked in a little girl voice.

He didn't quite know what to say. As far as he could remember he'd never told her he loved her, but he might have done in the aftermath of some particularly satisfying sexual coupling. 'You're beautiful,' he said, knowing that this was usually a good get-out line.

'I didn't ask if I was beautiful,' she said crossly. 'I asked if you still loved me '

'Hell it's a bit late for one of these agony-aunt style conversations, isn't it? We've never exactly been Romeo and Juliet, Pam. If you're asking whether I still fancy you or not, sure I do. I thought we'd have some fun now, but since you feel that I'm using you as a sex object we'd better not.'

'You like Kate better, don't you?'

Allan felt his back stiffen. 'Oh cut the crap,' he said. 'She's a married woman.'

'That doesn't mean you can't fancy her.'

'Look, Pam,' he said patiently. 'This isn't the first time that we've had fun with friends. Why are you getting paranoid about Kate?'

'Because you're obsessed with her,' she retorted. 'You watch her all the time and whenever you're touching her or having sex with her you're really tender, the way you used to be with me. I didn't mind when you took Lucinda in the sea tonight, that's the way you always behave, but you're different with Kate.'

'Kate's a novelty. I've had sex with Lucinda more times than I've had hot dinners.'

Pam started to massage between his shoulder blades. 'Now I've made you angry, haven't I?'

He wished she wouldn't keep putting on the little girl voice, he didn't find it at all sexy. 'I don't like nagging women,' he agreed.

'I'm sorry,' said Pam, reaching round him and rubbing her hand up and down his chest. 'You can take the nightdress off if you like,' and now she gave her throaty giggle.

Allan swung his legs onto the bed and pushed her down so that she was lying beside him. 'You're sure about this? You don't feel I'm using you as a sex object any more?'

She shook her head, her eyes smiling and her lips parted invitingly. Allan wasn't fooled. He knew that she was trying to placate him, to make amends for showing what he had a nasty suspicion was her true self to him. Just the same she was very sexy and, as he'd been anticipating some fun, he saw no reason to turn it down, although he was rapidly revising his opinion of her.

Carefully he eased the long nightdress up over her body and she lifted her arms above her head to make it easy for him. As usual the sight of her naked body swiftly aroused him and he pushed himself up to the head of the bed so that he was sitting against the pile of pillows. Pam knelt facing him and then lowered herself backwards so that the backs of her thighs were supported by the front of his and she put her hands down on the bed, letting her head hang back until her long blonde hair tickled the tops of his feet.

Allan gave a groan of pleasure at the sight of her stretched so taut and athletically before him. Placing his hand under the small of her back, he began kissing her breasts and stomach,

164

letting his lips travel around each full globe, taking his time as he nibbled at the delicate flesh. When he drew his tongue down the centre of her breasts and lower across her ribcage and upper belly, her body began to jerk and the veins on her neck stood out prominently.

Now he pulled her upright and she clasped her hands behind his neck, cupping his head while he drew each nipple in turn into his mouth, grazing them gently with his teeth as she whimpered and murmured with mounting excitement.

Gradually Allan eased himself back onto his elbows and Pam leant forward more, lightly stroking his shoulders and chest, tweaking at his nipples and running her fingers across the skin at the side of his armpits. He was so hard that it was almost painful now and, supporting himself on one elbow, he reached between her outspread thighs and slid a finger inside her moist entrance, spreading her juices up and down between her sex lips.

Pam was panting, her body tense, her breasts swollen and the nipples hard. Unable to wait any longer he put his hands beneath her hips and lifted her onto him, pulling her down hard and feeling her close about him, contracting her muscles tightly in the way that she knew he loved.

Pam's eyes were bright, her pupils dilated and her cheeks flushed. She leant back a little and he let her control the depth of penetration by her position as she moved her body up and down over his rigid cock, occasionally rotating her hips which drove him into a frenzy.

He could feel the tension building to the point of no return. All around the glans he could feel the tingles of mounting excitement as the pressure built within him and every muscle in his body went rigid. Pam, who knew the signs well, reached forward and scratched on his tight belly with the tips of her long fingernails. He moaned in ecstasy, feeling the inexorable tightness, the almost unbearable build-up before release, and longed to hold on to the feeling, to retain the glorious sensations longer, but it was impossible.

Moving above him, Pam gave a cry of delight as she reached her own climax and her body arched back and then doubled forward, her hair falling over her shoulders and brushing against his face. Lost in her own pleasure she stopped moving. Frantically Allan grabbed hold of her hips and moved her urgently up and down over his throbbing shaft, savouring every delicious moment of pre-ejaculatory tension. Then the wonderful hot tingling exploded in his first spasm of release and his hips jerked uncontrollably.

After a few seconds, as he was still groaning with relief, Pam tightened herself around him, milking him as hard as she could. His body jerked again as he spilt the last of his hot seed inside her until all the tension in his body dissipated and he collapsed back against the pillows with one final groan.

Pam eased herself off him and then snuggled up next to him. 'Was it good?' she asked.

'Great,' he enthused.

'I know how to make you happy, don't I?' she persisted.

'You sure do. I trust you got a little pleasure from it as well?'

She laughed. 'You always make me come. You're the best lover I've ever had.'

'I bet you say that to all your men.'

'I do not.' She sounded quite affronted, but Allan wasn't misled. He was beginning to suspect that Pam's motives weren't as genuine as he'd first thought. He'd have to get some of his people to run a check on her, he thought, as his hands moved idly over her soft flesh. She'd probably got a lot of debts or came from a very poor background and was after his money. It wouldn't be the first time but normally he spotted the gold-diggers straight away. It seemed that Pam had been cleverer than most of them. Not that it mattered, he'd greatly enjoyed their time together and the sex tonight had been deeply satisfying.

He felt her hands moving over his body and gently moved them. 'That's it for tonight, honey.'

She pressed her skin closer to his and wriggled her hips

166

provocatively. 'Can't I have one more?' she asked.

'Talk about greedy,' he groaned in mock despair.

'I can't help it if you turn me on.'

'That's not much good if I can't satisfy you, is it?'

'You do but I'd just like one more.'

Allan wondered why she was being so persistent. It seemed like a desperate move to prove how much she wanted him. For a moment he thought of refusing but then decided it would be unfair. Maybe she was just feeling extra sexy, turned on by the cold Cornish sea despite her protestations to the contrary. Slowly he slid down the bed, parted her thighs, then, as she hooked her knees over his shoulders, he began to devour her with his mouth. Her moist flesh was still sensitive from her orgasm and he felt it leap beneath his tongue, her clitoris was quickly hard and he swirled the tip of his tongue around it feeling her thighs tremble each side of his head. 'That's right, that's right,' she urged him. 'Just lick the top, please.'

He had no intention of being told what to do by her and deliberately slipped his tongue lower instead, swirling it around the entrance to her vagina where his erection had so recently been sheathed. She tasted delicious and he plunged his tongue inside, swirling it around and lightly caressing the tiny G-spot which made her jerk and groan.

She was arching her hips higher now, frantically trying to force him to lick her clitoris but still he made her wait. He licked the creases at the tops of her thighs, moved his head upwards and swirled his tongue inside her bellybutton until she was almost sobbing with frustration. Only then did he return to the centre of all her pleasure. For a few seconds he continued to circle it and then, as her hands beat a frantic tattoo against the bed, he finally moved his tongue over the head of the clitoris itself, trailing it up and down in firm steady strokes until he felt her muscles begin to contract. Then she was screaming his name aloud as her pleasure spilled over a second time.

When he was certain that she'd finished, Allan got back into bed beneath the sheet and draped one arm around her shoulders. 'Think you can sleep now, Pammie?'

She sighed with satisfied delight. 'Yes,' she murmured.

'Good,' he said, and within minutes of closing his eyes he was fast asleep.

As soon as Pam was certain that Allan was asleep, she eased herself away from his body, climbed out of bed, pulled on a robe and padded quietly along the landing to Lucinda's room. Before tapping on the door she listened for a moment and heard an all too familiar humming sound. Clearly Allan hadn't satisfied her in the sea and she'd now resorted to her vibrator. Pam tapped twice on the bedroom door.

'Who is it?'

'It's only me, Pam.'

'Oh, come in,' called Lucinda.

Pam was surprised that Lucinda didn't bother to stop what she was doing as she walked into her room. She was sprawled across the bed widthways, her knees drawn up, one hand stroking her breasts whilst the other was holding a large vibrator inside herself. 'Won't be a minute,' she gasped, her breasts and chest flushed with sexual excitement.

Pam stood uncertainly by the side of the bed. She was fascinated but at the same time felt she was invading the other woman's privacy. Group sex was one thing, private masturbation another, although clearly it didn't disconcert Lucinda because with a sharp cry she climaxed and her body twisted around in sensual abandonment.

'That was good,' she gasped, leaning up on one elbow and staring at Pam. 'Do you want a go?' She held out the long, thick and very realistic-looking vibrator.

Pam shook her head. 'No thanks, Allan and I have been busy ever since we got back.'

'Lucky you,' said Lucinda. 'Unfortunately James spends his nights with his wife. Naturally it's what she expects.'

'I suppose it's what he wants to do as well,' said Pam innocently.

She was surprised to see a look of annoyance in Lucinda's eyes. 'It's not meant to be but I'm beginning to think it is.'

'Why isn't he meant to want to sleep with his wife?' asked Pam curiously.

'It's a long story and I can't explain,' said Lucinda. 'The only thing I can say is, the marriage isn't quite what it seems.'

Pam sighed and sat down on the padded stool in front of Lucinda's dressing table. 'Maybe that explains why she's interested in Allan,' she said slowly.

'Do you think she is?' asked Lucinda.

'Yes, and even if she isn't he's certainly interested in her.'

'Are you sure?'

Pam was surprised by Lucinda's eager questioning. 'Pretty sure. I tried to get him to commit himself to me tonight but he wouldn't. Besides, I'm not a fool, I can see the way he is with her and the way he watches her when someone else is pleasuring her. She fascinates him.'

'Good,' murmured Lucinda.

'There's nothing good about it,' said Pam indignantly. 'It's taken me years to catch a millionaire, I don't want some English girl snaffling him from under my nose.'

'Ah, I see,' said Lucinda quietly. 'Unfortunately it would suit my purposes rather well.'

'I don't think James will be pleased,' said Pam.

'No, I don't think he will, although there was a time when he would have been,' said Lucinda.

Pam frowned. 'Don't you feel a little strange sharing their honeymoon with them?' she asked.

'I was enjoying it at first,' confessed Lucinda. 'It's been great fun watching Kate learning to be obedient and discovering a great deal about herself in the process, but the fun seems to have gone out of it recently, thanks to James.'

'I've enjoyed myself here,' said Pam quickly. 'It was great in the summer house this afternoon.'

Lucinda looked thoughtfully at her. 'I enjoyed it too, but I really prefer men I'm afraid.'

Pam nodded. 'I was thinking about that while Allan was making love to me earlier and I think perhaps I do too. The thing is though, women take it at a better pace, they understand your body better. Perhaps what I need's a young male who I can train like James has been training Kate.' She laughed.

'That's not such a bad idea,' agreed Lucinda.

'The reason I came to talk to you,' explained Pam, 'is because I'm worried about Allan. You don't think he'll go off with Kate do you?'

'No I don't,' said Lucinda confidently. 'But I might as well admit that James thinks it could happen.'

Pam had a terrible sinking feeling in the pit of her stomach. 'So I'm not imagining it all?'

Lucinda sighed. 'Maybe not but I can't see the two of them together. For a start Allan's much older than her and he's always liked experienced women.'

'Kate's experienced now,' Pam pointed out.

'Yes, but not in the way he likes. Everything she knows, she knows because she's been made to learn it.'

'Allan thinks she's still got lots of untapped sexuality,' confessed Pam. 'He knows everything there is to know about me now. I'm not exactly deep. I know what I like and I'm willing to try most things but I never try and hide my feelings. Also, I couldn't possibly have behaved like Kate. I'm not into this obedience thing. Like I say I wouldn't mind training someone myself but I wouldn't want to be trained.'

'That can't be why Allan wants her,' said Lucinda. 'Now that James has trained Kate there'd be no point in Allan taking over. If he does want her it must be for completely different reasons.'

'I think he's falling in love with her,' said Pam miserably.

Lucinda groaned. 'He can't be! James thinks he is as well.'

'Well of course James is in love with her, he's her husband.'

'Yes but he wasn't meant to be in love with her,' explained Lucinda.

Pam frowned. 'Can't you tell me what their marriage is really about?'

Lucinda shook her head. 'Not right now. I will later, when it's finished.'

'When what's finished? Not the marriage I hope?'

'Of course not,' said Lucinda soothingly. 'It's a kind of project we're doing.'

Pam wished that Lucinda could tell her more. Nothing was making sense, and, if anything, she felt more confused than when she'd left the sleeping Allan. 'Do you think there's anything I can do to stop Kate and Allan getting together?' she asked.

'Why is it so important?' queried Lucinda. 'Are you madly in love with Allan?'

Pam shook her head. 'No, not at all, although he's fantastic in bed. It's his money I want. I grew up with nothing at all in some two-bit shanty town. I had nothing going for me but my looks and I decided early on that I was going to exploit them to the full. There've been a lot of men along the way but none of them were quite rich enough, I always knew that. Allan is and I want to marry him.'

'Just marry him? If I remember rightly you're not too bothered if the marriage doesn't last, is that true?'

Pam nodded. 'But I still need to get him to the altar,' she pointed out. 'Kate could mess that up for me.'

'I really don't think there's much we can do about Kate,' said Lucinda briskly. 'Since we're being so honest with each other I may as well admit that it would suit me very well indeed if the pair of them got together. As it's money that you're worried about I think there's another way you could get rich, in your own right too.'

'You do? But how?' asked Pam incredulously. 'I'm not even well educated.'

'That won't matter.'

'Can you give me a hint of how I could do it?'

Lucinda sighed. 'I'm not trying to be difficult but right now

171

that isn't possible either. Trust me though. If Allan and Kate do get together then don't panic. I'll help you and believe me you won't starve.'

Pam supposed that she would have to be satisfied with that. 'Do *you* love James?' she asked Lucinda.

Lucinda paused. 'I suppose I do in a way. We've had some good times together and we share the same tastes. I wouldn't call it love though, neither of us are into that kind of thing.'

'I didn't think Allan was,' said Pam. 'I wasn't trying to make him fall in love with me, just fancy me so much he wouldn't want to lose me.'

'It seems that Kate has a curious effect on men,' said Lucinda. 'James has never shown any sign of falling in love before.'

'I don't think she's anything special,' muttered Pam. 'She hasn't even got decent-sized breasts.'

Lucinda laughed. 'I don't think that's got a lot to do with it.'

'Well mine have helped me,' said Pam.

When she crept back into bed beside Allan, Pam snuggled up against the comforting warmth of his back and wondered if she'd been telling the truth when she'd said that she wasn't in love with him. She'd certainly grown extremely fond of him and she'd miss him terribly if he left her, but at the back of her mind she couldn't help thinking about what she'd said to Lucinda. It would certainly be exciting to train a young man to satisfy her every desire. The only problem was, she couldn't imagine how that would ever happen.

Chapter 9

The following morning Lucinda was up early. She'd spent most of the night thinking about what Pam had told her and trying to work out what might happen to them all in the future. There were several possibilities but the most likely one she feared was that James was going to attempt to regain Kate's love. Once the book was completed he might decide that it was Lucinda he no longer needed and choose, instead, to settle down with Kate. The more she thought about it during the night the more determined Lucinda became that this wasn't going to happen.

She knew that James could be persuasive when he wanted to be, that he was capable of charming Kate so much that she forgave him everything that had happened. Also Lucinda realised that James truly believed he was in love with Kate, which made the situation all the more dangerous. The solution had come to her in the early hours of the morning and after that she'd been unable to sleep for excitement.

Now, she prowled around downstairs, nibbling on a croissant and awaiting her opportunity. It came sooner than she expected. Clearly Kate had found it difficult to sleep as well because by seven o'clock she was in the kitchen, plugging in the kettle. She had faint smudge-like circles beneath her eyes.

'You're up early,' said Lucinda brightly.

'I couldn't sleep.'

'Too much excitement last night.'

Kate shot a glance of dislike at Lucinda. 'I do wish you wouldn't keep up a running commentary on my private life.'

'I'm sorry, but I can't help it. I suppose I see it as part of my job,' said Lucinda, knowing that this would catch Kate's attention.

'Part of your job? What on earth do you mean? You're his literary agent.'

'That's precisely why I'm involved in your marriage.' She saw a look of confusion on Kate's face and pressed home her advantage. 'I suppose James has been telling you all night how much he loves you?'

Kate nodded. 'Not that it's any of your business, but yes he has.'

'You shouldn't listen to him,' said Lucinda sweetly.

'Why not?' demanded Kate.

'Because he doesn't mean it.'

'I think I'm the best person to be the judge of that,' retorted Kate. 'And I believe he does.'

'He's just terrified of losing you before it's finished.'

'Before what's finished?'

'I'm not supposed to tell you,' said Lucinda slowly.

Kate stirred her coffee, the spoon clattering against the side of the cup. 'I'm sick and tired of everyone's secrets,' she snapped. 'Either you've got something to tell me or you haven't.'

'I'm beginning to think you ought to know,' said Lucinda, making her voice as sympathetic as she could.

'Know what?'

'Everything,' replied Lucinda.

'And are you in a position to tell me?'

Lucinda smiled sweetly. 'Yes. Because it was all my idea.'

'What was your idea?' Kate made no attempt to disguise her intense irritation.

'Come with me,' said Lucinda swiftly. 'Come quickly, before James wakes up.'

She saw the younger girl hesitate for a moment but then, as she'd guessed it would, curiosity overcame her and when Lucinda hurried towards James' study, Kate was at her heels. 'I didn't think we were meant to go in there,' whispered Kate.

174

'I've got a key,' explained Lucinda. 'I need it in case the publisher rings about his work and he's out.'

'Why should they ring? He hasn't done anything yet.'

'Oh yes he has,' said Lucinda.

She saw Kate looking round the study and watched as her eyes fell on the pile of printed paper lying next to the computer. 'What's that?' she asked curiously.

'His novel,' said Lucinda.

'But he's done a lot.' Kate was obviously shocked.

'Just one of his little white lies to you,' Lucinda tried to sound sympathetic.

'What's his novel about? Why is he so secretive?'

'I'll show you,' said Lucinda and she held out the title page for Kate to look at.

Kate's eyes widened. 'It's called *Obedience*,' she said in astonishment.

'Read the beginning,' Lucinda urged her.

Kate shook her head. 'I don't want to.'

'Then I'll read it to you,' said Lucinda crisply. '"The man stared across the crowded nightclub floor. The girl was quite perfect, he thought to himself. She was young, tall and slender, her blonde hair cut in an attractively tousled style and when she laughed her face positively shone with innocence. He knew then that he was going to marry her. For years now he'd been searching for her, only she'd had no face. He travelled the world searching in vain, always knowing that when he saw her he'd recognise her. Now he had. All he had to do was introduce himself, court her and marry her. Then, once she was his, he would finally find satisfaction. At that moment he thought that he was the luckiest man alive".'

Lucinda stopped reading and looked at Kate. 'Do you recognise yourself?' she asked.

'Yes, of course I do. That's how I met James, in a nightclub. But I don't understand what it means.'

Lucinda flicked through the pages, searching for something that would finally bring the truth home to Kate. 'Ah,' she said at last. 'Let's see if this explains it a little more. Are you sure you don't want to read it for yourself?' Kate shook her head. 'Perhaps I should explain that the girl in this book is called Caitlin,' explained Lucinda. 'Now, here's another extract.'

'"He parted the cheeks of Caitlin's bottom and moved his fingers between them, drawing one fingertip in circles around the outside of her rear entrance. She tensed and he knew that she was afraid. His excitement increased as he continued to move his finger insistently round and round while her body trembled with fear. Abruptly he slipped one oil-covered fingertip inside her and began to circle it around the inside. 'Don't,' cried Caitlin, trying to draw away from him.

'"He was tremendously excited by her fear and reluctance and inserted another finger. Immediately Caitlin's entire body went rigid. 'Please don't do this to me,' she begged him. He loved it when she begged and, watching the leather belt dig deep into her flesh as she tried to move herself away from him, he nearly came there and then." Do you recognise yourself?' asked Lucinda sweetly.

Kate's cheeks were bright red and she looked as though everything she believed in had been taken away from her. 'He's been writing about me all the time,' she whispered. 'He's been using me for his book, hasn't he?'

'That's right,' agreed Lucinda. 'He didn't marry you because he loved you, he married you because I suggested he did. He got a big advance for this book, but he didn't know how to write it. You see, it isn't easy to find a girl like you, Kate, a girl so sexually inexperienced and naive. The problem was the book wouldn't have worked if it hadn't had a heroine like that. So he needed you and the only way he could get you in his power was to marry you.

'It was really lucky you were so besotted with him because it meant that you'd do anything he asked of you. You've been brilliant, and so's the book.'

'How does it end?' asked Kate.

'In the outline he didn't give an ending. He couldn't because

176

he had no idea what would happen.'

'What about now?' Kate looked stricken.

'I haven't asked him,' said Lucinda carelessly. 'But I imagine he's got something worked out.'

'So he never loved me at all?'

'No. Did he say he did?'

Kate shook her head. 'He wouldn't say it at first, but lately he has done.'

'Ah,' said Lucinda, 'that must have something to do with the ending he's got planned.'

'Was he ever going to tell me?' Kate's voice was barely audible.

'I suppose he would have had to, once the book was finished,' said Lucinda carelessly.

'And then was he planning on a divorce?'

'Do you know we've never discussed that,' lied Lucinda. 'Maybe he thought that when he told you, you'd just go off and leave him.'

'Or maybe he thought I'd be flattered,' said Kate thoughtfully.

Lucinda nodded. 'Possibly, his ego's big enough for that.'

'Is it all there?' asked Kate.

'Everything.' Lucinda couldn't keep the satisfaction out of her voice.

'You're both sick,' said Kate, her anger flaring. 'I bet you were behind it. James would never have thought this up on his own.'

'I'm his agent, it's my job to help him think of things that will make him money.'

'But you've enjoyed it haven't you?' persisted Kate. 'No wonder you've never liked me. You never really wanted him to get married but it was the only way that you could make sure I was trapped here. It must have been hell for you watching some of the things that went on.'

'It's been a bit disconcerting,' confessed Lucinda. 'But I've never felt there was anything to worry about.'

'What about me?' cried Kate. 'What about my feelings?'

'Well sexually your feelings were the things that interested us,' explained Lucinda.

'I didn't mean sexually!' Kate shouted.

'They were the only feelings I was interested in,' said Lucinda smoothly.

'And James?'

'I don't think James was overly concerned with emotions to begin with. He may be now, but then I'm not sure what direction the book's taken. Would you like me to have a look? See where he's got up to?'

Kate picked up the manuscript and flung it across the room, the pages flying in all directions. 'No I would not,' she shouted. 'I'm not some animal in a laboratory, to be used in an experiment. I'm a person and I loved him. You both knew that and you exploited it.'

'I just thought you ought to know,' said Lucinda quietly. 'It was all right when James wasn't trying to pretend it was more than it really was but lately . . .'

'Yes, lately he's tried to be more romantic about it,' said Kate, her voice tight with anger. 'Thank you so much for telling me the truth, Lucinda. It's certainly helped to clear my mind.'

'I'm so glad.'

She watched as Kate stormed out of the study and up the stairs. Then Lucinda carefully picked up the pages of the manuscript, put them back in order and laid the tidy pile down next to the computer. She wished that she could hear what was going on in the bedroom upstairs but it didn't really matter. She had a pretty good idea.

'Wake up!' shouted Kate, shaking James' shoulders vigorously. 'I want to talk to you.'

He stirred sleepily, opening his eyes with difficulty. 'What on earth are you playing at? Pack it in, Kate.'

'How dare you,' she screamed, beside herself with fury. 'It was all lies wasn't it? You've lied to me right from the beginning!'

He looked dazed as she continued to pummel his bare shoulders and chest while he struggled to sit upright and fend her off. 'I don't know what you're talking about. Kate, control yourself.' With this he finally managed to catch hold of her wrists and, gripping them tightly, pulled her down onto the bed next to him. 'Have you gone completely mad?'

'No, but no thanks to you,' she shouted, the words of his book still seared into her memory. 'I can't believe it, I just can't believe it.'

'Can't believe what?'

'That you've been using me to write your bloody book.'

He stared at her in dismay. 'How did you find out about the book?'

'So you're not denying it?'

He didn't seem to know what to say. 'I've told you not to go into my study. It's a great pity that I still haven't taught you obedience.'

'Don't you talk to me about obedience,' she shouted. 'I've seen the title of the book. It's all there, isn't it? Every single thing that you've done to me is in the book. You bastard! To think I loved you, that even when I got up this morning I was hoping we could make it work. Well I hope you got some satisfaction from it all.'

'*You* did,' he retorted. 'I was astonished at the way you took to it. I've lost count of the number of times I've watched you writhing around, helpless in the throes of another orgasm. It didn't take much to bring you out of your shell.'

'But I was in love with you,' she cried. 'I thought it was all for love, but you betrayed me. You never loved me. You and Lucinda set me up so that you could write the book. What were you going to do when you'd finished it, kill me off?'

'Don't be so ridiculous,' he snapped. 'I haven't any idea what's going to happen at the end.'

'Well that's a pity because I'm not going to hang around long enough for you to find out.'

Now he looked alarmed as well as dismayed. 'Kate, for God's

sake give me a chance to explain.'

'Lucinda's already done that.'

Understanding crossed his handsome face. 'Lucinda told you all this, did she?'

'She didn't just tell me about it she showed me. That was even worse. How do you think I felt reading about myself? And it's hardly changing my name to call me Caitlin is it? All my friends will recognise me.'

'Don't you see, Lucinda's done this because she's jealous of you,' he explained, releasing her wrists and moving his hands up and down her arms. 'It's true, I admit it, I was using you and when I married you I wasn't in love with you but that's all changed. You've made me realise that sex isn't just about sensations it's—'

'You needn't bother.' Kate's voice was full of scorn. 'I know you need an ending, that's the only reason you're changing your tune now.'

'That's a lie. I suppose Lucinda's put that idea into your head but it simply isn't true.'

'And why would she lie?'

'Because she's jealous. She chose you after rejecting loads of girls. I realise now that she wanted someone who wouldn't pose any threat to her. She was my mistress, obviously she didn't want me marrying someone that I was going to fall madly in love with.'

'You've never fallen in love with anyone in your life,' said Kate.

'Not until now, but I do feel differently about you, Kate, and that's the truth.'

'I don't think you'd recognise the truth if it bit you,' said Kate. 'How can I believe a word you say after all this? When I think of the things you've made me do.'

'But you enjoyed them didn't you?' he said softly. 'You've had more pleasure since we've been married than you dreamed possible, and that's what I promised you. Do you really think that you'll get that with anyone else?'

'I don't see why not. There's nothing that special about you except that you're a liar.'

'Of course there is. Half of your excitement came from the fact that you were being submissive, dominated by me. You need that, you need to be pushed to the limits, to be forced to do things that otherwise you'd reject. Some nice everyday husband who works in an office nine to five, comes home and rolls on top of you twice a week isn't going to satisfy you now, Kate. We've trained your body too well for that. I need you, but you need me too.'

Kate shook her head. 'I don't believe you need me except for the book.'

'I do,' he protested vehemently.

'So how's the book going to end?' she asked sharply.

James frowned. 'What's that got to do with it?'

'Just answer the question.'

'I'm not sure yet. I haven't written up what happened last night and obviously that changed a lot of things. It looks as though the man's going to fall for the heroine. It's not what I'd expected but I've got to be truthful.'

'You're trying to please everyone, aren't you?' said Kate. 'This way women and men will enjoy the book because women care about relationships as well as sex and men want the sex. I expect Lucinda's already told you that.'

'Lucinda's my agent, she doesn't do my writing for me! Kate, please listen to me. We could have a great life together. Lucinda won't always be around. I can get rid of her today if you like. As for Allan and Pam . . .'

'I don't want you to get rid of Allan and Pam,' said Kate flatly.

James' brown eyes darkened. 'What do you mean by that?'

'Exactly what I say. I like having them here.'

'You mean you like having Allan here.'

'Doesn't that fit very well into your book?' she asked mockingly. 'I suppose not. It will throw quite a spanner in the works if Caitlin falls for someone else, won't it?'

'But you haven't, have you?' he said thickly, his hands deftly unbuttoning her blouse and unfastening her bra so that he could caress her breasts. 'Look, you still respond to me. I know I've hurt you and I'm sorry, but this book's going to make me rich. I want you to share my success. So what if people guess that you're Caitlin. I'd have thought that would make you proud. And we can do a follow-up, I can write about our life after your initiation. Naturally I'd have to wait and see what particular path your sexuality takes but—'

'Do you really think I'm going to provide a sequel?' she asked incredulously.

'I adore your breasts,' he murmured, his fingers tweaking her nipples. 'They're so sensitive. At first I thought they were too small but I've grown to adore them.'

Kate wished that her body wouldn't respond but she knew that her nipples were hardening.

'It isn't you I'm responding to,' she muttered. 'It's just that my body . . .'

'Likes the pleasures I can give it,' he finished for her.

'Let me go,' said Kate. 'Whenever you touch me now I know it's just another chapter for the book.'

'Stop talking about the damn book,' snarled James, throwing her onto the bed and then stretching her arms above her head, imprisoning her wrists in one hand while with the other he stripped her naked. 'You know you want me,' he continued, his hand moving between her thighs. 'There's no point in denying it, you're already wet.'

Kate tried to jerk herself away from him but he was too strong and pressed the full length of himself on top of her. He was very aroused and she could feel his hardness against her thigh as he pressed his pubic bone against hers, sending tiny currents of electricity sparking between her hips and deep inside her belly.

'Please don't do this,' she begged him. 'I don't want you any more.'

'But you do, I can tell you do,' he persisted. 'You feel so

good.' He lowered his mouth to her breasts, licking them gently at first. As she struggled to get free, his teeth nipped sharply on the point of one tender nipple and she gasped at the swift pain, but then moaned as it was followed immediately by the tight pressure of mounting excitement and she knew that her body did want him.

She could feel the tip of his erection pushing blindly between her thighs, searching desperately for her opening, and, to her horror, she felt her hips move to make it easier for him. As he slipped inside her he was murmuring to her, and soon he was moving in a wonderful easy rhythm that matched her rising desire, and the delicious hot heaviness centred itself between her thighs while every muscle was tense with arousal.

'I knew it,' he said triumphantly. 'You're going to come, aren't you?'

'No,' she cried furiously.

'There's no point in lying,' he laughed, and to her despair she felt the first tiny tremors begin.

Clearly James felt them too because now he was moving more swiftly. His tongue licked and flicked at the aching nipple until, at exactly the right moment, he drew it into his mouth, sucking hard, and the delicious pulling feeling seemed to draw the pleasure up from between her thighs so that it spread over her whole body and suddenly she was coming, groaning with pleasure.

As she climaxed James came too. He came with a shout of mingled pleasure and triumph and when it was over Kate turned her head away unable to meet his eyes, shamed by her body's response.

'That looked good,' said a voice from the doorway.

'How long have you been standing there, Lucinda?' asked James softly while Kate struggled frantically beneath him.

'Long enough. She really is putty in your hands, isn't she?'

'Get her out of here,' hissed Kate.

James looked down at his wife. 'That's not what you really want.'

'Yes it is. You promised me you'd get rid of her today. Well if you meant what you said, do it now.'

'You need another good chapter, James,' said Lucinda.

James looked helplessly at Kate. 'It isn't just the book,' he explained. 'It's what I like. This is what turns me on. And it's what I like best about you. You're so wonderful the way you try to pretend that you don't like things when you do.'

'Get her out of here,' repeated Kate, raising her voice. 'I've told you, it's over. I'm not helping you with your book any more.'

'But you're my wife,' he reminded her. 'I'm entitled to make love to my own wife.'

'Not like this,' protested Kate, unable to believe what was happening to her.

'Turn her on her side,' said Lucinda, advancing into the room. 'I've got a real treat for her here.'

With horror Kate saw, in Lucinda's hand, a double vibrator. She realised that they intended to use it on her. They were going to force her pleasure to spill again and again, filling her front and back and shaming her yet more, increasing her humiliation and taking pleasure from it. And all the time she realised, struggling as James tried to part her thighs, her husband would be watching her reactions, memorising them for his book.

'This is obscene,' she shouted. 'I don't want to do it. Let me go.'

'She doesn't mean it,' said Lucinda as James hesitated.

'I do,' shouted Kate. 'I want you both to let me go.'

Lucinda continued to advance towards the bed and Kate's heart sank. Clearly James had given up all hope of saving their marriage and instead was desperate to finish the book, even if it meant ignoring Kate's wishes. 'Please, please don't do this,' she begged them. 'Surely the whole point of the book is that the heroine obeys because she wants to, not because she's forced to?'

'It seems to be changing,' said James regretfully.

'You'll enjoy this,' Lucinda promised her.

'Let me go,' screamed Kate.

'You heard what the lady said,' said a blessedly familiar voice. 'I prefer consensual sex myself, even if it is between husband and wife. Are you going to let her go or do I have to make you?'

Both Lucinda and James looked flustered. Lucinda turned away and walked over to the window while James pulled a sheet over his wife. 'It was only a game,' he said quickly.

'It wasn't,' sobbed Kate.

'It sure as hell didn't look like one,' agreed Allan. 'Do you want to come with me, Kate?'

She didn't need asking twice. Pushing back the sheet, she stumbled across the room and when he caught her in his arms she realised that she was sobbing with relief. 'Guess I'll take her back to my room for a while,' he said to James. 'I'm sure you and your agent have a lot to talk about.'

'Let go of my wife,' snapped James.

'She's free to do as she likes,' Allan pointed out. 'It seems to me that she's gone off you.'

'Kate, come back here,' said James. 'You said you wanted to make me happy, so prove it. I don't want you to go to his room. I want you to stay here.'

'I was never making you happy,' said Kate. 'I was simply writing your book for you. I'm sorry, James, it's all over.'

'But what about the ending?'

'This is your ending.'

'I can't be,' shouted James.

'Don't worry about it,' said Lucinda, still with her back to James. 'It will be an unexpected twist.'

'But it's not the ending I want,' shouted James.

'Too bad,' said Kate and then she let Allan lead her away.

Much to Kate's relief there was no sign of Pam in Allan's bedroom. She was still shattered by what had happened between her and James and brushed away a tear as Allan led her over to the bed and sat her down on it. 'What the hell's been going on?' he asked.

Haltingly, unable to look him in the face as she talked, Kate explained what she'd learnt that morning and how she'd confronted James with it. 'I thought at first he wanted to forget the book, to make our marriage work properly,' she cried. 'But then it all changed again and I could tell he was using me. I think he'll always be a detached observer, it's his nature.'

'Lucinda told you about it, did she?' asked Allan.

Kate nodded. 'I know she did it because she's jealous but I'm glad she told me. The trouble is I feel so ashamed of myself, as though I've been used.'

'But you haven't have you?' said Allan gently. 'You've enjoyed yourself. You never did anything you didn't want to and now you're a woman instead of a girl.'

'But I did it out of love for him,' she explained.

Allan shook his head. 'You've gotta be honest with yourself, honey. It looked to me from the moment I arrived as though you were having a ball. Sure, you told yourself you were doing it out of love but you got a kick out of it, didn't you?'

Kate sighed. 'Yes. What on earth must you think of me?' she added hopelessly.

'I'd already found out about the book,' Allan confessed.

'When?' asked Kate.

'A couple of days ago. I knew something wasn't right here and in the end James told me the truth. Lucinda didn't know, and he was terrified she'd find out.'

'Why didn't you tell me?' cried Kate.

Allan shrugged. 'It wasn't my place. He told me in confidence and I don't break promises.'

'It's all gone so wrong,' said Kate sadly.

'Your marriage you mean?' She nodded. 'Sure, that's not worked out the way you intended but some good's come out of it all. If you'd never married James we wouldn't have met and that would have been a pity.'

'Do you mean that?' she asked.

'I'm not like James, I never say things I don't mean.'

'James is jealous of you,' Kate blurted out.

Allan's eyes gleamed with amusement. 'Has he got good cause?'

Kate fidgeted uneasily on the bed. She didn't know how to reply. It would be dreadful if she let Allan know how she felt about him and embarrassed him. So far he'd said nothing to indicate that he felt anything more for her than sexual attraction, despite the fact that he'd rescued her from James and Lucinda. 'Maybe,' she muttered.

'I sure as hell hope so,' he said, crouching down in front of her naked body. 'It's been a nightmare watching you and knowing you were his wife. When I heard that the marriage was a sham I was mighty relieved. I felt that you were fair game. I'm not the kind of man who breaks up marriages normally, but this wasn't a normal marriage.'

'You didn't break it up, James did,' said Kate.

'I'm going to make sure the split's permanent,' said Allan, his hands lightly stroking her shoulders and arms. He stroked her hair for a few minutes, his fingers light against her scalp, then he started to kiss her. His lips were firm, insistent, and she opened her mouth, her tongue darting into his as their excitement mounted.

For a long time they continued kissing and cuddling, Allan moving his hands all over her body, stroking her back, the insides of her elbows, even her fingers one by one, and she grew more and more aroused. When he lifted her legs onto the bed she gave a soft murmur of pleasure and as his mouth travelled between her thighs her hips started to move restlessly.

He kept his tongue soft and supple at first but then curled it at the edges and used it more firmly against her, the tip of it brushing unexpectedly over the entrance to her urethra which made her gasp and jerk as the paper-thin skin revelled in this unexpected touch.

Eventually he moved his head upwards, kissing her lower belly and swirling his tongue inside her naval, while his fingers moved relentlessly from her clitoris to her labia and on to the vagina.

As she moaned and whimpered with desire, he dipped one finger inside her, spreading her own juices upwards over the pulsating clitoris until she thought she'd explode, so great was the sexual tension within her.

She was nearing an orgasm now, her hips arching off the bed as she tried desperately to get him to apply firmer pressure, the kind that she needed if her pleasure was to spill. She was thrilled to realise that Allan understood what she meant because now his fingers moved in a stronger, regular rhythm around the whole area between her sex lips. With his free hand he stroked her belly and breasts.

'Let it go,' he whispered. 'Just enjoy yourself.'

She couldn't have stopped even if he'd told her to, so great was the tension, and now she was moaning louder. 'That's so good, so good,' she cried. His fingers continued their clever, knowing movements and then suddenly there was a flash of white light behind her eyes and with a cry of joy she spasmed in an ecstasy of release.

As soon as she'd finished Allan lay down beside her, cuddling her and uttering small murmuring sounds that both soothed and excited her. As Kate's body calmed, he swung himself onto the edge of the bed, putting his feet on the floor and lifting her easily on top of him. Now she was sitting facing him with her feet on the bed. He ran his fingers around the entrance to her vagina, spreading her moisture once more and then, confident that she was ready for him, he lowered her onto his erection. Together they moved slowly and rhythmically as the sexual tension built.

His hands were gripping her buttocks, the thumbs digging in to the backs of her hip bones, and she could tell by the tension in his body that he was nearing the point of no return. Her breasts were aching and she gripped them with her own hands in order to increase her pleasure. At the same time she tightened her vaginal muscles around him and he groaned.

She could see that his chest and neck were flushed with excitement and guessed that she was the same. 'Come on, honey,' he urged her. 'We're nearly there.' She shivered as the delicious tightness increased. Both of them were breathing rapidly and suddenly, without any warning, her climax began and she felt herself contracting around him.

Her body arched backwards as the pleasure crashed over her and she flung an arm round his neck in order to steady herself. The contractions seemed to be spiralling outwards from her pelvis to her vagina and the tendons of Allan's neck were like whipcords as he threw his head back just seconds before she felt his sperm spurting into her. They both cried out with excitement, clutching each other with desperate hands, frantic to savour every last second of this delicious coupling.

As their breathing quietened and their heartbeats slowed, Allan lay down on the bed, keeping Kate close to him so that her head was on his chest, their mouths only inches away from each other. His left arm was tucked beneath her, resting protectively in the middle of her back. All the tension had eased away now. She felt sensual and languorous, content to lie against him replaying the pleasure in her mind. She saw that Allan's eyes were half closed, his limbs limp while his breathing was once more deep and slow. Their bodies were warm and she wished that she could stay like that forever, safe in the comfort of his arms. At the same time though, she knew that this was only one aspect of him. He, like James, enjoyed complex sexual games too.

After a long time Allan spoke. 'What are you thinking about?'

'Us,' she admitted.

'Just us?'

She smiled, her eyes looking directly into his. 'Us and sex,' she confessed.

Allan nodded. 'That sounds even better. Come away with me,' he added.

Kate looked intently at him. 'You mean to America?'

'Yeah, California to be exact. I spend most of my time in California although I've got an apartment in New York and a house in Cape Cod.'

'I'd soon bore you,' said Kate, determined to be honest.

Allan shook his head. 'No way. I can think of lots of things we can do together. By the time you bore me I'll be too old to worry.'

'The way we made love just now, it was great,' said Kate. 'That's what I never got from James, tender sex, sex with love, but it won't always be enough for me.'

'Hell, why should it be? Variety's the spice of life,' said Allan cheerfully. 'If you want the truth I'm very keen on S & M and bondage but you wouldn't have to join in if you didn't want to. You might find it fun simply to watch.'

Kate's pulse quickened. 'I think I'd probably like to join in,' she confessed. 'Once I would have thought that good, uncomplicated sex was all a woman should want, but I know better now. I'm not sure if James was corrupting me or . . .'

'Who's talking about corruption?' asked Allan. 'You're a normal woman and you've discovered your own sexuality, which is great. I've told you what I like but we'll do the things you like too if they happen to be different.'

'I suppose I've got used to being dominated,' she confessed.

'Yeah, well I'm not exactly a submissive male.'

'And you really want me to come away with you?' asked Kate, unable to believe her luck.

'I sure do. I think Pam guesses, which is probably why she isn't here right now.'

'What about my marriage?' asked Kate.

'What about it?' Allan sounded almost bored. 'You can end that in a couple of years' time. It's not as though I'm trying to drag you to the altar straight away. We'll have to see how things go once we're together.'

'Isn't this going to hurt Pam badly?' asked Kate, determined to be fair to the other girl after the way James had treated her.

'It's not my body Pam's after, it's my money,' said Allan. 'You don't need to waste any sympathy on her. She's done pretty well out of me and we've had some good times together, but I never promised her more than that.'

'I see,' said Kate.

'I'm offering you more though,' he continued. 'I think we've got a future together. What do you think?'

Kate stretched lazily and as her hand slid down his body she realised that he was becoming aroused again. 'I think you're right,' she laughed. 'It's lucky we didn't meet earlier. A few months ago I wouldn't have interested you.'

'Then that's something we can thank James for when we leave,' said Allan.

'How soon can we go?' asked Kate.

'Hey, you're in a rush.' Allan was clearly taken aback.

'It's just that after what happened with James earlier I really don't want to have any more to do with him,' explained Kate.

'Then pack an overnight bag and we'll go,' said Allan.

Kate was stunned. 'It doesn't have to be quite that quick!'

'When I make up my mind about something that's it,' he said firmly. 'There's no point in us hanging around here any longer. Let's go. It'll add a neat little twist to the end of James' book.'

Kate laughed. 'Perhaps we're doing him a favour.'

'I doubt if he'll see it like that,' said Allan.

Kate knew that he wouldn't but she didn't care. Suddenly she was free, free to go where she wanted with a man she'd chosen, whose feelings for her were genuine. At this moment it was Allan she wanted to be with. She had no idea what she'd want in six months' time but for now this felt right and she was going to follow her instincts. 'I'll get my things,' she said.

When she walked back into her own bedroom James and Lucinda were sitting on the window ledge talking. James jumped to his feet. 'Kate, you've come back.'

'It's all right I'm not stopping,' she said briskly. 'You two keep talking. I've just got to throw a few things into an overnight bag.'

'What do you mean?' he asked.

'I'm leaving you,' said Kate calmly.

'You can't!'

'Just watch me.'

James' astonishment turned to anger. 'Where do you think you're going?' he demanded.

'To California.'

'That shit Allan's taking you away from me.'

Kate shook her head. 'No he isn't, James. I've chosen to leave you and go with him.'

'It won't last,' said James petulantly. 'He's incapable of being faithful for five minutes.'

'You're a good one to talk,' retorted Kate, walking into the bathroom to collect her toothbrush.

'Kate, please don't do this to me,' he begged her. 'I'm sorry about what happened earlier. I got carried away. It was the excitement of it all, but—'

'You don't need to apologise. In fact, I should thank you because that's what really decided me. At least that was partly what decided me.'

'What else made you change your mind then?' he asked.

'What Allan and I have been doing in his bedroom since I left,' she said, deliberately running her hands sensuously down the sides of her body. 'Thanks for all you've taught me, James, but now I'm off.' Putting her hands on his shoulders, she kissed him gently on both cheeks and walked out of the bathroom.

'Are you really going?' asked Lucinda curiously.

'Yes.'

'And does Pam know?'

'I imagine Allan's telling her right now. Unlike James he doesn't care to deceive people,' said Kate.

'He doesn't mind dumping them though, does he?' said Lucinda. 'One day it will be your turn.'

'I might tire of him first,' said Kate sweetly. 'It's kind of you to be so concerned about me, Lucinda, but really I think this is the best thing for all of us. I'm sure you can console James once I'm gone. Or isn't that a role that you care for?'

'You've certainly changed,' said Lucinda.

'I have,' agreed Kate cheerfully. 'I hope the book does well,' she added as James hovered uncertainly between bathroom and bedroom. 'If it gets published in America I'll make sure I buy a copy and I know Allan will get all his friends to do the same.'

'Please, don't do this, Kate,' cried James. 'You haven't thought it through.'

'Oh yes I have,' she assured him. 'I didn't think our marriage through properly. I thought that I could turn you into the person I wanted you to be. That was a mistake, I know that now. With Allan I know exactly what I'm getting and this time I know I'll be getting what I want.'

'When will I see you again?' called James as she reached the doorway.

'Probably in the divorce courts,' said Kate and then, with a brilliant smile at James and Lucinda, she left them.

Chapter 10

James sat behind the wooden table and looked at the long line of people waiting for him to sign their books. This was what he'd always longed for, always imagined. At last he'd achieved his ambition. *Obedience* was number one in the bestseller list and he, James Lewis, had arrived.

He looked up at the dark-haired woman standing in front of him. 'Would you put "to Kate with best wishes"?' she asked, smiling politely at him.

James' hand shook slightly. 'Kate?' She nodded. He signed, wondering why it was that even the mention of her name was enough to reduce him to total misery. He signed until his wrist ached. Men and women were buying the book in equal numbers, and they didn't mind admitting it. 'Breaks all boundaries, a classic for our time' the *Sunday Times* had called it. Of course he was grateful, but not as grateful as Lucinda felt he should be. The money was pouring in. Rights had been sold all over the world and now, he gathered, America had snapped up the film rights, yet success had a bitter taste.

Eventually the book shop closed and he was left in peace. 'I thought for one dreadful moment we were going to run out of copies,' said the manager, a bespectacled young man whose face was shining with excitement. 'You must be delighted with the way it went,' he added.

'It's very gratifying,' said James.

'What do you think your father would have thought?'

'Funny, I was asked that on television the other night. To be honest, I doubt if he'd have been at all interested. It isn't the sort of book he read.'

'Because of the sex? But it's far more than that, isn't it? I mean, it's a story about a woman discovering herself. My wife thought it was terrific.'

'That's nice,' said James, trying hard to sound pleased.

'What does your wife think of it?'

'We're separated,' said James shortly.

The other man was clearly shocked. 'I'm so sorry, I had no idea. The book's dedicated to her, isn't it?'

'Yes, but I don't imagine she's read it.'

'Are you driving yourself back?' asked the manager, now anxious to be rid of this dispirited author.

'My agent's picking me up.'

'Fine. You can wait in the staff room if you like.'

Wearily James put his pen in his pocket and then sat for another twenty minutes kicking his heels while he waited for Lucinda. 'How did it go?' she asked brightly as she breezed into the room.

'Very well. I must have sold over a hundred copies.'

'Brilliant! Where are you tomorrow?'

'I haven't a bloody clue.'

'Temper, temper,' she chided him. 'Honestly, James, I don't know what's the matter with you. You're famous, you're going to be rich and you've aroused controversy. It's all gone exactly as we planned and you look as though you've lost a five pound note and found a two pence piece.'

'I miss Kate.'

Lucinda sighed impatiently. 'There are plenty of other Kate's out there if you'd only go and look.'

'There's only one Kate,' he said coldly.

'You're thinking of the Kate you met. She doesn't exist any more,' snapped Lucinda as they got into her car. 'You may not choose to remember it, but you were the one who changed her. Besides, people keep commenting about the wonderful twist at the end of *Obedience*. If she hadn't gone off with Allan it would have been a much more typical erotic novel. You've described the man's shock well too. It's all helped make it the success it is, James. There's no point in making a fuss now.'

'She wasn't meant to run off with Allan,' he said angrily.

'What was she meant to do then? When we first talked about it you said you might have to drive her to some distant cove and dump her there,' said Lucinda with a laugh. 'She was never meant to figure permanently in your life.'

'I know that but things changed.'

'You changed, nothing else did,' pointed out Lucinda. 'For God's sake stop looking so bloody miserable, James. We're meeting your editor for dinner in an hour. At least try and look enthusiastic when she's talking to you.'

James had forgotten his editor. He wished that he could get out of the meeting but knew that he couldn't. For weeks now his publisher had been on at him about a sequel and he'd been evasive, telling them he was too busy promoting this book to think about the next, but tonight was crunch time. Tonight he'd have to come clean.

'Have you thought about what you're going to write next?' asked Lucinda casually.

'A little. I'll tell her tonight.'

'Great.'

A couple of hours later, over his crème brûlée, James faced the big question.

'When can we have an outline for the sequel?' asked his editor, Claire, leaning across the table eagerly.

'I'm afraid there isn't going to be a sequel,' said James.

She looked at him in astonishment. 'But we've had masses of letters from people wanting to know what becomes of Caitlin and the hero. It was clever of you not to give him a name, just to call him the man. Mind you, in the next book I think he'd have to have a name.'

'I've just said there isn't going to be another book,' said James quietly, taking a perverse satisfaction from the expression of horror on Lucinda's face.

'We've already announced it,' said Claire.

'You didn't consult me first.'

She gave a guilty smile. 'True, but I didn't really think that was necessary. After all, this is your big break. Besides, you wrote *Obedience* in less than a month. A sequel's hardly going to tax you, is it? People need to know what happens to Caitlin and the man.'

'I think,' said James slowly, 'that if they find out what happened to them they'd be very disappointed.'

'You mean you've already written it?' Claire's face lit up. 'For a moment there you had me worried.'

James shook his head. 'I haven't written it, but I know.'

Claire turned to Lucinda. 'Do you have any idea what he's talking about?'

'I think he's tired,' said Lucinda, kicking James' ankle under the table in case he was thinking of contradicting her.

'I hope that's all it is,' said Claire. 'The board won't be very happy if I go back and tell them he's not writing another book for us. I'm sure there must be a clause in the contract somewhere that mentions us being given first sight of his next novel.' All at once her expression changed. 'I suppose you've had a big offer from another publishing house, is that it?'

'No,' said James shortly. 'There's more than money involved here.'

'I bet you never thought you'd hear him say that,' said Lucinda, trying desperately to sound amused.

Claire shook her head. 'I certainly didn't. Is it because of the movie, James? Are you worried they're going to ruin the book?'

'They can do what they damned well like with it,' he snapped.

'Listen,' said Lucinda soothingly to Claire, 'I'll send you a copy of the outline within the next week, how about that?'

Claire shot a dubious glance at James who looked down at his pudding. He didn't intend to say any more. Let Lucinda flap about trying to save the situation. It was all her fault anyway.

'All right,' she agreed, 'but remember, follow-ups are notoriously difficult. We want the same freshness, and the same element of shock.'

'You'll get it,' Lucinda promised her.

'What the hell were you thinking about?' she demanded as she drove James back to his London hotel. 'You've never said anything to me about stopping writing.'

'You've never asked me.'

'The money won't keep coming in forever you know. No one can live off one book, however big a success it is. In any case, if you don't write what will you do?'

'Go to America and try and get Kate back.'

Lucinda shook her head. 'James, you're wasting your time.'

'If I get her back then I can write a sequel,' he said. 'If I don't then I can't, it's as simple as that.'

'You don't need Kate,' shouted Lucinda. 'You can use your imagination can't you?'

'When will you understand that I'm in love with her?' asked James. 'All this means nothing to me. Even the money doesn't compensate for what's happened. If you hadn't told her about the book when you did she'd never have left me, so it's your fault as much as mine.'

'Do you know what I think it is?' asked Lucinda, drawing the car up outside the hotel and leaning across him to open his door. 'I think you're scared of success. Some authors are, but I didn't expect you to be one of them.'

'Aren't you going to come in with me?' asked James.

Lucinda shook her head. 'You don't turn me on any more, James. Besides, if you're so desperately in love with Kate I can't believe you're interested in me.'

'We could still have sex.'

'We could,' she admitted. 'But I don't fancy you any more. You're mooning around like a love-sick teenager and it does nothing at all for me.'

'What's going to happen about this outline?' he asked. 'I'm not going to do one.'

Lucinda shrugged. 'Don't worry about it. I've got other ideas up my sleeve.'

'But I shall be too busy to write, even if it's a different sort of book. As I said I'm going to America and—'

'My ideas don't involve you at all,' said Lucinda sweetly. 'In fact, I don't think my life does any more, not unless you smarten up your act. Goodnight, James. Ring me when you've got over losing Kate and maybe we can get together again.'

Exhausted and miserable, James shut himself away in his hotel bedroom and lay awake all night wondering what Kate was doing and how he could track her and Allan down.

Exactly one week later Lucinda and Claire were dining together again in the same restaurant, only this time it was Pam and not James who made up the group.

'Have you brought the outline for the sequel with you?' Claire asked as she ordered for them all.

Lucinda shook her head. 'I'm sorry but James is absolutely adamant that there isn't going to be one. His idea is to leave his readers wanting more.'

'I'm afraid that isn't very good publishing policy,' said Claire sharply. 'The original contract made it quite clear that—'

'James isn't writing for anyone else,' Lucinda assured her. 'It seems as though he's got a bad attack of writer's block.'

Claire frowned. 'How much time do you think he's going to need?'

'I don't think it's a question of time,' said Lucinda. 'To be honest, I'm not certain I'm ever going to get another book out of him.'

Claire was clearly stunned. 'Why's he behaving like this?' she asked. 'He's the last person on earth I'd have expected to panic when he found success. It's always been his one aim in life. What's he going to do, live like a hermit in Cornwall? It isn't as though he's got a wife any more.'

'I think his domestic situation's got quite a bit to do with it,' explained Lucinda. 'Listen, Claire, I realise what I'm going to suggest is unusual but once you've thought about it I know you'll feel just as excited as I do.'

'What is it?' Plainly Claire was suspicious.

'Pam here has written a proposal for a book that I'd like you to look at,' said Lucinda, sliding a folder across the table.

Claire raised her eyebrows. 'How many books have you written, Pam?'

'She hasn't written any,' said Lucinda, who'd already decided to be perfectly frank about this. 'That won't present any problem though because I'm going to help her.'

'You mean *you're* going to write it?' asked Claire.

'I shall ghost write it,' said Lucinda.

'But what's this got to do with *Obedience*?' queried Claire.

'When you look at the proposal you'll see. I thought that after the huge success James has had it would be wonderful if you published a book from a woman's point of view.'

'*Obedience* did put the woman's point of view,' Claire pointed out.

'Yes, but this woman won't be obedient. This time the book would be about a woman who picks up a young man and then trains him to be exactly the sort of lover she wants. It's role reversal and the sexual theme would be slightly different.'

'In what way?'

'The man would be more of a slave, more dominated. I think a lot of women would find the idea of having their own sexual slave incredibly exciting, especially if he was young, strong and overeager. Imagine the wonderful situations you could have when he lost control, came too soon, that kind of thing?'

Claire glanced around the restaurant. 'There's no need to tell everyone the whole plot.'

Lucinda smiled. 'Sorry, I suppose I got rather carried away.'

Claire nodded. 'All the same I have to agree it does sound good. There's just one thing that I can't make out, why don't you write it yourself under a pseudonym? I don't mean any offence to you, Pam, but I'm not certain why you're needed.'

'Pam's had some experience of this kind of thing,' explained Lucinda. 'Also, because she came up with the idea, I think she should have a share of the money.' It was a complete lie but Lucinda knew that she couldn't possibly tell Claire the truth about the book.

'I'll read this through and see what I think,' said Claire, slipping the proposal into her briefcase. 'It's a pity about James,' she added wistfully. 'We're having to reprint *Obedience* all the time.'

'This could be even bigger,' Lucinda assured her. 'Think of all the women out there who spend half their lives fantasising about having the perfect lover. It isn't just the women either, lots of young men would give their eye teeth to spend their lives satisfying a beautiful woman, even if it did mean being treated like a slave. That's part of the turn-on, just like obedience was for James' heroine.'

Claire nodded. 'You could be right.'

'I know I'm right,' said Lucinda. 'Trust me, Claire. You could market this as the female equivalent of *Obedience*, that way you'd score extra points for being politically correct.'

'You really think this is going to work, don't you?' said Claire. Lucinda nodded. 'And Pam's going to help you?'

'Yes, she's going to do a lot of research.'

'Well I'll have to run it past some of the others, but if James really isn't going to come up with anything we've got to produce something, and we've got to announce it pretty soon. I'll call you next week.'

When the meal was over Lucinda and Pam climbed into a taxi and set off for a nightclub. 'She didn't seem too sure,' said Pam, her short black skirt rising up her thighs.

'Publishers never like to get overexcited in front of agents,' explained Lucinda. 'They're too worried about the kind of advance they might be asked to cough up. Claire's lucky really. James could have demanded a huge advance. Obviously we'll have to set our sights a bit lower. It won't matter, in the long run you'll earn a fortune.'

Pam's eyes were bright with excitement. 'Are you sure?'

'Absolutely,' said Lucinda. 'Believe me I'm never wrong about this kind of thing. Now let's start hunting.'

Two hours later they entered their fourth London nightclub of the evening. 'This is more difficult than I expected,' said Pam. 'When you told me the truth about Kate, James and his book it sounded easy as well as exciting.'

'Patience,' counselled Lucinda. 'It's vital that we get the right person. I don't want to make another mistake.'

'Kate couldn't have been a mistake, think of how well the book's selling,' said Pam.

'True, but she was a mistake on a personal level.'

'That's not going to matter here though, is it?' asked Pam. 'Hey! Look at that guy over there, standing watching those two girls dancing. He looks kinda neat.'

Lucinda looked. He was about six foot tall with fair hair and dark-brown eyes. It was clear from the tightness of his T-shirt and jeans that he was extremely well built. Lucinda thought that he probably worked out a lot and estimated that he couldn't have been more than nineteen. 'You move in on him,' she shouted, trying to make herself heard above the music. 'See how it goes. He certainly looks promising.'

'What if he gets off with me?' asked Pam. 'Where shall we go?'

'You can take him back to the hotel and try him out,' said Lucinda. 'I'll kip down with a friend for the evening if I see you leave together. Remember, right from the start you've got to make it clear that he has to satisfy you before he gets his own satisfaction. If he's not interested then we'll just start looking all over again another night.'

'I'd love him for a slave,' said Pam, moistening her lips with the tip of her tongue and, as Lucinda watched, she swayed provocatively across the dance floor, her eyes fixed on her prey.

Half an hour later the pair of them left, their arms wrapped tightly round each other and Lucinda gave a small sigh of relief.

She had a feeling he was going to be absolutely perfect. 'Bad luck, James,' she whispered as she went to ring a friend and book a bed for the night. Not that she really minded, training this young man was going to be a job for two and she couldn't wait to begin.

As the maid pulled back the curtains from the huge picture window overlooking the sea at Cape Cod, Kate stirred sleepily. The sun was already streaming into the room and the maid placed a tray of orange juice, fresh croissants and apricot preserve beside her mistress' bed before leaving quietly. Allan was already awake and Kate nestled up to him. 'I'm getting thoroughly spoilt,' she whispered.

'Then let me spoil you some more,' he suggested, lifting her left leg over his hip before reaching over her buttock and beneath her, his fingers tickling and teasing her exposed clitoris. This was a position she loved. Immediately she felt the warning prickles of impending orgasm and wriggled sensuously. 'That's so good,' she murmured.

He continued manipulating the tiny bud, rubbing lightly around it, occasionally dipping his fingers inside her and spreading her juices around until she was soaking wet with excitement, gasping and panting as the tension built and her belly started to contract.

For a moment his fingers stopped and she gave a cry of despair. 'Don't stop now,' she begged him.

'You're sure you're not too tired after last night?' he teased.

'Please, please,' she urged him. 'Touch me like you were before.' Once more his fingers resumed their knowing rhythm and within seconds she was flooded with sweet release. She writhed against him, groaning with delight.

Once she'd come he slid inside her, his hands firm in the small of her back as he moved her back and forth on his erection. 'The best way to start the day,' he groaned, and she felt her pleasure beginning again. 'I can't wait much longer,' he warned her.

'I'm nearly there,' she cried and then she felt one of his fingers tickling the entrance to her rectum before sliding inside. Immediately she was consumed with the dark forbidden passion that she'd grown to love and contracted violently around him.

Allan gasped, the veins standing out on his neck and forehead as she milked him remorselessly, her contractions savage and uncontrollable. 'A great way to start the day,' he gasped when it was over and they lay with their limbs entwined until Kate's breathing had slowed and her body began to descend from its state of excitement.

Later, when they were propped up and eating their breakfast, he teasingly tweaked one of her flaccid nipples until it grew rigid. 'What are you doing?' she asked.

'Just trying to get your attention, honey. I thought you might like to hear about my latest investment.'

Kate knew very little about Allan's investments or business interests. Once they were in America she was surprised at how busy he was, although he never neglected her, but neither did he confide in her about his money-making schemes. It was plain that he was highly regarded in the business world and she had seen him featured in an article in *Time* magazine, but she was still surprised that he was offering to discuss an investment with her.

'What is it then?'

'I'm going to be one of the backers for the film of *Obedience*,' he said slowly.

Kate gasped. 'But why? You're just helping James make more money.'

Allan picked up the copy of the book that was beside their bed. '"For my wife",' he read out. 'Now, if he means what he says it seems to me it's only fair you should get something out of it, financially that is. If I'm a backer then that's one way of making sure you do.'

'It's one way of making sure you do,' she retorted.

Allan shook his head. 'Nope, any money I make from this will go straight to you. What do you think?'

'Is the film really going to be made?'

'Sure is.'

'I suppose you're right,' she agreed. 'After all, without me he wouldn't have had a book.'

'I'd like to see the film when it's made,' said Allan. 'It'll be interesting to see what the heroine's like.'

'You won't have any say in casting, will you?' asked Kate.

'No, honey, I'm a backer not a casting director, but I'm sure they'll get someone who resembles the heroine in the book physically.'

'You don't think anyone will guess it's me?' she asked anxiously.

Allan didn't have the heart to tell her that everyone already knew it was her. That from the moment the book had come out it had been assumed that his wife had been the role model for Caitlin. 'Shall I go ahead then?'

Kate nodded. 'Will James know you're a backer?'

'Hell yes, I'll make sure of that. Nothing like rubbing his nose in it.'

'Who's he using for the follow-up?' she asked curiously.

'I've heard he isn't doing one,' said Allan.

Kate was genuinely shocked. 'Why on earth not?'

'The way I heard it he's lost interest in the project.'

Kate said nothing. She supposed that it was her fault, that without her James couldn't work, but she didn't feel any guilt. 'He won't come over here if they make a film will he?'

'Of course not,' said Allan soothingly, but he knew that wasn't true. He'd already heard through friends in England that James was determined to come to America and try and win back his wife. He didn't have a chance in hell, Allan knew that and he saw no reason to worry Kate. As far as he and she were concerned those days were behind them. In any case, she was having a far more exciting time here in America than she'd had in Cornwall, and he was delighted at the way she'd accepted his particular sexual preferences.

'I've got a dinner guest coming tonight,' he told Kate as he started to dress. 'A good-looking guy from South America. Very dark-haired, tall, slim, wears silk Italian suits. Your sort of guy.'

He saw Kate's cheeks flush. 'Do you want me to help entertain him?'

'I think it would be a good idea,' said Allan slowly.

Kate nodded. 'I'll make sure everything's ready. What time are you bringing him home?'

'About seven.'

He bent down to kiss her and she wound her arms round his neck, their lips meeting as they kissed deeply. 'See you then,' she murmured, and he knew that she was very excited.

Dinner that evening was served at seven-thirty. Kate, wearing a tight-fitting ankle-length red silk dress, high at the front but backless, had been the perfect hostess. Over pre-dinner drinks she'd chatted vivaciously to Juan, answering all his questions about England and telling him how much she was enjoying living in America. Just before they ate Allan excused himself and disappeared upstairs. Kate knew what he'd be doing, he'd be preparing the upstairs room for later.

As she continued talking to Juan she felt herself start to shake with mounting excitement. She enjoyed these evenings more than she could describe, and they only made her more certain that when she'd chosen Allan she'd done the right thing. Their life together satisfied her far more than life with James would ever have done.

They drank their coffee outside on the veranda, looking across the water, until Allan cleared his throat. 'Perhaps Juan would like a little entertainment now, honey,' he suggested.

Kate got gracefully to her feet, smoothing her hands down over her hips and noticing how Juan's piercing dark eyes followed her every move. 'Let's go upstairs then,' she murmured.

Allan led the way up two flights of stairs to the large room set in the roof which he liked to call his entertainment room.

The windows were blacked out and when he flicked on the wall lights only a subdued glow illuminated the room. Kate was used to it now but she heard Juan's swift intake of breath as he looked about him.

'Juan shares our tastes,' said Allan quietly to Kate. 'Take off your dress now.'

She moved across the room to their visitor and then turned her back on him. Immediately his fingers found the long zip and, with one swift movement, he unfastened it, lightly shrugging the dress off her shoulders and allowing it to fall to the floor so that she could step out of it. Beneath it she was naked apart from a red G-string which their visitor didn't touch. Allan pulled her away from Juan and into the middle of the room where a tall metal frame had been bolted to the floor. Silently, compliantly, Kate lifted her hands and Allan slipped the dangling handcuffs over them before tightening a chain, which meant that Kate was balanced on tiptoe, her breasts thrust forward and her slim body cruelly stretched and totally exposed to the watchful gaze of the two men.

'She is very beautiful,' murmured Juan.

'She sure is,' Allan agreed. 'Before we start understand this, you're only allowed to touch her when I say and you're only allowed to do what I tell you. If you step out of line you'll be out of here before you know what's happened and there'll be no place on the board for you either.'

'I understand,' Juan assured him.

'Great,' said Allan and then he began to caress Kate's body, with his hands running lightly up and down her back, caressing her buttocks and stroking the backs of her knees. Because she was stretched so tightly every sensation was intensified and it felt to Kate as though butterflies were dancing over her. She started to shake, knowing what was coming, longing for it and yet still slightly afraid.

The frisson of fear was necessary to her, both she and Allan knew it, and these games in the presence of strangers which were videoed by Allan's concealed camera were like an addiction for her now. Even as she hung there helpless and waiting, she couldn't help anticipating watching the film later, after Juan had gone.

Both the men undressed and when they were naked Allan switched off all the lights except for one single beam high above the frame which held Kate in the spotlight, trapped and waiting to see what they intended to do with her. Juan walked slowly around her, very occasionally allowing his long tapering fingers to touch her in unexpected places, on the side of her neck or the outside of her thigh, and each time her muscles quaked and she uttered tiny mewing sounds of nervous pleasure.

'Bring her to an orgasm,' said Allan thickly.

'Using what?' asked Juan.

'Your cock, but you mustn't penetrate her.'

Their visitor nodded and then Kate felt her husband's large hands tear off the G-string before opening her up for their visitor and the delicious full feeling returned between her thighs as she felt her clitoris swelling. Juan pushed his hips forward and she felt the velvety softness of his glans brushing between her sex lips, moving up and down the already damp channel until, with unerring precision, he started to rotate it around the head of her clitoris.

Glorious tendrils of anticipatory pleasure were snaking through her belly and thighs and she glanced down at the dark head of the stranger. His cock felt long and lean but supple, gliding back and forth over her excited flesh, driving her into a frenzy, while Allan held her open and used his thumbs to tease at the creases at the tops of her thighs.

She began to moan as her pleasure mounted. Thrusting her hips forward for a second she felt the visitor slip inside her, but immediately he jerked his hips and removed himself, anxious not to break the rules before the fun had even begun.

'That was her fault not yours,' Allan conceded, and he slapped Kate sharply on the buttocks, causing her body to rock to and fro and intensifying all the wonderful sensations that were sparking through her.

Juan grasped the base of his erection in his right hand and carefully manipulated the tip so that he was travelling up and down the hot hungry length of her before circling the head once more. Then he pressed himself firmly against the side of the clitoral shaft while Allan held her tightly in his grip. The steady pressure caused a dull ache to begin behind the bunched mass of nerve endings, an ache that grew and grew before abruptly exploding into a climax that made her cry out with delight.

For the next fifteen minutes the two men covered her with oil, their hands probing into every crevice, lubricating every centimetre of flesh, yet never once did they allow her pleasure to spill. She felt as though she was on fire, her skin burnt with desire, and she heard herself pleading with them, begging them to allow her fulfilment.

'We'll both take her at the same time,' said Allan. 'But first I'll cover her eyes,' and the by now familiar black mask was slipped over Kate's head so that she had no idea which of the men would penetrate her where. It was only when Juan's long slim cock entered her vagina that she knew it would be Allan taking her from behind. She started to twist in a panic because he was so large that the pleasure was always tinged with pain. Nevertheless, it was a pain that she adored, worshipped, and it made the ecstasy even greater.

'I want you to get right to the edge, Kate,' Allan whispered in her ear. 'I'm going to let Juan do that to you, but don't come until I'm inside you.'

She felt his huge erection nudging between her buttocks. She could hear their visitor's heavy breathing as he slid in and out of her, using his hands on her belly and breasts, and soon she began to ache with the tension of her internal muscles.

When Juan sucked on her nipples, pulling his head away whilst keeping them imprisoned between his teeth, lances of ecstasy streaked through her whole body. It seemed as though he was pulling on the back of her clitoris at the same time because all the sensations started to focus in on one central point between her thighs, and her body arched in preparation for its climax.

'Withdraw,' Allan ordered Juan and the visitor obeyed, his own frustration only obvious to Kate by his heavy ragged breathing. 'Now I'm going to enter you too,' Allan whispered in her ear. 'We're going to fill you right up until you can't bear it any longer.'

In her imagination she could picture the scene so well – the two men, complete opposites in build and colouring, both lusting after her, frantic for pleasure and possession, her lithe honed body driving them into a frenzy equalled only by her need – and she felt herself becoming even more aroused at the erotic images her brain was conjuring up.

Allan's hands gripped her waist tightly, his fingers digging into the tender flesh, and she flinched. His fingers dug deeper. 'That's not a movement we've practised,' her reminded her.

She said nothing. She was only grateful that he was willing to share his dark side with her at times like this rather than exclude her, grateful that she was being allowed to enjoy the strange forbidden pleasures that she'd first learnt at Penrick Lodge and which her body now craved. She subdued her disobedient flesh, forcing herself not to wince again as his large fingers continued to dig into her. Only when she was still did he start to penetrate her.

Juan eased himself into her vagina, his hips quickly picking up the rhythm he'd been forced to abandon earlier. Allan moved more slowly, keeping her in a state of fearful tension as his huge cock slipped between her oiled buttocks and into her tight rectum, gradually filling her while her muscles spasmed furiously, almost unable to bear what he was doing.

At one point she heard herself cry out, pleading with him to stop, but immediately the pleasure started to exceed the pain until soon there was only pleasure as the two men worked in unison, Juan's hands fondling her while Allan's kept her still, and they drove in and out of her as her long-delayed orgasm came nearer and nearer.

'Yes, I'm coming!' she screamed and suddenly it was as though someone had thrown a switch and an electric shock seemed to course through her entire body, sending tingles to the tips of her toes and the ends of her fingers, the shock waves travelling through her breasts, belly and thighs. Deep inside her, where previously there had been the despairing ache of frustration, now there was just incredible flooding warmth and endless contractions of orgasmic pleasure.

She was vaguely aware that both the men were climaxing as well, the visitor muttering in his own language, words that were meaningless to her, while Allan's teeth nipped at the flesh of her left shoulder in a mark of love and possession. A few minutes later the mask was removed and she blinked in the spotlight. Allan was standing in the corner, his face in shadow, but Juan was only a couple of feet in front of her, his nearly black eyes still surveying her hungrily, appreciatively. 'Is the entertainment over?' he asked Allan.

Kate waited for the reply, waited to see if she was to be allowed anything else or if Allan had tired of the game.

'You can make her come again if you like,' said the American.

'Any way I like?'

'Sure.'

With a nod the visitor moved towards her and she stared at him, trying to work out what he had planned. When he fell to his knees and pushed her aching legs apart, her flesh leapt in readiness. As his tongue licked and probed at her damp swollen flesh, her head fell back in languid delight. His tongue was soft at first, caressing her gently, but soon he hardened it, using the point like the end of a feather, jabbing at her most sensitive places so that her body began to jump and leap and she twisted helplessly in the handcuffs.

To her surprise Allan remained in the corner. Normally he would have come forward and supported her body but he let her sway back and forth, her muscles aching, and she realised that this time he was going to let things go further, allow her to be at the mercy of the visitor. Juan knew what he was doing.

212

Time and again he brought her to the very brink of release until she was sobbing with frustration, her hips thrusting helplessly back and forth. Every time she moved he would turn his head away, only returning when she became still once more.

She was shamingly damp, so desperate now that she began to plead with him. 'Juan, Juan, let me come, let me come,' she cried and saw Allan stir in the shadows.

The visitor remained silent. His only answer was to tweak one distended nipple and the fierce shard of pleasure-pain was nearly enough to give her release, nearly but not quite. Just when she thought she'd go mad, Juan began to suck rhythmically on her swollen clitoris and she felt as though every muscle was starting to dissolve as the liquid pleasure began to spread and the heat mounted. She was nearly there, approaching that blissful point of no return, whimpering like some mindless animal in her search for satisfaction.

'Finish her off now,' called Allan from the shadows.

Kate waited for the final swirl of Juan's tongue around her clitoris but instead his teeth closed around the delicate flesh, just grazing the skin, and her whole belly caved inwards with fear and anticipation.

Suddenly, after endless seconds, he nipped at the pulsating flesh. With a scream Kate felt her body spasming helplessly as wave after wave of dark-red pain-tinged ecstasy threatened to tear her apart and she heard herself sobbing aloud at this incredible new sensation.

'Get dressed,' said Allan from the shadows, and she was vaguely aware of the visitor moving away from her. She couldn't see him because of the brightness of the light in her eyes but she could hear the sounds of him dressing and waited for Allan to release her. Instead he dressed as well and the two men left the room and she heard the door click closed behind them.

She had no idea how long Allan left her there but when he finally returned and walked over to her she began to cry with relief. 'I was afraid you were going to leave me here,' she sobbed.

His hands cupped her face and he kissed the tears away

from her cheeks, fondling her lovingly. 'Honey, I'd never do anything like that. I just wanted to see what it made you feel like.'

'I can't explain,' she said. 'It was terrifying and yet . . .'

'And yet?'

'It was exciting too,' she confessed.

Allan slid a hand between her thighs. 'Yeah, I can tell.'

He lifted her up to ease the tension in her body and automatically she fastened her legs around his waist. Then, as he undid the handcuffs, she buried her head in his neck. He walked across the room with her, pressing her back against the wall, one hand fumbling to unzip his slacks. She couldn't wait to feel him inside her once more. 'What did you think of our visitor?' he asked as he moved steadily to and fro.

'I can't wait to see the video.'

He chuckled, his breath warm against her breasts. 'Neither can I.'

'Oh God, I'm going to come again,' she cried.

'That's the idea,' he said encouragingly. Within seconds she was climaxing again, her legs gripping him tightly, and she heard him call her name when his pleasure finally spilled.

That night, just as she was about to fall asleep, Allan rolled over so that his mouth was against her ear. 'I forgot to tell you, Pam rang me. She's writing a book.'

'A book?' asked Kate sleepily.

He laughed. 'An erotic book.'

'What's it about?' asked Kate.

'I don't know,' said Allan. 'But whatever it's like I'm sure you could write a better one.'

'I'm not interested in writing books,' said Kate. 'I prefer fact to fiction.'

'Me too,' agreed the huge American, his arms enfolding her. 'And I'll tell you another good thing about that, we don't have to keep to any guidelines.'

Kate shivered as she realised that it was true. Together they could do anything they liked, she could be whatever she wanted to be. For a moment she spared a thought for James, knowing that without him and *Obedience* none of this would have been possible.

'I hope the book does well,' she murmured.

'Our videos are better than any book,' he reminded her and, with images of the scene that had been played out earlier that night still in her mind, Kate closed her eyes.

'If I ever write a book,' she mumbled. 'I shall call it *Satisfaction.*'

Allan gave her a squeeze of appreciation. 'America suits you then, huh?'

'Absolutely,' she said with a smile, but she knew really that it was Allan who suited her, and always would.

Dangerous Desires

J. J. DUKE

*In response to his command, Nadine began
to undress. She was wearing her working
clothes, a black skirt and a white silk blouse.
As she unzipped the skirt she tried to keep
her mind in neutral. She didn't do this kind
of thing. As far as she could remember, she
had never gone to bed with a man only
hours after she'd met him . . .*

There's something about painter John
Sewell that Nadine Davies can't resist.
Though she's bowled over by his looks
and his talent, she knows he's arrogant
and unfaithful. It can't be love and it's
nothing like friendship. He makes her
feel emotions she's never felt before.

And there's another man, too. A man
like Sewell who makes her do things
she'd never dreamed of – and she
adores it. She's under their spell, in
thrall to their dangerous desires . . .

0 7472 5093 6

More Erotic Fiction from Headline Liaison

Vermilion Gates

Lucinda Chester

Rob trailed a finger over Rowena's knee, letting it drift upwards. She slapped his hand. 'Get off me,' she hissed, 'or I'll have you for sexual harassment.' Nevertheless, part of her wanted him to carry on and stroke the soft white skin above her lacy stocking-tops . . .

Rowena Fletcher's not having much fun these days. She's a stressed-out female executive with a workload more jealous than any lover and no time, in any case, to track one down.

Then she is referred to Vermilion Gates, a discreet clinic in the Sussex countryside which specialises in relaxation therapy. There, in the expert hands of trained professionals, Rowena discovers there's more than one way to relieve her personal stress . . .

0 7472 5210 6